COVER DESIGN: Shasti O'Leary Soudant

EDITING: Wendy Chan, The Passionate Proofreader

DEVELOPMENTAL EDITOR: Ashley Cestra

This is a work of fiction. Names, characters, places, and incidents either are the product of the author's imagination or, if an actual place, are used fictitiously and any resemblance to actual persons, living or dead, business establishments, events, or locales is entirely coincidental. The publisher does not have any control and does not assume any responsibility for author or third-party websites or their content.

 Created with Vellum

INTRODUCTION +
ACKNOWLEDGMENTS

I began writing this book over a year ago, when the idea came to me (quite literally) out of nowhere. At the time, I had contracts and other deadlines taking priority, so I placed this project aside—though not once did I ever stop thinking about it. This year, I was finally able to carve out enough time to finish this passion project of mine, but it was no solo endeavor. Once the initial draft was finished, the fun and games were over and it was time to get down to business and shape this thing into the story it was always meant to be!

None of that would have been possible if it weren't for the brutal honesty, blunt feedback, and beautifully talented minds of fellow authors Alex Gates, Rachel Hargrove, and Marin Montgomery or my amazing beta reader, Ashley, who never fails to ask all the hard questions.

Shasti O'Leary Soudant—thank you for a knock-out cover. I

never tire of looking at it! And to my editor, Wendy Chan, thank you for your patience and unfaltering professionalism. To all of my bloggers, bookstagrammers, and ARC readers—thank you for your contagious enthusiasm and willingness to read and review. I hope my love for this story came through as you read it, and I hope it's a tale that will stay with you for a long time.

Last, but not least, to my readers: thank you for choosing/reading/buying/borrowing this book. You've officially made the dreams of a seven-year-old girl with an 80s perm come true.

xo—Sunday (aka Minka Kent)

DESCRIPTION

She has every reason to hate her ex. It doesn't mean she wants him dead ...

Every day on her way home from work, Dove Damiani drives past her ex-house, where her ex-husband lives with her ex-dog and her ex-yoga instructor, next to her ex-neighbors and the ex-life she once affectionately described as "frighteningly perfect."

To outsiders, Dove is bitter and resentful. The divorce left her alone, with nothing but a set of car keys and fifty percent of a paltry savings account. So when the lifeless body of her former husband is discovered in the birch grove outside Dove's apartment on what would have been their fifth wedding anniversary, investigators waste no time making Dove a person of interest.

She swears she didn't do it. She's never so much as killed a spider in her thirty-four years.

But as evidence mounts against her, Dove finds herself questioning her memory, her sanity, and finally—her innocence.

1

DOVE

IT'S BEEN three hours since you died. Well, more like five. It was five hours ago when they found you cold and lifeless in the birch grove outside my apartment. But it was three hours ago when they knocked on my door and asked me when I'd last spoken to you.

I type my password into my work computer—one-zero-one-four.

October fourteenth.

Today's date.

What should have been our fifth wedding anniversary.

The screen flickers to life and plays its joyful chime as a picture of us populates the desktop wallpaper pixel by pixel. We were baby-faced in this one, both of us just having finished our junior years at Holbrook College and venturing on a cross-country road trip to celebrate. We stopped at some hole-in-the-wall ski town east of Telluride. Neither of us had ever skied before, but we loved the idea of being skiers someday.

We were staring down the barrel of forever back then, weren't we?

"What are you doing here?" Noah—Dr. Benoit—stands in the doorway of my office in his white dental coat, a paper mask hanging from his neck and a file under his left arm, and I'm ejected from my melancholic trance. His brows come together and his thin mouth is agape.

"Sorry I'm late." I double-click on the insurance software icon: a smiling tooth against a sky-blue background.

"I didn't think you were coming in today." He speaks with the kind of carefulness one might exercise when handling a delicate china tea cup.

"How'd you find out?" I'm not in the mood to explain something he couldn't begin to understand, so I deflect with a question.

"The clerk at the gas station was talking about it," he says. "Did you get my text?"

"Yeah," I say. Now that I think about it, he did text about an hour ago to check on me. But the last few hours have been a hazy blur. "Thank you for that."

If good news travels fast, bad news travels faster, especially in Lambs Grove, Kansas, where nothing tragic ever happens.

We always used to joke that there was some kind of magnetic force field surrounding our hometown, an invisible blanket that shielded us from things like natural disasters, mass shootings, and scandal—political, professional, or otherwise. But sometime between midnight and four AM, the protective force field was shattered when you were left to die in the birch grove outside my apartment.

Noah examines me with his dark hooded eyes and an

unreadable expression on his boyish face, and I imagine he's wondering why I'm not crying.

I would if I could.

Numbness, disbelief, and a cocktail of mood stabilizers will do that to a person.

"I thought maybe you'd want some time to ... process everything," he says, his cadence like a gentle tap dance as he avoids weightier words like death and grief and murder and loss.

"These insurance claims aren't going to file themselves." I manage a flicker of a half-smile before my gaze moves toward the name plate on the edge of my desk. *Dove Damiani.* I never changed my last name back to Jensen, and I never intended to because you were going to come back for me. "Oh. And here's your almond milk hazelnut latte. No sugar. Extra foam. The balance on your card is getting low. FYI."

I slide the coffee toward the edge of my desk. He hesitates before retrieving it.

"If you change your mind ... if you want to go home later ... if you want to take a couple of days," he says, "we can handle things around here."

"I'll be fine." *Home* is a sorry excuse for an apartment on the north side of town—4.7 miles from the cozy brick ranch we used to share—and today it's the last place I want to be. Five-hundred square feet of contractor-beige, assemble-yourself furniture, and clearance-bin candles to cover the cat urine-scented carpet. I never bothered to feather this nest because it was only supposed to be temporary.

I gather the stack of encounter forms from the top tray of my desk—last Friday's appointments that I wasn't able to file since the system was down for maintenance that day.

Noah lingers. I'd be annoyed at him if he wasn't coming

from a good place. It's a shame you two never got to meet. I think you would've been friends.

"Pretty sure you're booked solid this morning," I remind him as I type in the name of the first patient and press enter. The machine whirs and the software 'thinks' as it tries to process my request. I reach for my coffee, taking a sip out of my glittery, rose gold-colored reusable mug—the French Press Café gives a thirty-cent discount when you bring your own.

"Right," Noah says, pressing his lips into a flat frown until his dimples show. They make me think of your dimples, the ones I'll never get to see again, the ones that gave you a youthful, playful sort of look and made waitresses, sales clerks, and strangers on the street do double-takes.

My desk phone rings—a transfer from the receptionist.

"We'll chat later," I tell him before spinning in my chair until my back is toward him. Lifting the receiver, I cradle it on my shoulder. "Benoit Dental. This is Dove."

"Is this the office manager?" a woman asks. Her piercing voice sends a shock of pain to my eardrum.

I tap the volume down several notches. "Yes it is. How may I assist you today?"

"My daughter was just there for a cleaning last week and when she got home, she realized some *jackass* slipped a card in her goodie bag," she says. "Some referral for some shrink or something? I want to file a complaint against the hygienist. You're a damn dentist office. You clean teeth. You're not qualified to tell people they need mental help."

A torrent of cold bursts beneath my skin and my middle tightens.

I don't tell her that the "jackass" was me, I don't tell her how I consoled the crying young woman in the hallway for a solid twenty minutes, nor do I tell her the enamel of her twenty-one-year-old daughter's teeth is destroyed from years of the bulimia she kept secret from her hypercritical mother.

It was I, not her hygienist, who slipped the card for Dr. Deborah Schermerhorn into the bag.

"I'm so sorry to hear about that," I say. "I'd be happy to share your concern with Dr. Benoit on your behalf."

"That won't be necessary. I want to talk to him myself."

"I understand, but he's scheduled with back-to-back patients this week and as the clinic manager, I handle these matters." I speak quickly, before she has a chance to talk over me. "I can assure you I'll address the responsible staff member as soon as possible, but please know that we're terribly sorry for upsetting you and your daughter."

It's a lie. I'm not sorry.

Sometimes people aren't capable of acting in their own best interests, sometimes they need a gentle nudge—or a good hard push—in the right direction.

It's times like these that I think about you and your students, Ian. All those instances you went above and beyond, staying long after the final school bell rang to hold study sessions or volunteering to take the history club to Washington, D.C. for a week every summer and paying for your expenses from your own pocket so there would be extra money in the budget for more sightseeing.

Remember when you donated your clothes to that family with all the boys when their house burned down?

And how could I forget all the times you'd give school rides to neighbor kids when they missed the bus after their parents had left for work?

There's a reason you won the prestigious Greenleaf-Montblanc Education Association's *Teacher of the Year* award your first year at Lambs Grove High. You were an angel, Ian. A saint of an educator. And you left a legacy no one will ever be able to outshine.

It's funny how people expected me to hate you after the divorce. They assumed I was bitter, told me I had every right to be angry with you, to curse your name and air your dirty laundry. But it was going to take a lot more than a piece of paper and a naked ring finger to make me fall out of love with the man who'd made the last twenty years of my life the best ones I'd ever known—frighteningly perfect.

I glance at your vintage LeCoultre aviator timepiece on my left wrist—the one I snuck into a small box of mementos when I moved out six months ago. The second hand is motionless, the time stuck at 1:43. It needs a battery and a tune-up, but the idea of parting with it for a week doesn't appeal to me, not now.

You treasured this watch, and it was one of your favorites—a gift from Grandpa Damiani before he passed. But as soon as it stopped working, you placed it in your top dresser drawer for safe-keeping and never got around to getting it fixed. I took it when I left, planning to get it serviced and give it back to you when the time was right.

But the time was never right.

And then you requested all communication be handled directly through our lawyers—which was right before you started dating my then-friend, Kirsten Best.

You weren't yourself this year, Ian, but I loved you too much to hold that against you. I knew you too well to take it personally. It was a phase. A whim. A funk. You were going to come back to me.

Returning to my screen, I finish e-filing the first of Friday's claims. The scent of your citron and vetiver cologne wafting off the collar of my blouse fills the air with a subtle transporting softness. I'd taken one of your travel-sized bottles from the bathroom the day I moved out, thinking it might help to spray it every once in a while when I was feeling particularly blue and nostalgic. It only took a month for me to use it up and I ended up opening a charge card at the department store so I could buy a new bottle. When the woman behind the counter told me it was a limited edition, that they were going to stop carrying it soon, I bought two of the larger bottles.

I still can't believe you're gone but I swear to you—I'm going to find out who did this.

You have to believe me.

2

DOVE

"KIRSTEN DID IT." Ariadne points a splintered chopstick at Noah from her side of my kitchenette table after work Monday. "My money's on her."

"And you know this how?" Noah counters.

Ari lifts a shoulder before readying a bite of sesame chicken. "She was the closest person to him. And nine times out of ten, it's the significant other. Maybe he pissed her off? Maybe he cheated on her and she snapped? Women snap all the time. That's why there's that show about it ... what's it called? Oh, yeah. *Snapped*."

Noah exhales, mouth pressed flat, as he considers Ari's theory. "They hadn't been together that long. You have to have more invested in a relationship to snap like that."

"Unless you're crazy," she says without pause. "And someone who steals their friend's ex-husband the second he's single ..."

"Doesn't make them crazy," Noah cuts her off. "Self-serving? Yes. Coldhearted? Absolutely. Insecure? Very much so. But crazy? I disagree with you there."

My kitchen table is a panorama of opened wine bottles and paper boxes of savory Chinese takeout, but my hunger has yet to show its face today. During my lunch break earlier today, I grabbed a deli salad out of habit, sat in my car with the box in my lap, and didn't take a single bite. Ninety minutes went by before I realized I'd been sitting there, dazed, and I hurried back to the office, sneaking in the back door before anyone realized I was late.

"Fine, *Detective Benoit*, what are your theories?" Ari angles her body toward him, her elbow resting on the table.

"He knew something," he says. "And someone wanted to keep him quiet."

Ari rolls her eyes. "So you're basically saying he was a mafia informant. In Kansas. Who moonlighted as a history teacher."

"No. I'm not saying that at all," Noah says.

I glance behind me toward the muted TV in my living room, only to find them reporting on the upcoming pumpkin festival.

"Maybe he was making meth? Like that chemistry teacher in that Breaking Bad show?" Ari's mocking him now, her lips wrestling a smirk.

Noah ignores her sarcasm. "I'm just saying he probably knew something about someone, something really awful, and that someone wanted to make sure their secret was safe. Forever."

"You guys," I interrupt them. "He was a small-town high school history teacher, not an FBI informant or a drug dealer or mob informant."

"Maybe we shouldn't be talking about this right now?" Noah's elbows settle on the table as he studies me. He's been doing this all day, looking at me like I'm two seconds from falling apart.

I almost left work early today because I'd finished my claims for the day, but also because Noah wouldn't stop checking on me.

And I get it.

To the outside world, it looks strange that my ex-husband was murdered in the middle of the night and I went into work like it was any other day, but it's not like there's a manual on this sort of thing.

All I knew was sitting at home in isolation, pacing my apartment wasn't going to find your killer.

When I got home tonight around a quarter past five, they still had the birch grove girdled in yellow tape, and an officer in a squad car had taken up residency outside the entrance to the hiking trail, keeping people from stepping foot inside. The scene was night and day from this morning when the parking lot was packed full of police and DCI and news vans.

Locals have been coming out in droves. I watched them from my car for a few minutes when I pulled in. Everything from rusty conversion vans to shiny white BMWs crawled and creeped through the parking lot, trying to steal a glimpse of ... well, there isn't much to see anymore.

By the time I parked in my assigned spot, I noticed a sunny-blonde newscaster from Channel Seven standing in front of the birch thicket as a heavy-set camera man filmed her giving a report. I don't know what she could possibly be reporting on. Seems like all they do now is recycle the same information fifty different ways until it almost sounds new again.

Anything to sell ads, right?

You always said the news was in the business of spinning tragedies as entertainment to make a few bucks, and you weren't wrong.

"You doing okay, Dove?" Ariadne places her hand over mine, pulling me out of my thoughts. "You're quiet."

"She's always quiet." Noah winks at me from across the table.

"You know what I mean," Ari snaps at him. She reaches for her wine glass, throwing back a liberal swig. "This whole thing is wild. I mean ... stuff like this never happens here, and then for it to happen to someone we know?" She glances down. "*Knew*."

Noah says nothing. He doesn't know you and he never knew you, only the version he gleaned from stories. I painted you in the best light I could, but Ari couldn't resist getting her digs in when the opportunity arose. You weren't her favorite person to begin with, and you didn't do yourself any favors by breaking my heart. I'm sure Noah sees through it though. He's good at reading between the lines. You were too.

"Anyway, are there *any* leads?" Ari asks, changing the subject.

I sigh, releasing a lungful of tension. "I wouldn't know. I kind of want to call his parents, but I don't want to overstep."

Ari scoffs. "You were married to the man for almost five years and you've known him since you were fourteen. You have every right to call and ask what's going on. Screw what they think."

If only it were that easy.

I have nothing but love for your parents despite no longer being in touch. I'll reach out at some point to offer my sympathies, but not today. I imagine they're raw, and the last person they want to hear from is their former daughter-in-law.

"I just had a thought," Ari says. "Remember a couple of years ago when Ian volunteered to chaperone his AP History class on a trip to St. Louis? And you wanted to tag along and he said you couldn't because they had enough volunteers?"

"Someone needed to stay back with Lucy," I say.

"Is that what he said?" she asks.

"Kennels are expensive, and we'd just replaced the alternator in my car."

"But he had money for a hotel room ..." she says. "He paid for it from his own pocket, right? Because he wanted to make sure the kids could go to some extra museum or something?"

"He split the cost with a couple of the other teachers," I say.

"Didn't one of them back out at the last minute?" she asks, brows lifted. "I swear you told me that."

"Jeannie McNamara's mother was in hospice," I say. "She had no choice. By the way, what are you trying to imply?"

"That maybe if you stop making excuses for him for two seconds, you might realize that the signs were there all along." Ari crosses her arms in her lap, shoulders squared with me.

"Signs for what?" I ask.

"That he was up to something," she says. "That maybe he wasn't as perfect as you always thought? That maybe he wasn't always giving you the full story? That there might have been more going on than you realized?"

"I think I'd know my own husband," I say. I resist the

urge to scoff and remind her we were together for twenty years.

"And what about all those grad courses he was taking? All those night classes semester after semester, with no degree to show for it?" she asks.

I don't need to explain to her that you took a few terms off here or there and that graduate degrees take years to finish when you're chipping away at them one class at a time.

"The man is dead. Are you really going to criticize his academic shortcomings?" My voice is higher, louder than I intended.

We trade a hard stare for a moment, a silent standoff.

"It's tragic," Noah finally speaks, his gaze secured on me as he cuts through the tension with his placid attempt to moderate. "Regardless of the fanfare and excitement coming from our end of the table, I hope you don't think we're making light of any of this."

He reaches across the table, navigating through white boxes of fried rice and chicken, and he places his hand—which is soft like the powdery insides of a latex glove—over mine.

Sometimes I think he *likes* me, but as my boss and a new dentist with a budding reputation to protect, he's never once acted on it—thank goodness. I never wanted to have to explain that I was waiting for you to come around. He's too pragmatic to understand.

"Speak for yourself," Ari says, getting up from the table to take her dish to the sink. She swats her hand at him. "Ian was a selfish prick. Maybe now you can finally start moving on."

The small space is engulfed in a quietude so heavy it

sinks into my shoulders, rendering me motionless as I lean back in my seat.

"What is wrong with me?" she asks with a self-directed sneer. "That was a shitty and insensitive thing to say. I just mean, maybe now you can find someone who will treat you better. Someone who'll actually appreciate you."

Ari peers at the empty plate in her hands.

"I'm horrible at this kind of thing ... death," she adds. "I never know the right thing to say. Sorry if I'm all over the place."

I don't fault her for any of it.

She's the kind of person who laughs at funerals and cracks jokes in uncomfortable situations. You always thought she was excessively sardonic and coldhearted, but I've been around her long enough to see that that side of her is nothing more than a coat of emotional armor.

On the inside, she's as vulnerable and sensitive and full of heart as anyone else. It's too bad you never got to experience that side of her, but it was always easier for me to keep the two of you separate.

"It's okay." I lean across the table and top off her wine glass to show her there are no hard feelings.

"Shoot," she says as she watches me. "I can't stay, babe. I have to let my mom's dog out. She's on her fifth cruise of the year. The woman can sail all over the world on luxury cruise liners but God forbid she opens her Givenchy pocketbook for a proper pet sitter."

"No worries," I tell her.

She leans in, giving me a quick side hug. "Call me if you need anything, okay? I mean it. I don't care what time it is. My phone's always on for you."

"I know," I say. "Thank you."

She heads toward the door, stepping into her neon cross

trainers before snatching her bag off the console table. Ari's a vision in blue, still dressed in her dental hygienist scrubs. It means the world that she came straight here after work, not bothering to stop at home for a quick change.

Before she leaves, she turns back and offers an apologetic wave, lips pursed.

"Everything's going to be okay," she says. It's rare for Ariadne to offer any sentimental (if not cliché) words of advice. She isn't the world's most optimistic woman, as you know. "We'll get you through this."

Her attention moves to Noah, then back to me, and with that, she's gone.

The door closes with a firm click, and I look to Noah, who's dabbing the corners of his mouth with a paper napkin, so polite. You were always proper like that. Over-dressed and well-mannered was the unspoken Damiani family motto. In all our years together, I think I saw your father in jeans all of three or four times.

I miss your parents.

Your mother reached out once, after the divorce papers had been filed, and I ran into your father with a few of his golfing buddies at the Mexican restaurant in town a few months ago. I think it was more awkward for them than for me. You were their son, their loyalty naturally belonged to you. But they also loved me like a daughter and love—in any form—doesn't just go away, it doesn't dissolve into thin air.

Your mother didn't say this explicitly, but I think she disagreed with your decision. Your father, if you're curious, offered nothing but avoided eye contact and small talk about the weather as we'd had a massive heatwave that day. He's always been one to deflect and change subjects that are too uncomfortable for him. I was glad he didn't ignore me or look through me the way you look at a former acquaintance who has since become a stranger. That would've stung.

Before we parted ways, I never had a chance to tell them what they meant to me, and I regret that. If it weren't for them, I might never have known what a lasting, functional marriage looked like or how a "normal" family environment operates.

That was one of the things I loved most about you, Ian.

Everything about your life was ordinary in the best of ways.

Your parents didn't fight. Your house was always clean and smelled permanently of cinnamon potpourri. You had a dog and a cat and an older sister who didn't make your life a living hell. Your parents had stable, white-collar jobs and your mom drove a Chrysler minivan until you left for college. You never smelled of second-hand smoke and your clothes were always wrinkle-free and dryer-fresh. You were amazing at baseball and soccer and your parents never missed a game, whether it was home or hours away.

You had the perfect family, and I was blessed to be a part of it. I'd never experienced so much love and inclusivity. The Damiani home became *my* home. Even during our college years, when everyone was homesick for their childhood bedrooms, I was homesick for your mother's chicken cacciatore and your father's dry sense of humor and the way the hall by the laundry room smelled after your mother had just switched a load of white towels into the dryer—Downy April Fresh with a hint of chlorine bleach.

But I digress.

From where you are now, I'm sure you know these things.

"You need to eat something," Noah says as he clears the table.

"Not hungry." My stomach is as hard as a rock, braced to reject anything I might attempt to offer it.

He pours what's left of one of the wine bottles down the sink, his back to me. I shouldn't be drinking with my meds anyway. It could cause seizures and black outs. It says so right there on the labels, in neon yellow stickers with bold print.

"I can't imagine what's going through your mind. I wish I had some sage advice for you, but I've never lost anyone close to me before."

"It's enough that you're here," I say. If he wasn't, I'd probably be poring over old photo albums of us while our wedding video played on the TV screen in the background.

Remember our wedding dance and how we practiced every night for an hour the month leading up to the big day? You wanted it to be perfect. And it was. Every choreographed step, every camera flash, every grin plastered on the faces of our friends and family as they watched you twirl me and toss me while the live band performed a medley of swing songs.

I rise from the table and place what's left of the food cartons into the fridge where they'll likely remain untouched. It was kind of Noah to spring for dinner like that, and I don't want to come off unappreciative.

"You want to take a walk? Maybe get some air?" Noah asks when we're finished cleaning up a few minutes later. It doesn't take long to clean a kitchen so compact it could fit in an RV. It's not like the kitchen we used to share in our house on Blue Jay Lane. There's no island, no stainless-steel hood vent. No oversized side-by-side refrigerator humming between built-in cupboards and cabinets, ready to spit crushed ice with the press of a button. "It's kind of chilly, but I've got a jacket in my car I could throw on."

In many ways, it's like someone else's kitchen and I'm just borrowing it for now ...only "now" has turned into an indefinite and non-specified amount of time.

I contemplate his offer for all of three seconds before saying, "I think I'm going to stay in tonight."

Noah lifts a dark brow. "Are you sure?"

You were never a worrier, Ian. I loved that about you. You were a doer. A restless soul. A fearless embracer of change, taking on every plot twist life threw at you as if it were an adventure. That was the Sagittarius in you.

Noah yawns, covering his mouth with the back of his hand.

"You should go home," I say. "Get some rest."

Noah lingers in front of the kitchen sink for a moment before dragging a hand through his short, dark hair.

"Yeah, all right," he says. His eyes lift to mine. "I'll have my phone on all night if you need anything. And if you want tomorrow off—or the rest of the week—take it. Take all the time you need."

"Appreciate it," I say, leaving it at that. As of now, I fully intend to be at work in the morning, but I'm not psychic. I'm not sure what tomorrow will bring.

None of this feels real yet, and honestly I'm still waiting for reality to sink its teeth deeper into me, all the way to my marrow.

I escort Noah the full five steps to the door, standing back as he slips on his shoes and checks his pockets for his phone and keys. He's an organized type and there's something deliberate about this, like he doesn't want to go yet, and I wish he would because if he asks me if I'm okay one more time ...

"Thanks for dinner," I say, arms folded as I lean against the wall. "And thanks for coming by."

"Dove, of course," he says, eyes squinted almost as though my show of gratitude offends him.

We exchange wordless goodbyes as he leaves, and I lock up behind him.

It's funny—growing up in Lambs Grove, no one ever locked their doors at night, but ever since moving to this apartment and living alone for the first time in my life, I've made a quick habit of it.

Making my way to my room, I take a seat on the floor beside the bed and fish the wooden memento box from beneath the box springs. It's the mahogany one you made in your high school woodshop class with Mr. Pierson, the one with your initials cauterized into the bottom. A minute later, I'm flicking through stacks of old photos of us as a myriad of your things surround me on the floor. Faded shirts. Ties. Your watch. Ticket stubs. A dried prom boutonniere.

Grabbing the empty bottle of your cologne next to my left ankle, I lift the nozzle to my nose and inhale your scent, dragging it into my lungs again and again until I can no longer smell it.

The fact that someone wanted to kill you is one that I can't wrap my head around. You were smart and kind and educated, involved in your community and your parents' church. You went above and beyond for your students, put in long hours without so much as a single complaint. You never forgot a birthday and always made sure to equally divide Mother's Day amongst your mother, my mother, and all the grandmothers. Your best friends were the same ones you'd had since childhood, and I've always thought that said a lot about the kind of person you were—loyal, nostalgic, dependable, and reliable.

I can't imagine anyone feeling such animosity toward you that it would drive them to take your life.

It had to be random ... that's the *only* logical explanation.

This had to have been the work of an opportunist—maybe the kind of opportunist who swoops in like a vulture to feed on the remains of her best friend's marriage?

Rising, I fish my car keys from the bowl by the door.

I'm going for a drive.

3

DOVE

SHE SAW ME.

But in my defense, I wasn't trying to be inconspicuous. I wasn't trying to sneak by unnoticed. It's not illegal. I wasn't harassing her. I would never do those things. This isn't about me getting revenge, this is about you getting justice by any means necessary.

I slowed to a crawl when I got to the house, trying to grab a quick mental snapshot before speeding off. But all I gleaned was that she was home—evidently alone—and she was peering out the living room window, her body poorly masqueraded behind a curtain panel.

Hands gripping the wheel, I turn off Blue Jay Lane and head back to my side of town, the window half rolled down and the radio tuned to some Top 40 station.

I find it interesting that your parents aren't there to console her—or to be consoled by her. If we were still together, your parents and I would've been inseparable from the second news broke.

It makes me wonder what they think of her, if they find it odd that you spent twenty years with me and the instant you bring someone new into the picture, you're mysteriously murdered. Of course Michael and Lori are too kindhearted to make their opinions known to anyone but themselves, but I can imagine the connection they're drawing and I can imagine it matches the one I'm drawing myself.

In less than ten minutes, I'm back home.

I strip out of the day's clothes and wash up before crawling beneath the chilled covers of my lumpy used mattress. My thoughts go to her. To Kirsten. The way she peered out from behind the curtain as if the backlit living room wouldn't give her silhouette away. It's like a cat that thinks it's hiding beneath a chair, tail sticking out to give it away.

I stare at the ceiling for several endless minutes, mind spinning, before I relent and grab my phone off my nightstand. The screen flashes to life and I wince as I dial down the brightness and tap in my code. A second later, I type your name into a search engine to see if there are any new developments. The top result in an article on CNN, but the timestamp shows it was posted earlier this morning. No updates. I check the articles on the three local news stations in the area, but the information is stale and recycled.

They still don't know who killed you and they haven't released an official cause of death.

I can only pray it was quick.

I don't like to think about you suffering.

A yawn hits me out of nowhere and the phone turns to

dead weight in my hands. Looks like I might get some sleep tonight after all.

In the seconds before retiring for the night, I decide to perform one last search ...

... on Kirsten.

Why I never thought to do it before is beyond me. Then again, I've always taken people at face value. The first time we met was when she came to deliver some mail of mine at my paint-n-sip and introduced herself as my business neighbor, the owner of Best Life Yoga. Everything about her was Zen and graceful and centered, the way a yoga instructor should be. We met again after that at a mixer for local business owners. She ran up to me, excited to see a familiar face, and we talked all night like two people who'd known each other their whole lives.

Our close friendship spanned two years, and not once did I ever think she would do what she did. *Not once.*

You think you know someone, Ian ...

She duped us both, I'm afraid.

I type "Kirsten Best" into the search bar and the results assume I'm searching for "Kirsten Dunst." Sighing, I type in "Kirsten Best Detroit, Michigan" and try again. Results populate the screen in seconds, and I start at the top with an unused LinkedIn account, before continuing to an article about a legal aid under scrutiny for embezzling—the photo does not match. The third result is a memorial. I click on the headline.

A black and white photo of a good-looking man with dark hair and dimples, unquestionably too young for an obituary, takes the upper left-hand corner. I scroll down and find his name—Adam Nicholas Meade. And then his age—twenty-seven. His obituary is brief, mentioning that he grew up in Detroit, worked as a welder, and passed unexpectedly.

There's no mention of parents or siblings, just that he had a lot of friends ...

... and that he is survived by his *fiancée*, Kirsten Best, of Detroit, Michigan.

4

DOVE

I TAKE an early lunch on Tuesday and stop by the pharmacy on Cardinal to pick up a refill on my medications,
though half of me is tempted to wean off them. I don't like
being so anesthetized, so unable to properly mourn you or
experience the deep void of this loss.

If it doesn't feel real, will I ever be able to accept it?

There was this book I read once, not long after the
divorce, *Feel It to Heal It, Girl!*. You always hated self-help
books, especially the ones with the overenthusiastic titling,
but I was desperate, and the book called to me from its
polished oak shelf in the back corner of the bookstore where
down-on-their-luck souls could browse in peace.

Settling in line, I count two people ahead of me, so I
reach for my phone to kill some time.

I can't stop thinking of that obituary I found last night.
I've read it so many times I've lost track. In fact, the thing
haunted me in my dreams. As soon as I pulled into the staff

parking lot at Benoit Dental this morning, I called the police station and asked to speak to the detective on your case. They gave me someone's voicemail and I've yet to hear back.

I don't want to say the Lambs Grove police are incompetent, but they're not exactly experienced in the whole murder-solving department.

I pull up the obituary on my phone again. By now Adam's black-and-white grinning image is imbedded into my mind. I can't close my eyes without it taking center stage. I attempted to dig up what I could on him last night as well, but all I found were a few honor roll mentions from his community college days as well as a new hire announcement at Van Wyk Welding in Detroit. Other than that, the man didn't have so much as a Facebook profile.

How can you be best friends with someone for two years and not once mention you had a dead fiancé back home? One that died young and unexpectedly? I ended up shelling out fifty dollars (that I had no business spending) to some shady-looking website so I could take a look at his death certificate.

Are you ready for this, Ian?

It claimed his cause of death is "homicide."

Homicide.

And on top of that, some quick math put a mere six months between the time Adam Meade died *suspiciously* and the time Kirsten opened Best Life Yoga in Lambs Grove, Kansas.

"Next?" The woman behind the pharmacy counter calls out and I step ahead.

"Dove Damiani," I say before fishing in my purse for my wallet. The insurance Noah provides for us at the office isn't as great as the insurance I had when we were married, but it's better than nothing. I wouldn't be able to afford these if I had to pay cash each month.

"Dove?" A woman's voice beckons from behind me. "Is that you?"

Turning, I find your mother standing a couple of feet away. She looks smaller than the last time I saw her, more delicate, and the creases beneath her eyes have deepened. Gone is her trademark matte red lip and hair-sprayed hair, and in their place is nude pink lip balm and a low ponytail twisted into a bun.

"Lori." My mouth goes dry. I wasn't expecting this. "H ... hi."

I want to go to her, to wrap her in a hug the way you would want me to, but I find myself paralyzed as I think about everything that has changed, everything that has happened. This interaction means different things to each of us.

"Oh, Dove ..." she tries to speak but her lips tremble.

I've never seen your mother so frail, so colorless. A shapeless beige cardigan hangs off her shoulders, the sleeves running past her wrists. I can't tell if she's wearing leggings or if they're simply tight sweatpants, but this is not the Lori Damiani I knew.

Your mom tries to speak again, only nothing comes out and a second later thick tears begin to roll down her cheeks.

Ignoring my earlier instincts, I decide to comfort her.

It's what she needs.

And it's what you would want.

Throwing my arms around her, I inhale the familiar-yet-fading scent of her spicy Thierry Mugler perfume and let her cry into my shoulder.

I should have reached out before now, but I didn't want to bother your parents and I didn't know how it would've been received. I know now that my worries were silly.

I was a part of your family for almost twenty years, and in a strange way, I get the sense that I'll always be a part of your family, especially from here on out. They associate me with you and while I can't fill your void, I can still serve as a reminder of those beautiful, happy years we all once shared.

"It's horrible, isn't it?" she asks, her voice a whisper.

My eyes are dry but my chest is cannonball heavy. "The worst."

I release your mom and step back a small way. Our eyes lock and while we say nothing, there's a silent exchange happening, an understanding of sorts. I always had an unspoken connection with her since the beginning. And I know you know this, but I've always been more mothered by your mom than my own.

Losing her was one of the worst parts of the divorce.

"How are you holding up, dear?" she asks, wiping away her tears before running her hand along my arm. "Are you doing all right?"

My lip quivers for a second. There's so much love radiating from her in this moment it's almost enough to overpower the numbness.

"I'm still in disbelief," I say.

She clucks her tongue. "We all are."

"Dove?" the woman behind the counter calls me back.

"One second," I excuse myself from your mom, pay my co-insurance, and place the stapled paper bag in my purse.

"Are you free tonight?" your mom asks when I'm done. "We'd love to have you over, catch up a bit. We're about to go through photos for the funeral and I'd love your help with that. If there are any of your own you'd like to include ..."

The fact that she wants me to have a part in the planning of your funeral is all the confirmation I need to know that I still mean something to her.

"Of course," I don't let her finish. I'm one step ahead of her. "I'll be there. What time?"

"Sometime around six?" She offers a teary sniffle before coming in for one more embrace.

"I'll be there," I say before heading back to the office.

———

"DOVE DAMIANI?" A woman says my name the instant I shut my car door. When I turn to face her, I'm met with a police badge in my face.

"Detective Rhonda Reynolds," she says, lowering the shiny shield. Her bushy blonde-gray hair blows in the October breeze and her eyes soften as she examines me. "I need to ask you some questions regarding Ian Damiani."

I glance around. Fortunately there are no patients around to witness this. I can only imagine how this might look, the rumors it would spark.

"Right. Of course," I say. "I just need to finish up a few claims and then I can come down to the station if that works?"

She winces. "I'm afraid not. I think it's best we talk now."

Detective Reynolds points to the idling, unmarked Impala behind her. "Why don't you climb in. I'll give you a ride. Take you back when it's over."

I resist the urge to make a face, to show how taken aback I am at this. "I don't want to inconvenience you, Detective. I can just drive myself and meet you there?"

She chuckles once and the lines around her eyes

deepen. "You're not under arrest, Ms. Damiani, if that's what you're worried about. This is standard procedure. A courtesy if you will."

My hands tremble at my sides. What is it about being in the presence of authority that makes the most innocent of people wrought with guilt?

"All right then," I tell her with a smile. "I just need to let the front desk know I'm stepping out this afternoon."

"Perfect." She leans against the driver's side door, checking her phone as I head inside. When I return, she has the rear passenger door cocked open.

I slide in, my palms damp against the leather seats, and the detective climbs into the front seat. The radio plays some eighties song, upbeat and synthesized.

"You comfortable back there?" she asks as we pull out of the parking lot. I'm beginning to think Detective Reynolds is too nice. I only hope it's not an act. If it's an act, that means she thinks I'm guilty and she wants to make me comfortable so I'll open up.

"Let me know if you get too hot or too cold." Her reflecting smiles at me from the rearview.

"Will do." I clear my throat, sinking back as far as I can and praying no one sees me like this.

I take a deep breath, reminding myself that once she asks her questions and pieces her facts together, she'll realize I would never do anything to hurt you, Ian.

Never, never, never.

5

DOVE

"APPRECIATE you meeting with me on such short notice, Ms. Damiani," Detective Reynolds says as she pulls up the chair across from me. She's still smiling, almost like she hasn't stopped, but it feels genuine. She places a yellow legal pad in front of her, before uncapping her pen. Her gaze drifts to my hands for no more than two seconds, like she's studying them for a moment, and then she returns her attention to me.

"Of course." I say. I try to stay chipper, try to ignore the fact that I rode here in the back of an unmarked police car. I try not to focus on the fact that my Civic is on the other side of town in the clinic parking lot. I also try to remind myself that Detective Reynolds promised this is standard procedure. *A courtesy.* "Are there any new developments?"

She scribbles something on the upper righthand corner, a date I believe. "I'm so sorry, Ms. Damiani. It's an active investigation, so I'm not at liberty to share anything at this time."

"You said you got my message," I say.

"Yes. I sure did. Thank you for that." She doesn't look up from her notebook as she peruses her notes. She reminds me of an aunt. A sweet-natured, wholesome aunt. I wish I could ask her what made her get into this line of work, but that's neither here nor there.

"Have you done any checking into that yet?" I ask.

"You know, we've got a lot of ground to cover here," she offers an apologetic grimace, the point of her pen rapping against her paper as she peers across the plastic folding table between us, "so why don't I take it from here and start with a few questions? I'll try to make this as quick and painless as possible."

"I'm happy to help any way that I can." I sit straighter, hands folded in my lap. My palms dampen for some odd reason.

"Before we begin, can I get you some water? Coffee?" she asks.

"I'm fine, but thank you." I clear my parched throat, suddenly wishing I'd asked for some water, but I'll survive.

"Okay, then let's get started." She flips to another page in her notepad, eyes squinting as she reads something. More notes, maybe? "So I see here that you and Mr. Damiani divorced in March of this year, is that correct?"

"Yes. That's when it was final. *Legally.*"

"Would you say things ending amicably or was there tension?" Her blue-gray eyes rest on mine.

"He asked for the divorce. I didn't. But there wasn't any tension. We didn't fight or anything," I say. "He told me he wanted out of the marriage, and I packed up my things and left. I'm not really the dramatic type. After that, we communicated through our attorneys."

Her brows meet in confusion. "If there wasn't any tension, why would you only communicate through your attorneys? Seems to me that'd get expensive pretty fast, and on a teacher's salary no less."

She has a valid point, one I can't deny.

"That's what he wanted. He thought it'd be easier for both of us that way."

"Easier how?" she asks, her cadence light and inquisitive. I imagine she's trying to keep this from feeling like an interrogation.

It's a question I never had a chance to ask you, so I could only surmise. I imagine you didn't want to talk to me because you couldn't stand to witness the pain in my eyes or experience the hurt in my voice.

"We'd been together since high school," I say. "I think he wanted a clean break."

She jots something down, silent for a beat. "Okay, so back to the divorce. You said he was the one who wanted it, not you?"

"Correct." I nod.

"Would it be fair to say that you still had feelings for him after the divorce?" She rubs her lips together, face pained as she waits for my response.

"Of course. He was my first love. You don't stop loving someone, not like that." I snap my fingers. "I'll always love him."

Her thin lips press into a flat line. "So it must have bothered you that he was able to move on so quickly ..."

"It wasn't the best feeling in the world, no, but from what I understand, it was a casual thing. They were having fun. *Rebound*. She was a rebound."

"A rebound who also happened to live with the victim in the marital house the two of you shared," she says before splaying her hand. "Forgive the bluntness."

"Yes."

"It couldn't have been easy for you," she says, "watching your ex-husband move another woman into your house so quickly after leaving you."

I begin to say something and then stop. If I say no, she'll know I'm lying. If I say yes, it will make me look like a vengeful ex-wife and that couldn't be further from the case. I realize now they're looking for motives, which means they're not closer to finding out what happened to you than they were yesterday.

"And isn't it true that the victim's new girlfriend is a former friend of yours?" she continues, leaning in. I'm dying to know who's feeding her this information. "I imagine that has to be pretty infuriating. I know how I'd feel in your shoes, that's for sure."

My skin is hot and suddenly the room is ten times smaller than it was a few moments ago, but I look Detective Reynolds in her kind, hooded eyes. I want so badly to feel like I'm having a conversation with an aunt or a concerned friend, but then I remember why we're really here: to find out who murdered you.

She has a job to do.

Her kindness and courtesy and sympathy is all a part of that, no doubt.

"Kirsten *was* a very close friend of mine," I say. "I won't sit here and tell you it was easy, but what good would it have done for me to ruminate on it? To sit around being angry about something that was beyond my control?"

"So you didn't obsess over Ian or Kirsten or their relationship in any capacity?" she asks, her tone neutral.

"*No*," I say, voice louder than I intended. I'm getting defensive. I need to cool it.

"Then why did you drive past the victim's home every day for months?" she asks, point blank.

I try to respond, but the words get stuck.

I didn't see that coming.

Yes, Ian. I drove by every day, twice a day, but only because I wanted to make sure you were okay. If ever I saw something amiss, I'd know I needed to step in. But the flower beds were always weeded, the wreath on the front door was always swapped out according to the season, and the lawn remained manicured.

"You've been talking to Kirsten," I say. Of course. It makes sense. She's trying to point their suspicions in my direction to take the heat off of herself.

Reynolds doesn't confirm nor deny. "Why did you drive by the house, Dove? You're lucky they didn't report you for stalking or harassment. I'm not going to judge you for that, because that's not my job, but as a detective, I have to say it doesn't paint you in the best light here. So please, help me understand."

"Beech Road has been closed for repairs for months. Blue Jay Lane was on my commute," I say. "Besides, it's a main road. And it was on the city's detour route. But I never stopped by. I never bothered them."

"Fair enough," she says, nodding. "But if you weren't ruminating on your marriage, why did you keep photos of you and the victim in your apartment? Our officers counted four framed photos of the two of you in your living room alone."

Heat flushes my ears and my throat is too dry for me to swallow away the lump forming in real time.

Two uniformed Lambs Grove officers knocked on my

door at six AM yesterday morning. I invited them in and after asking me a few brief questions about you, they gave me the news. They couldn't have been in my apartment more than five minutes at most, but it turns out five minutes was enough time for them to get a good look at the place.

"The pictures remind me of better times," I say with as much guiltless confidence as I can muster. I can't let this shake me. I know what she's thinking, and she's wrong. "They give ... they *gave* me hope."

"Hope that what? That he'd change his mind and come back to you?" Her words are infused with such softness they take the tiniest edge off my defensiveness.

Damn, she's good at this.

"Yes." My gaze flicks to hers, and I give her a stronger, "*Yes*."

"Over the past six months, did the Ian ever give any indication that he planned to leave his girlfriend and return to you?"

I rub my lips together. "No. He did not."

I don't elaborate. I don't tell her that when you know someone inside and out, know all their whims and moods and tendencies, their heart and soul, sometimes you just *know*.

Detective Reynolds wouldn't understand.

I know that you were going to come back to me eventually.

I know you were going to get bored with Kirsten and her yoga pants and organic perfumes and tiny little micro car, and you were going to yearn for that nostalgic familiarity that you only ever had with me.

She was your retreat, your escape from reality, a brief break from the monotony that dulled your spirited soul.

But *I* was your home.

And everyone needs a home.

"Look, I'm not trying to back you into a corner here, Ms. Damiani," she says with a merciful sigh. "But woman to woman, I can tell you that I've been in your shoes. I know what it's like when your husband leaves you for another woman. Not only that, but a *beautiful* woman."

I don't like what she's implying.

Those kinds of things might matter to the average person, but I'm not the average person. I've never cared about looks—mine or anyone else's. I've always valued inner beauty over outer.

That said, I get what Detective Reynolds is getting at.

Kirsten isn't pretty.

She's stunning.

With her half-Puerto Rican, half-Swedish heritage, she has the kind of exotic looks you don't find in places like Lambs Grove. Full lips, angled chin, big brown eyes with a curtain of thick, velvety lashes that required not so much as a swipe of mascara. Long and lean from hours of yoga, she had the kind of physique most women would kill for—but not me.

I couldn't kill a spider if I tried. I've never had the heart.

"Were you aware that the Ian was killed on what would have been your fifth wedding anniversary?" she asks next.

I swallow. "Yes. The timing is ... upsetting, as you can imagine."

"And did you happen to know that the fifth anniversary is typically commemorated with some sort of wood gift?" she asks.

"Now you're reaching." I keep my tone light and read-just my posture after realizing I've deflated a bit. "Yes, it would've been our wooden anniversary. Yes, he was found in the woods. But you're wrong. It's a sick coincidence, but that's all. Maybe ... maybe I'm being set up?"

Reynolds doesn't laugh at my theory. She rests her pen and gives me her full attention. "And who would want to do that?"

I shrug. "I don't know ... maybe Kirsten?"

"Why her?" Her brows knit. She's curious, but she isn't on board with this yet. "She has what you wanted. Why would she want to get rid of him and pin it on you?"

"Again, I don't know. Maybe ... maybe this is what she does?" I stop short of using any terms like *black widow* because I want to be taken seriously. "You said you got my voice mail earlier. Did you check into the dead fiancé thing?"

"Yep. I've got someone looking into that right now actually." She flips to another page in her notepad. "Oh, before I forget ... your brother ... Slade Jensen."

"What about him?"

"It says here he was recently released from state prison after doing some time for breaking and entering." She glances down. "Amongst other things."

"That's correct."

"Have the two of you been in touch since his release?" she asks.

I shake my head. "No. He stole some things from Ian and me a few years back and we cut off all contact after that. We tried to help him several different times, giving him money and helping him find places to live, but he could never sort his life out. The last straw was when he broke into our house when we were at work and took a bunch of things to pawn for drugs. Irreplaceable things."

I never forgave him for pawning your uncle's rare coin

collection or the heart-shaped diamond necklace you got me for Christmas our senior year of high school.

She's quiet as she takes notes.

"I don't even know where he's living these days," I say. "My mom probably does."

"And your mom is," she scans the bottom of her page, "Cathie-Ann Jensen."

I nod. "I can give you her number."

"That'd be great. Thank you."

"I get that you're trying to narrow down suspects, but I can assure you my brother would have no reason to kill Ian," I say.

"And how do you know that? Since the two of you haven't spoken in a while?"

"Because Slade—drug problems aside—is a gentle person. Not a violent bone in his body. He steals things so he can buy heroin, but he doesn't hurt people. And he definitely wouldn't have any reason to hurt Ian."

"That you know of." She angles her head almost as if to say, *"I've seen some things in my day."*

I sigh. "Correct."

She scrawls a few more sentences before dropping her pen and leaning back in her chair, but this can't be it ...

We haven't gotten to Kirsten yet.

"I'm sorry, can we go back to Kirsten's dead fiancé for a second?" I ask. "Don't you find it odd that the man dies under mysterious circumstances and within months she moves from Detroit to Lambs Grove—essentially the middle of nowhere—and starts a new life for herself?"

"Odd?" she asks. "Or tragic?"

I don't mean to, but I make a face.

"Not to discredit your theory because it's definitely something we're checking into, but when you've been doing what I do for as long as I have, you see a lot of tragedy. People are allowed fresh starts. It doesn't make them criminals. She deserves the benefit of the doubt just as much as you do. Remember that."

"I don't disagree. I just think it's odd, given the circumstances, that her last boyfriend is murdered and the first guy she dates after that is also murdered." I lean forward. "We were friends for *two years*, and not *once* did she tell me about her fiancé's death. Tell me that isn't shady."

Reynolds stares through me, unblinking as she digests my words.

"Valid point," Detective Reynolds caps her pen before placing it aside and rising from her chair. "Anyway, I think that's all I need for now. If anything else comes up, we have each other's numbers."

I stand, slowly exhaling a lungful of relief despite knowing that I had nothing to do with this.

"Meet me up front by the reception desk. I'll be up there shortly to take you back," she says, gathering her things.

———

I DON'T HEAD into the office when I get back. With all the thoughts swimming in my head and the emotional rollercoaster I rode over the past hour, I'm in no shape to file insurance claims, so I head home to gather some photos for your mom and to start getting ready so I can make it to your parents' house by six.

I wish I could ask your parents what they think of Kirsten, but I know it wouldn't be appropriate given the circumstances. If I get the chance tonight, though, I'm going to tell them all about her and her dead fiancé. They deserve to know who she really is so they can protect themselves.

Maybe I couldn't protect you, Ian, but I can protect your family.

And I will.

I promise you, I'll keep them safe from her.

6

DOVE

"LET ME TAKE THOSE, LORI." I gather the stack of your suits and shirts and ties from your mother's arms and lay them neatly across the back of a floral armchair in the sitting room before taking a seat on the settee.

I'd only been here a handful of minutes when Kirsten showed up.

I stayed back, planting myself in the far corner of the living room next to the piano, watching the awkward exchange. Apparently your mother told her to come by tomorrow with the suits, but she dropped by tonight ... unannounced.

Was she watching me?

Did she time it perfectly?

Was she afraid of what I might say to your family about her?

Thank goodness they didn't invite her to stay. That would have been beyond uncomfortable for everyone involved. She couldn't have been here more than two minutes before they thanked her and sent her on her way. They even told her when the funeral service was going to be and your dad said, "We hope you can make it."

"We hope you can make it?"

Who says that to their son's girlfriend?

Maybe you didn't bring her around much? I could see you not wanting them to get attached—especially your niece and nephew. And if the two of you weren't serious, there's no point in doing that whole song and dance.

Your mother takes the spot beside me, reaching for a stack of photos I had printed at the one-hour photo before coming here.

"I probably brought too many, but I wanted you to have copies of everything I had," I say. Most of these are photos from college, from various road trips and vacations you and I enjoyed over the years, but I imagined she would want them.

"Don't be ridiculous, sweetheart. I'm so glad you did this. So thoughtful of you." She places an arm around my shoulders and squeezes me against her. "You know, there aren't a lot of people like you in this world. I told Ian that, too, when he told us he was wanting ..." She doesn't finish her sentence, she doesn't have to. "I tried to talk him out of it. I told him he's going to regret it one of these days." Her lip trembles. "I can't help but think if you two were still together, this never would have happened."

I don't tell her we have no way of knowing that. She's allowed to believe whatever she needs to believe.

"The police questioned me today ... about a lot of things ... but we talked about Kirsten," I say.

She's silent for a moment. "They asked us quite a few questions about her as well. I have to admit, Michael and I thought she was nothing more than a summer *fling,* so we didn't try too hard to get to know her. I'm kicking myself for that now."

"Are the police saying anything?" I ask. "About Kirsten?"

Lori lets her hands fall in her lap. "They're not saying a whole lot. Just that they're looking into everyone."

"Yeah." I exhale. "They were trying to paint me as a jilted ex-wife who wanted revenge."

Lori turns to me, eyes watery, and then she laughs.

Your mother *laughs.* Hysterical. Uproarious.

"Oh, my," she says, eyes wet. "They don't know you at all, do they?" She takes my hand in hers. "I know you would *never* do anything to Ian. In fact, I told the police that you were the last person who would want to hurt him."

My shoulders relax as I bask in the relief that washes over me in real time, grateful I can actually feel it.

"He was strangled," she says a second later. "I don't know if you knew that or not."

Tightness fills my chest, and an image of you gasping for air fills my mind despite my attempts to will it to go away. "I didn't."

"The police are keeping a lot of the details private, you know, for the investigation," she says.

"What else do they have to go off? Any actual evidence?"

"There were shoe prints," she says. "Nike sneakers, I believe."

"Male or female?"

"They aren't sure yet. They said they could've belonged to a male with smaller feet or a female with larger feet. Still waiting to hear back on that."

"Any DNA? Did he fight back? Was there anything

beneath his fingernails?" I've been watching too many crime shows, I know. "I'm sorry. I just want to find out who did this."

And why.

"They've gathered everything they could and sent it off to the state crime lab, that much I know," your mom says. She releases my hand and reaches for a stack of photos, slowly flipping through them, lingering on one of the two of us in Niagara Falls on our two-year wedding anniversary.

I don't want to tell her this next part, and yet I'm compelled.

They say information is power, but in this case, information might be the difference between life or death.

"Did Ian ever tell you about Kirsten's last boyfriend?" I ask.

Lori turns back to me, one brow lifted. "No. What about him?"

"Fiancé, actually," I correct myself. "He died several years back, when she was living in Detroit. He was murdered."

Your mother gasps as she makes the connection, and then she lets the stack of pictures fall from her hands to the top of the coffee table.

"But why would she ...?" Her voice dissipates. "What reason would she have to ...? It doesn't make sense."

I shrug. "I don't know either. I just thought you should know."

Your mother shivers and her face drains of its color. A moment later, she upswings from the sofa and begins to pace the living room, her fuzzy socks wearing tracks into the plush ivory carpet.

"I didn't mean to upset you, Lori. I only thought you should know ... in case ... for safety reasons. You can't be too

careful with who you let into your life these days. I mean, I
don't think she would be capable of doing anything like that
and what reason would she have, you know? But two in a
row? It's suspicious. And until we know more, I think we—"

"Michael!" Lori calls for her husband. She's never inter-
rupted me before. "Michael, get in here."

Your father appears almost instantaneously, as if he
were waiting in the wings should his wife need him.

"I *knew* it." Your mother throws her hands in the air, her
eyes narrow and face pinched.

Your dad looks to me then back to your mom. He has no
idea what's going on.

"It was Kirsten," your mother says.

I come to a slow standing and lift my palm. "Wait a
minute, Lori, we don't know that for sure."

"What do you mean *it was Kirsten?*" your dad asks.

"Two months ago, remember what I told you? I saw her
at the pharmacy buying pregnancy tests." She buries her
face in her hands.

My stomach drops.

Is it true, Ian? Was she pregnant?

"That doesn't prove anything," he says.

"I know it doesn't," she says. "But if she *is* pregnant, the
child would get *everything.*"

You had a six-figure life insurance policy and a million-
dollar trust fund your grandfather left you after he passed—
one that can't be accessed until next year when you were to
turn thirty-five. Technically, the money would go to your
sister or your parents—whatever you declared in your will
after the divorce (assuming you changed it). But if you have
an heir, everything would go to the child—*and the child's
mother*.

I can't think of a more damning motive than that.

I'm going to be sick.

Before I realize what's going on, your father has his phone pressed to his ear, asking for Detective Reynolds. "Hi, yes. This is Michael Damiani ..."

Your mother clings to his right arm, lifting on her toes to catch the other side of the conversation.

I sit in silence as I listen to him share their theory with the detective, and I can't help but think about the house key I still have. It was a spare that I'd kept in the bottom of my purse for years—ever since that time I locked myself out of the house when you were out of town about a month after we moved in. I'd forgotten about it after I moved out, and when I came across it months later, I decided to keep it in a safe place—mostly for sentimental reasons but also in case I ever needed it again for any reason.

You never know ...

"Thank you, Detective," your father ends the call after sharing this information.

Your mother looks toward me, exhausted, defeated, but mostly terrified.

I hate seeing her in pain.

I hate having theories but no answers.

I hate how long it takes the police to unearth evidence and clues.

I hate how your killer is out there, roaming free ...

Looks like I'm going to be using that key again after all.

7

DOVE

THE CODE on the garage is still our anniversary. You never changed it. Maybe you were busy or it never made it to one of your millions of to-do lists, but I like to think it was an intentional slip.

I park my car in the left stall Wednesday morning, but not before circling the block a couple of times to make sure no one else is around—no unmarked cars or nosy neighbors to be specific. Pulling in, it feels like coming home. To the right is your silver Passat, stock-still as it collects dust. There's a weight in my center when I look to the door. If I sit here a little longer, I can almost convince myself I've gone back in time and I'm two seconds from heading into my home. *Our home.* I picture you standing over a pot of simmering spaghetti sauce and Lucy is two seconds from barreling into me and you've got a bottle of white wine chilling in the fridge as you sing along to the Frank Sinatra station streaming from a Bluetooth speaker by the sink. The ordinary days were some of the best. I wish I realized that at the time.

I don't linger in that memory for too long. I can't afford to.

I checked the Best Life Yoga class schedule online earlier. Kirsten should be starting her eight o'clock class any minute now, which means she'll be occupied on the other side of town for at least another hour.

Climbing out of my car with gloved hands, I make my way to the back entrance and hit the button to close the garage door. Darkness swallows our cars and I retrieve my key from my pocket. There's a chance you changed the locks after I moved out, but if you didn't bother changing the code on the garage, I'm doubtful.

Taking a long, slow breath, I insert the key into the lock and give it a gentle twist.

The lock pops.

The door swings open.

The house is dark, all the curtains pulled.

The scent of this morning's coffee fills my lungs and as I step into the kitchen, it looks like it hasn't been used in days. I imagine Kirsten is too upset to eat. She's probably wasting away, more skin and bones than before.

"Lucy," I call out with a whisper. I suppose it's silly to whisper when no one's home.

I peek my head into the living room and find Lucy curled up on her favorite sofa cushion along with what appears to be one of your t-shirts. She pops her head up when she sees me, climbs down reluctantly, nose low as she approaches me the way she used to approach complete strangers at the dog park.

It breaks my heart.

I place my hand out and let her sniff me. A moment

later her tail wags, faster and faster. And then she rises on her hind legs. Stooping low, I let her lick my face as I scratch her soft ears.

"I missed you," I say before retrieving a treat from my pocket and handing it over. A small rawhide cookie shaped like a cowboy hat that I grabbed from the dog bakery this morning. She gives it a sniff before accepting it and wandering back to her spot.

I try to think of all your hiding spots. You were always putting things in random places. Coins in one spot. Cash stash in another. Loose buttons in a candy dish. I start in the kitchen first, with the junk drawer. It looks the same as it used to, nothing out of the ordinary. I check the cupboards above the lazy Susan next, reaching back until my gloved fingertips brush the tin Beechnut coffee canister. Sliding it out, I pop off the plastic lid and find it shoved full of cash. Small bills mostly. You always liked to keep them on hand in case a Girl Scout came knocking or we needed to tip the pizza delivery man. Carefully, I return the can to its spot in the back of the cabinet and shut the door.

I head to our old room next, then I'll make my way to your office—you never hid anything in the bathrooms or guest room.

Both closet halves are wide open, your suits and cash-mere sweaters a stark contrast against the sea of athleisure that hangs from Kirsten's side. You once told me that you hated the athleisure trend, that wearing black leggings outside of a gym was tacky, amongst other things. It was all Kirsten ever wore—except once, when we had that barbeque. She showed up in a creamy linen romper, sleeveless with tortoiseshell buttons. Lips the color of candy apples. And her hair, which was almost always in a messy topknot, cascaded down her shoulders in shiny dark waves.

You couldn't take your eyes off her all night. Here it was because I thought you couldn't get over how different she looked. I wonder, now, if it was because you couldn't get over how beautiful she looked.

I've never been a jealous woman, Ian, but I got jealous that night. I'm not proud, but sometimes we can't help the way we feel, you know? Sometimes it's too strong to shove away and it overpowers us.

I take a step toward your half of the closet, over-whelmed by the familiar scent that greets me. Everything inside me is dark and heavy, weighted with emotion too deep to surface. I'd give anything to have a good cry. I think it would be good for me. You once told me that after we cry, our brain produces feel-good chemicals, and that's why crying is like a mental cleanse.

I take a seat on your half of the bed. At least I think it's your half. For all I know the two of you switched sides, but I don't want to think about that right now.

Closing my eyes, I pretend for a moment that it's one year ago.

Everything was wonderful then, wasn't it? At least it was for me—aside from having to close down my shop. I had you. I had Lucy. I had our home. I had my friends. I had a life. I had love.

So much love.

It was abundant back then, coming from every which way. But mostly coming from you.

My biggest fear after we split, Ian, was that no one would ever be able to love me the way you did. I never told you that, of course, and I never told Noah or Ari because Ari would've made fun of me and Noah would have put his pragmatic spin on it and told me how wrong I was, but it's the truth.

You loved me for me. You never judged me. You were always there for me. My biggest cheerleader. My soft place to land. My sweet escape. My refuge from the maelstrom that is life.

Until you became that maelstrom ...

But again, I've forgiven you because that's what you do when you love someone.

I sit up from your bed and head to the closet, checking suit coat pockets before searching for that old dusty shoebox you always kept in the back of the top shelf. I pull it down and place it on the top of the dresser, removing the lid to reveal love notes from our high school years, a dried boutonniere from our first prom, and the promise ring you gave me when we turned eighteen, still nestled in its red velvet box.

The fact that you kept all this only confirms what I already knew.

I place it back, ensure the doors are in the same position they were when I came in, and then I smooth out the dip on the comforter. I give the room one last look before heading to your office. The door is closed, so I make a mental note, and I head in, flicking on the overhead light before taking a seat in your leather desk chair.

Your computer is gone, as is your iPad. I imagine the police have confiscated anything that could contain evidence, but they don't know all your secret hiding places. Surely there's something that got left behind.

Rising, I move to your bookshelf, which is filled with thick, dusty historical biographies and tomes galore. You loved to read. You could binge read one of these books in a day if you tried and still make time for things like mowing the lawn, grilling steaks, and making love to your wife.

How you did it all, I'll never know, but I always adored that about you. You never seemed overwhelmed or spread thin—you were always doing your thing. So easy, so free. Living in the moment and enjoying your life.

I scan the rows upon rows of books and remember you had a phone book in here with the middle cut out. You used to keep important things in there like spare keys to your parents' house, birth certificates, and Social Security number cards. It takes me a few tries, but I manage to locate it. The code on the side is still unchanged—our anniversary. It pops open without problem a second later, and I fish around, looking for anything out of the ordinary.

And then I see it.

A black cell phone no bigger than a deck of cards.

My pulse quickens as I examine it. At first glance, it looks like someone's antiquated flip phone—the kind we used to have in high school back in the day. You were sentimental, but we traded our phones in over a decade ago, and you would have no reason to keep a phone like this hidden in your secret book.

I flip it open. I don't recognize the brand.

Pressing the power button, I wait for it to boot up, but it's dead. I decide to slip it into my purse and check into it more after I leave. I'm running out of time and the sooner I can get out of here, the better.

I place the book back on the shelf and head to your desk next. Tugging open drawers, I fish through your files as quickly as I can. Thank goodness you were always so meticulous about keeping things in order.

I find a file labeled DOVE and peek in to find a copy of our divorce decree along with a photo of the two of us from several years ago. Your arm is around me. I'm looking at you. We're both mid-laugh. I think one of your work friends took this. We were at a birthday dinner at Chanderley's, I believe, and the wine was flowing.

Look how happy we were. You can't fake that kind of bliss. We weren't pretending to be in love—we *were* in love.

I tuck it back into place before moving to the next file, labeled ESTATE. Surely you updated this after the divorce, but whether you're leaving everything to your parents or your sister remains to be seen. If Kirsten is pregnant, she can't be very far along. I'd imagine if the changes to your will are recent and line up with the pregnancy, that might be damning in the case against her.

The estate file is thin, only a few pages inside, and I pull out the stapled papers on your legal team's letterhead.

But the date on the cover sheet is over three years old.

Did you not update this after the divorce?

Flicking to the next page, I scan the type until my gaze settles ... on my name.

You didn't change a thing.

Which means ... you left me everything.

This doesn't look good. Not at all. Not with what happened to you.

The scratch of Lucy's claws on hardwood pulls me out of my stupor. She barks next, excited, like someone's home.

Shoving the file drawer shut, I dash to the office window, peek through the blinds, and spot Kirsten's mint green Fiat idling in the driveway.

What is she doing home?

I scan the office. In a desperate moment of non-thinking, I consider hiding in the closet—and then I remember my car is in the garage.

The distant rumble of the garage door follows next.

I head to the living room, take a seat in your favorite chair, and wait.

8

DOVE

NOAH'S HANDS grip the steering wheel, perfectly placed at ten and two as he drives me home from the county jail Wednesday night.

"Can we have some music?" I ask from the backseat. "Or something?"

The silence is too much. Nothing but road noise and the strained energy of unspoken thoughts. The last several hours have been an adrenaline-fueled blur. After Kirsten came home unexpectedly, I waited in the house for some kind of confrontation—only she stayed outside, and within five minutes a police officer showed up to whisk me away for breaking and entering.

She didn't even have the nerve to look me in the eyes as he hauled me off, hands cuffed behind my back. She looked down and away and over, her arms crossed as she leaned against the side of her mint-colored car like a coward.

"What the hell were you thinking?" Ari asks from the

passenger seat up front. "I mean, seriously ... *what the hell were you thinking?*"

She bailed me out of jail, the least I can do is give her some semblance of an explanation. But I know what she'll think, what she'll say, and it won't change any of what happened.

Besides, I don't regret it.

"He wasn't worth it when he was alive," Ari continues, "and he sure as hell isn't worth it now."

"Did you know Kirsten had a fiancé in Detroit?" I ask.

Ari whips around, eyes wild. "What does that have to do with you breaking into the house?"

"He was murdered," I say.

She faces front, throat bobbing as she swallows. Noah readjusts his grip on the wheel.

"He was murdered, and within months she moves here and starts a new life for herself," I add. "Did either of you know that?"

They give me a soft "no" in unison.

"I find it odd that we were close friends for years and not once did she bring that up," I say. "What was she trying to hide?"

The two of them exchange looks before Ari turns back to me again. "That's ... wow. I don't know what to say. Pretty damning, I guess. But what does that have to do with you breaking into the house?"

"I was at Ian's parents' yesterday and Lori said she saw Kirsten buying a pregnancy test a couple of months ago," I say. "And that got me thinking that maybe he changed his will and maybe Kirsten had something to do with what happened because she was financially motivated, and I still had a key to the house so I—"

"—so you took it upon yourself to break into the house

and look for his will to confirm this," Ari interrupts me, ever the impatient soul.

"She was supposed to be teaching a class. She came home early. I didn't mean to scare her. I was going to be in and out. I made sure to put everything back exactly the way I found it. She never would've been able to tell I was ever there." I pick at a hangnail on my left thumb until it begins to bleed. I can't remember the last time I had a manicure. They didn't exactly fit into my budget after the divorce and I was never good at the DIY versions. My right hand always looked like a preschooler painted it.

"Did you find it?" Noah meets my gaze in his rearview mirror. "The will?"

"I did," I say, pausing. "And it turns out ... he didn't change it. As it stands, he left everything to me."

Ari gasps. Noah's jaw sets.

"I talked to a detective yesterday," I say. "She was pretty clear about the fact that Ian being was killed outside my apartment on what would have been our fifth wedding anniversary doesn't paint me in the most flattering light—and when they see that he left me everything and that I stood to profit from his death ..."

"Okay so they have a body and they have a potential motive," Noah says, "but there's no murder weapon, right?"

"He was strangled," I say, swallowing the knot in my throat. "So I don't know that there is a weapon."

"Unless they used something ... a wire or a cord," Ari mutters, thinking out loud. We ride with nothing but the sound of road noise for another mile before Ari turns around to face me. "Dove, I wasn't going to tell you this, but Kirsten came in last month for a cleaning and check-up. She was scheduled with Tori. I overheard her say she couldn't do the x-ray because she was pregnant."

This information would come as more of a shock to me if I hadn't been blindsided by Lori's information yesterday.

Ari's eyes hold a silent apology, but I can't be upset with her. Legally she can't share patient information outside the clinic, and as my best friend, she probably knew the news wouldn't go over well with me.

"If you didn't do it, you didn't do it," Noah says, flicking on his turn signal as we stop at a red light a block from my place. "Without DNA evidence or witnesses, you have nothing to worry about."

I've watched far too many crime shows to know that isn't always the case. It isn't always that simple. Just last year a son was implicated in the murder of his mother simply because he was the one who found her body and he was the one who stood to inherit her multi-million-dollar estate. There was no DNA. There were no witnesses. He was found not guilty in the end, but he still lost everything. His home. His reputation. His friends and family. He may not have been sent to prison, but he still paid dearly for a crime he didn't commit.

Noah stops outside my building's entrance and shifts his Volvo into park.

If I didn't have these two, I would have nothing.

They're all I have left.

"I drove by the old house every day on my way to and from work," I add. It's out of the blue, but it's something they should hear from me while we're getting everything out in the open. "In my defense, it was on the detour route."

"There are a hundred ways to get from here to your office." Ari sees through my weak excuse.

"Do the police know?" Noah asks.

I pause. "Yes."

"Jesus, Dove." Ari shakes her head, giving an incredulous snicker of a laugh. "You realize how this looks, right? Jaded ex-wife kills husband on their wedding anniversary and inherits a stupid amount of money."

"Ari," Noah shoots her a look.

"What?" She tosses her hands in the air. "I'm just saying, this doesn't look good. *At all.*"

"I didn't do this," I say with as much conviction as I can. "I didn't kill Ian. You have to believe me."

They're quiet.

Ari's eyes are on her lap now and Noah's attention is to his left, toward the woods that are still blocked off with yellow tape.

Ari drags in a hard breath, shoulders rising and falling. "Of course we believe you. It's ... we know you never got over him. And we never said anything about all the pictures you have around your apartment because we thought maybe that was your way of dealing with this and we knew you missed him. But now to hear that you drive past his house twice a day, every day? And then suddenly we're bailing you out of jail after you broke into his house? Those aren't things you would normally do."

"So you *want* to believe me ..." I say.

"I'm not saying I don't believe you, I'm saying—" she says until Noah interrupts her with the lift of his hand.

"Okay, so let's say that Dove is being set up. The only question is why? How would it benefit someone to set her up? Even if everything was left to Dove in his will, if there's a child in the picture, the child's mother would be able to contest that in court. If you ask me, that keeps the motive in Kirsten's hands."

I exhale the lungful of stale car air I'd been harboring, thankful for the calm and rationality Noah brings to this conversation.

"Fair point," Ari says.

Noah turns back to me. "Everything's going to sort itself out. Let the cops do their thing. If you didn't do it, you didn't do it. But in the meantime, no more illegal activities."

He manages a chuckle out of me, though it's born of exhausted relief more than anything.

"I'd tell you to take some more time off work, but I think you're less likely to get yourself in trouble when you're in the office," he adds with a wink as I grip the door handle and begin to climb out.

I thank the two of them again for posting my bail and then I dig my keys out of my purse.

"The police impounded my car earlier so I'm going to need a ride to work in the morning," I say when I climb out.

"Pick you up at eight," Noah says.

A few moments later, I climb the two flights of stairs to my apartment and jam the key in the tarnished lock. Once inside, I'm swallowed by the darkness of my living room and met with the tireless tick of the kitchen clock. I lock up behind me, place my bag on the back of a nearby chair, and click on a table lamp.

My eyes immediately go to one of the many framed photos of us, and I get it. None of this is normal. It looks damning, especially given what transpired today. Having these pictures of the two of us scattered around my apartment isn't doing me any favors.

With a heaviness in my chest, I go around the room and gather them in my arms before carrying them to my bedroom. Once there, I slide the wooden box out from under the bed and place the photos inside along with a few of your t-shirts from a dresser drawer. When I'm finished, I put everything on the top shelf of my closet and shove it all the way to the back before covering it with a stack of chunky cable-knit sweaters and a few pairs of jeans I can no longer squeeze myself into.

I still love you, Ian, and I'll cherish every memory and memento for the rest of my days. But the last thing I want is to be implicated for something I didn't do. My time is better spent finding justice for you, not worrying about defending myself against false accusations.

Closing my closet, I grab a change of clothes and hit the shower to wash the musty scent of jail cell and metal handcuffs off my skin.

When I'm finished, I climb into bed, reaching for the pillow on the empty side and pulling it against me, wrapping it in a hug and pressing my cheek against its cool fabric the way I once pressed it against your shoulder.

But then the strangest thing happens.

The hot sting of tears fills my eyes before dampening the pillowcase below.

I'm crying.

I'm crying for you.

It's suffocating and wonderful, painful and cleansing all at the same time, an intense rainbow of emotions, things I haven't felt in years.

When I'm finished, I realize that because of everything that took place today, I forgot to take my medications.

In fact, it's been over twenty-four hours since the last dose. I debate gathering myself out of bed and shuffling to the kitchen to take this morning's pills, but I change my mind.

For the first time in years, I can feel again, and there's nothing wrong with that, Ian.

Right?

9

Kirsten

I FIND a folding chair in the back row of the funeral parlor Thursday evening and take a seat. Ian's casket is up ahead, surrounded by a plethora of floral bouquets and blocked by a small group of family members paying respects. I haven't gone up to see him yet, though I'm not sure what I'm waiting for.

I've never been good with death. At least not since I was twelve and found my mother and her boyfriend dead in our apartment living room after school one Monday, both of them with heroin needles hanging from their arms.

Bodies stiff, neither warm with life nor ice cold.

Eyes half-open.

Lips the color of muted violets.

The moment was so surreal I could have sworn I was dreaming. In an instant, CPS hauled me off to my first foster home (of dozens to come). I became so focused on surviving that I never had the chance to process what happened.

I learned early on not to get attached to anything or anyone.

And to always leave the past in the past.

Always, always, always.

All of this—the scent of roses and baby's breath, the low hum of idle chit chat, the stomach-turning swirl of heady perfumes and spicy colognes and peppermint gum—brings me back to Adam's funeral.

My eyes sting and there's a tickle in my nose as I fight back a wave of nausea, morning sickness intensified by the bazaar of scents surrounding me and heightened by the anxiety flooding through my veins.

In the far corner stand Mr. and Mrs. Damiani —and Dove.

It's funny—I spent yesterday morning missing Dove's friendship, regretting the choice I made to have coffee with Ian after running into him shortly after the divorce. He wanted to catch up. It was innocent—until it wasn't.

But to come home and find her inside my house, her car in my spot in the garage?

I'm still creeped out by it.

I don't think I slept more than a couple hours at a time all night, and even then, I left every light on in the house and barricaded my bedroom door with the dresser, just in case.

Supposedly she told the officer she simply wanted to spend some time in the house she once shared with Ian because she was overwhelmed with grief. She claimed she didn't mean to frighten me.

But what was with the gloves?

After the officer hauled her off, I inspected every square

inch of the house and found nothing to be missing or misplaced. The cop told me when he went inside, she was just sitting there ... in Ian's favorite chair.

I don't want to believe she had ill intentions, but I don't know what to believe when it comes to her.

Losing Ian, losing her business, losing me ... it changed her.

The Dove I knew wasn't obsessive.

The Dove I knew would never drive by someone's house multiple times a day, every day, for months on end.

The Dove I knew wouldn't have broken into anyone's house for *any* reason.

One thing's for sure, though. She won't be breaking in again. At least not with her key. I had a locksmith come by yesterday and change the locks. While he was there, he placed glass sensors on all the windows. If anyone tries to physically break in, an ear-piercing alarm will go off and deter them. He then suggested I install a security system with Wi-Fi connected cameras. As much as I'd love something like that, I don't have the extra money—and any day now, I expect Ian's parents to kick me to the curb.

I assume the house will go to them, being his next of kin, and they'll have every reason to sell it. Besides, if I move, I'm finding a place with a secure entrance and cameras on every corner of the building and parking lot—nothing like that rat's nest complex where Dove lives.

The group of mourners blocking Ian's casket clear away and for a second, he's alone up there. Gripping the back of the chair in front of me, I push myself to a standing, and then I smooth my palms over the charcoal fabric of my pencil skirt.

I make my way to him, the faint sound of organ music playing from hidden speakers in the ceiling, and a few eyes drink me in as I pass pockets of unfamiliar faces. I'm sure many of them are wondering who I am or what I'm doing here all by myself. Ian never introduced me to many of his friends and family. Our relationship was still so new and coming fresh off the heels of his divorce. Living together was a financial move. We kept the relationship casual and low-key.

He was going to start bringing me around this Thanksgiving—next month.

I approach his casket, my eyes glued to his hands folded near his waist. I can't look at his face. Not yet. His hands look sub-human, almost. Deflated and painted, distorted. Adam's were the same.

Of everything I dropped off Tuesday night, Lori chose the navy suit and green checkered tie—one of Ian's favorite combinations and LGHS's school colors. His white shirt collar is high and buttoned to the top. I heard he was strangled. I'm glad they were able to hide the marks.

Dragging in a difficult breath, I lift my gaze and force myself to take a closer look at him. With his mouth formed into a permanent straight line and his eyes glued shut and his skin caked in makeup, the motionless figure lying in the casket resembles nothing of the Ian I knew.

"Kirsten." A man's voice startles me, sending my heart into my throat. I turn and find Ian's father standing behind me, hands in his suit pant pockets. "Thank you for coming."

"Of course," I say. I never met his parents more than a handful of times since we started dating, but I could never get past his father's formal presence. Tuesday, when I dropped off the suits, he told me when the visitation was going to be and then he added, "I hope you can make it."

His eyes move to his son's body before returning to me. "He looks good, doesn't he?"

No. No he does not. "Yes. They did a great job."

He takes a step closer, staring down into the casket, and then he places a hand on Ian's.

It makes me think of my mother's visitation, when I reached in to touch her hand and some grown-up I didn't recognize slapped it away, telling me not to do that again. I spent the rest of that night crying in a bathroom stall until my foster mother found me and told me to toughen up, to never let anyone make me cry again.

Michael turns to me, and for a split second, I swear his gaze falls to my mid-section before meeting my eyes.

There's no way he knows about the pregnancy ...

Ian swore he wouldn't tell them yet. In fact, it was his idea to keep everything quiet until we got out of the first trimester. He explicitly stated he wanted to introduce me to his family at Thanksgiving and then drop the news on Christmas.

"Lori and I are having a family dinner next week," Michael says. "Something small. Close family only. We'd love if you could make it."

I'm speechless at first. I'm being invited to a dinner for close family? Two days ago he was saying he hoped I could make the visitation ...

I want to ask if Dove will be there as well, but it isn't appropriate to ask as we're standing over his son's dead body.

"Sure," I say. "I wouldn't miss it."

"Great. Tuesday. Six o'clock," he says.

Giving me a stiff shoulder squeeze I can't interpret, Michael returns to his wife's side.

I step away from Ian's casket and take a seat in the empty front row of the visitation area. I've only been here maybe ten minutes. It wouldn't be right to leave this soon, not to mention I'm sure it'll work its way around the Lambs Grove rumor mill—*Ian's girlfriend only stayed at his visitation for ten minutes. Scandalous!*

I can only imagine the things people are saying about me now. Judging by the number of clients who have paused their studio memberships this week and the instructors who have quit on me, I'm sure none of it is pretty.

Crossing my legs, I pull my shoulders back and stare ahead, focusing on the flowers. From the corner of my eye, I spot Ian's mother wrapping Dove in a lingering hug. They must not know about yesterday's incident. Would they be this warm and gracious with her if they knew what she did?

Lori's eyes light as she speaks to Dove, and a moment later she fetches her a clean tissue. There's a mother-daughter sort of dynamic between them, and I can't help but recognize the tiniest envious twinge burrowing beneath my skin.

Dove's relationship with her own mother was complicated at best and I know she and Lori have known each other for decades, but what I wouldn't give for a piece of something like that.

Lori has always been lukewarm toward me. The first time I thought it was in my imagination. The second time I thought she was having an off day. I stopped being so naïve the third time.

The warmth of another human body fills the chair beside me and for a moment I find myself displeased. This entire row is empty and they had to sit right next to me?

"You're the girlfriend, right?" the man asks. He wears a gray suit and a black tie, both of which coordinate well with his dark hair and salt-and-pepper temples.

"I'm sorry, have we met?" I ask.

"David Hobbs," he says, his eyes a warm shade of blue.

The lines around his eyes and across his forehead place him in his early forties. "I live up the street from you. And no, you and I have never met. Not officially. Just seen you around. In passing."

"Kirsten Best," I say.

"Looked like you could use a little company."

"You're right. I could," I say. Any other time I'm fine being alone, but with the Dove show going on across the room and the memories of Adam forcing their way to the surface, I could use a distraction. "Did you know Ian well?"

"Define well." David releases a friendly huff through his nose. "Nah, we were neighbors since he moved to the block about five years ago. And my kids go to the high school, so some of them had him for history." He scans the room. "They're around here somewhere. Probably ran into some friends I bet."

I take another look around. I didn't realize how packed this place was with teenagers. Or maybe they all showed up at the same time, coordinating their arrivals via group texts.

"Pretty horrible what happened though," he says, lips pursed and eyes softening. "Can't imagine what you must be going through."

There's something reassuring about his presence. Broad shouldered and soft bellied. He reminds me of some sitcom dad, always ready to lend a helpful hand or a sympathetic ear along with the occasional words of wisdom.

Out of sheer curiosity—and nothing more—I glance at his hands. His left ring finger is bare. Divorced, middle-aged, single dad.

You learn to do that when you grow up like I did. You learn to size people up. Pick up on little details that tell you more about them than you could learn through casual conversation.

"Yeah, it's pretty surreal," I say, because what else can I say?

David nods in agreement, his attention moving around the room until it settles on the Damianis. "Hey, isn't that his ex-wife?"

I nod. "Yep. And his parents. She hasn't left their side once."

"That should be you over there."

"Yeah, maybe."

"No. There's no maybe about it. You were his girlfriend. You lived with him. You were his person." He says it all with a couple of huffs and a shake of his head. "I'll be damned if I die and my ex-wife is up there schmoozing next to my parents like she gives a rat's behind that I'm gone."

"It's different," I say. "She grew up with them. I think they're still close. Plus I don't think his parents like me all that much. I think they blame me for the divorce."

He gives me side-eye, though it doesn't have judgmental energy.

"There was no affair," I say, voice low. "Nothing like that."

"Then why would they blame you?"

I shrug one shoulder. "Maybe because it's easier than blaming their son?"

David glances at a group of high schoolers in the corner. "Yeah. We parents tend to think our kids are incapable of ever doing anything wrong. We can be jerks like that. But don't let it get to you. Remember, they only had a birds' eye view of that marriage. I'm sure to them she was the perfect wife to their son, perfect daughter-in-law. My ex was always good with that kind of thing—putting on a show around family. She made damn sure that anyone who came along after her wouldn't be able to hold a candle."

He leans back in the small folding chair, which creaks with his weight. He isn't a large man, but he has broad shoulders and a soft belly.

"You live on the same street as someone, you tend to notice when they're checked out of their marriage," David says. "He checked out a long time ago. It's like they had two separate lives. He was always coming and going. Keeping busy. Probably trying to avoid her for whatever reason. And I'm speaking from experience, not speculation."

"He liked being busy," I say, thinking of all the extras he was always taking on. Working concession stands at school functions. Detention duty. His grad seminar. Helping with student council and homecoming committee. And those things were all over the last six weeks. He was almost never home.

"Don't we all?" he chuckles.

"And I think his parents just hate that he moved on so fast," I say. "So they take that out on me."

"Look, I know what it's like when a man is checked out of his marriage. He was checked out long before she packed up and left. If you put it in that context, he didn't move on that fast ... he moved on as soon as he was legally able to move on." David puffs out a breath and rolls his eyes. "Anyway, don't let them bother you. Some people are allergic to change. Especially people around here. You know how the locals are."

"What do you mean?" I ask. "I'm not actually from around here."

"Figured as much," he says. "Takes a transplant to spot a transplant."

"Why do you say that?"

"There are generations upon generations of families in this town. Some of them even live on the same block, all their houses lined up next to each other like a mini compound," he says. "And I swear, sometimes they all start to look the same."

I smirk through closed lips. Even if he's exaggerating, it's still pretty damn funny.

"Anyway, I should round up the crew and get them back to their mom's before she gets herself all worked up. God forbid I'm eight minutes late on *her* night." David's knees pop when he rises and he gives me a quick wave. "I'm sure I'll see you around. Let me know if you need anything, all right?"

Feels good to have a friend again.

———

AN EERIE SILENCE fills the house after Ian's visitation.

Lucy rustles from her spot by my feet at the end of the sofa before hopping down and stretching her long legs. She gives me her pleading brown eyes and the smallest of tail wags, and I get up, making my way to the back door to let her out.

Normally I wait inside, but I could use the fresh air, so I decide to join her. Hugging my sides, I stand on the back porch and pull in lungful after lungful of crisp autumn air, inhaling the inimitable scent of dying leaves and hibernating flora. Death and decay are beautiful in the right context and that irony is not lost on me, especially tonight of all nights.

Ian once mentioned fall was his favorite time of year. He said he lived for the changing leaves and pumpkin-spiced everything, and he always preferred his gingham-checked button downs and cashmere sweaters in rich, deep shades over his summertime t-shirt and shorts wardrobe.

Plus, as a teacher, fall meant back-to-school festivities. Football. Homecoming. Catching up with his favorite students. Student council elections. Coaching the debate team.

There was so much life in that man and now he's just ... gone.

There's a murky haze in the air today. Someone nearby must be burning leaves. I wonder if I'll forever associate the distinct, ashy scent of burnt nature with Ian's passing.

I peer across the deck railing, my eyes adjusting in the dark as I search for Lucy. I find her a few seconds later, doing one of her infamous perimeter checks where she runs along the fence line and sniffs at anything and everything before dashing inside.

Only she seems to be fixated on something.

"Lucy, in." A biting breeze wraps around me as I call for her, patting my thigh. But she doesn't budge. She's still as a statue, her nose glued to the ground and her tail pointing straight.

"Lucy!" I yell louder, stepping toward the end of the deck. "Inside."

She ignores me for another moment before rising on her hind legs and scratching at the wooden fence, going from statuesque to animated in the blink of an eye.

There must be someone on the other side.

I call for her a third time before marching out to get her myself.

She's going crazy, scratching and whimpering, jumping and whining. In fact, she's so caught up in whatever she's freaking out about that she doesn't notice me, startling and jumping back when I reach down and loop my fingers into her collar.

I get her to quiet down for a second, long enough to hear the unmistakable rustle of footsteps through fallen leaves on the other side of the fence. Through the quarter-inch slits that separate each wooden panel, I can make out the dark outline of a figure on the other side.

"I'm sorry," I say to the next-door neighbor. Ian introduced us once. I think his name is Will? He's a bachelor and a bit of a loner. Due to his work schedule at the tire factory, we don't tend to cross paths, but every once in a while I see him coming and going in his big black Ford with the chrome-tipped dual exhaust and depending on his mood, sometimes we exchange a wave or two. "She gets excited sometimes."

I loop my fingers around Lucy's collar until I have control, lingering for a second and waiting for a response that never comes.

Oh, well.

Will is the least of my concerns today.

I lead Lucy inside and lock the sliding door behind us, and then I make my way back to the living room to check my phone in case I missed any calls in the last few minutes. Only in the midst of reaching for it, I happen to glance out the picture window behind the couch—just in time to see Will pulling into his driveway and climbing out of his truck a second later.

I yank the curtains shut, violent chills running through my stiffened limbs.

That wasn't him.

10

DOVE

I STOP by Noah's after the visitation. I skipped my meds again today and I swear every part of me is vibrating with this restless, unsettled energy that I have no clue how to handle. Maybe it was seeing your lifeless body for the first time that did me in, but I don't think it's the best idea to be alone. I'm not myself.

"Here you go." Noah hands me a fresh pillow and a stack of sheets and blankets, and I place them on the edge of his sofa.

"Thanks for letting me crash here tonight. You going to the funeral tomorrow?" I ask. "It's at eleven at Saint Mary's."

He scratches at his temple. "I mean ... I can if you want? It's just, I never met the guy. I never knew him. Wouldn't that be weird? Would that even be appropriate?"

It's not like Noah to overthink these kinds of things, but I understand his position.

"I'll go for you. If you want me there," he says before adding, "if you need me there."

I think of his jam-packed schedule, all those appointments that would need to be rescheduled at the last minute, and I change my mind. "It's fine. Ari's going, so don't worry about it."

"You sure?" He angles a dark eyebrow before taking a seat in the leather armchair beside me. Two steaming cups of herbal tea rest between us, scenting the air with wisps of chamomile and peppermint.

"Of course." I reach for my mug before blowing a breath across the steamy top.

Noah slinks back into his seat, legs crossed wide, and he frowns as he stares at the blank TV screen over his fireplace.

"What? What are you thinking about?" I ask.

"I'm surprised Ari's going, I guess."

"Surprised? Why? She's known him almost her entire life. Why wouldn't she go?"

"It's just that, she hated him. Loathed the guy. Almost to the point where it was obsessive," he says. "Even when we weren't with you, all she would talk about was how much she couldn't stand him."

"Maybe you misunderstood her?"

He drags his hand along his jaw. "I don't think I did."

Noah's never been one for hyperbole or embellishments, but I've never known Ari to hate you. Sure you had your differences, but that's all they were. Differences. Plenty of people butt heads. And let's admit it, sometimes it was humorous watching you two go at it. By the end of it, we'd all be laughing.

"Maybe she was in a mood that day," I say. "You know how she gets."

"Dove, I'm not talking about one day. I'm talking

about several instances." Noah drags his straight white teeth along his lower lip before continuing. "Sometimes she'd bring him up out of the blue. Something would remind her of something he said or did and she'd go off about it, ranting and raving. Or if we'd hung out with you that day and you said something nice about Ian, that would almost always set her off. There was a very raw nerve there."

None of this sounds like the Ari we know, but I'm willing to hear him out. "What kinds of things did she say?"

His broad shoulders lift and fall. "All kinds of things. But mostly she'd talk about how selfish he was, how it was always about him and how he had everyone fooled into thinking he was a good person."

"Ari ... she can get intense sometimes."

His hand slicks against his angled jaw. "Right, but she seemed to take things to the next level. Red-faced. Spitting when she talked. That sort of thing."

"I've never seen her like that," I say. "Ever. She wasn't his biggest fan, but they always went back and forth. It was playful. They razzed each other. There was never any hate."

"I'm only telling you what I've experienced."

"Okay ... so what are you getting at?"

"I don't know." He hesitates. "Makes me wonder if there's something more to it."

"What are you talking about?"

"The incessant hatred toward Ian." He makes eye contact with me now, his expression stoic. "Why would she filter it around you but not me?"

"Out of respect? Plus we've been friends since second grade. She knows I wouldn't stand for that."

His temple pulses and he pushes a breath through

widening nostrils. I've upset him—not an easy thing to do to Dr. Noah Benoit.

"Do you know something I don't know? Is there something you're leaving out? Because you seem pretty convinced here but to me, it's just speculation."

I expect him to say no. I expect him to drop the subject, to admit his theory is ludicrous and implausible and he's reading into this too much.

"Yes," he says, shoulders falling as he exhales. "There is."

I swear my heart stops beating for a moment.

"What? Tell me," I say, sitting up, hand on my chest.

He doesn't speak at first, only readies his lips as he gathers his thoughts.

"*Noah,*" I say, the volume of my voice startling us both.

"I saw the two of them together," he says. "About a month ago."

"Are you sure?"

I think of Kirsten's shiny dark hair and bronzed skin and Ari's wild auburn curls and fair complexion—as much as I'd love to believe he got them mixed up, I know it would've been impossible.

"It was late," he says. "Maybe ten or eleven. And a weeknight. I had to run to the store and grab a few things. I saw them at a stoplight. I was right beside them. They were in her white Toyota. She was driving. It seemed like they were having some kind of heated discussion."

"Did they see you?"

He shakes his head. "The light turned green and they went left. Toward the highway, like they were going out of town."

I try to paint the picture of you and Ari in my head, but it refuses to come together. "Did you ever ask her about it?"

"No. I never brought it up. I didn't want to cause a rift between the two of you and I figured it was none of my business. Plus, I'm sure she would've denied it," he says. "She would've painted *me* as the liar and then you would've been upset with *me*. I was going to tell you, though, Dove. I just wasn't sure when. It's been bothering me ever since. I've lost sleep over it and everything."

I sit in stunned silence, thinking back to the beginning of my relationship with you and how the three of us used to be inseparable. Ari had a hard time adjusting to how much time we were spending together, so I always wanted to include her. I hated the idea of her feeling left out or pushed to the side as our romance blossomed, and we all know that teenage first love tends to take priority over everything else. But I refused to move Ari to the back burner. I thought I could give you both the same amount of time, love, and attention—only to have it backfire.

At first it was petty things, like who controlled the radio or which restaurant we went to or who got to pick the movie that Friday. Then it became accusations—Ari claiming she saw you flirting with someone or you claiming Ari was jealous and trying to break us up.

It wasn't until we set her up with one of your friends and started doing double dates every weekend that she seemed to ease up, but after a while, the two of you went back to bickering like an old couple in a sexless marriage.

When we all graduated senior year, I went off to Holbrook with you and Ari and Gage went to State. It wasn't until we all moved back to Lambs Grove and Gage dumped Ari that you two settled back into your ancient ways and I was back to keeping the two of you separate once again.

Ari is a good person. And she means well. But her jealous streak is only outweighed by her loyal streak.

I don't care how much Noah claims she hates you, she would never ...

She wouldn't do that to me.

The hot sting of tears begins to blur my vision before I realize I'm crying. When I glance down, Noah's handing me a tissue.

"I'm so sorry, Dove," he says. His eyes are wide and I realize he's never seen me shed a single tear the whole time he's known me. "I didn't want to tell you because I knew you'd be upset. But given what happened this week, I think you should know."

I try to speak, but I can't. The words are trapped, my throat constricted.

It isn't true.

It can't be.

But what reason would Noah have to make that up?

I think about Kirsten's pregnancy and the fact that you were always adamant about not wanting to have children. You always loved other people's kids and you loved your niece and nephew, but you never longed for any of your own. It was something we'd discussed for hours upon hours over years and years, and not once did your stance weaken or falter.

If you lied about wanting a family, Ian, did you also lie about your true feelings for Ariadne?

"What am I supposed to do now?" I ask Noah. "Act like I don't know this? I'm seeing her tomorrow. She's picking me up at ten."

The tears dry in an instant and the heat of anger creeps along my skin. I'm going on nearly forty-eight hours with no mood stabilizers. The urge to break something, to hurt someone, flashes through me, but I tamp it down.

"Dove," Noah says, inching toward the edge of his chair and reaching his arm to me. His fingertips graze the top of my knee. "Good God, I've never seen you like this before. You're flushed. Take some slow breaths before you hyperventilate."

I'm trying to take deep breaths, but my lungs refuse to expand, refuse to inhale the leather and cedar and perpetually spotless scent of Noah's condo.

"Here's what you're going to do," Noah says. He's on his knees now in front of me, his hands bracing my heaving shoulders. "You're going to get some rest. You're going to go with Ari to the funeral tomorrow. You're going to pay your respects to Ian. And then you're going to deal with this later."

He makes it sound easy.

He begins to say something more, but his phone vibrates from the coffee table.

It's in that moment that I remember finding your burner phone in your office. I'd stuck it in my purse which they took when they booked me, but when I got out, it was still in there. They must have assumed it was mine since it was with my things. Plus if Kirsten didn't know it existed, she wouldn't have reported it missing.

"I have to go." I pop up from the sofa.

"Dove, wait," Noah says, silencing his phone.

"No, no. I'm fine. Everything's fine. I want to sleep in my own bed tonight."

Noah rises, dragging his hand through his combed dark hair, mussing it up. He disagrees with me, but he's not going to try to stop me. That's not the kind of person he is.

I gather my things, flinging my purse over my shoulder

and stepping into my flats, and then I wrap my arms around him.

"Thank you," I say, kissing his cheek. "I'm glad you told me."

I can't place the strange look he gives me when I pull away. He's probably wondering how I went from denial to hysterics to calm in the span of a few minutes, but I don't have time to explain to him about my mood disorder.

"I'll get ahold of you this weekend," I tell him as I show myself out.

He gives me a wave, still wearing that peculiar look on his face like he doesn't understand what this is all about. But I can't tell him about the phone. I don't want anyone to know I have it until I know what's on it. If I give it to the police, they'll take it in as evidence and I'll never know what's on it—I'll never know if this is what you used to communicate with Ari.

Ten minutes later, I'm flying across town and all but skidding into my assigned parking spot in front of my apartment building. Sprinting up two flights of stairs, I make my way into my apartment, locking the door behind me. Breathless, I empty the contents of my purse on the tiled floor of my tiny foyer.

The black phone lands with a plastic thud, coming to a rest between spare change, lip balm, and my leather wallet.

I check the charging plug, which is different from that of my iPhone. Snatching the burner, I head to my kitchen and tear through my junk drawer until I find a random cord that fits. A second later, it's plugged in and a red lightning bolt fills the screen.

It's charging.

I chew my thumbnail as I wait, tasting salt and skin.

A solid fifteen minutes drip by before it has enough juice to power on.

My heart is beating so fast I think I might faint, and tiny beads of sweat begin to collect along my hairline.

I don't want to know what's on here, Ian.

I don't want this to change everything I believed about you, the beliefs I held deep down to my marrow.

Those things? Those are the things that defined me. Maybe it was wrong. Maybe we shouldn't let another person's love comprise our identity, but you were the only good thing I had going, Ian.

I lived for you.

I woke up every morning happy to see your face, and when I closed my eyes at night, I still dreamt of you even if you were right beside me because that's how much my soul couldn't bear to be away from you.

Using the arrow buttons, I navigate through the unfamiliar and generic-looking apps until I find the one that contains your text messages.

Upon first glance, they all seem to be coming from one number and one number only.

My hope deflates.

This is definitely a burner phone you used to communicate with someone in secret.

Why, Ian?

Why?!

I start with the first one, a simple "HEY, BABE. I MISS YOU" that came from your phone and went to hers. The date states that it was sent two Decembers ago.

We were still *happily* married then.

In fact, you'd given me diamond-and-sapphire earrings that Christmas and surprised me with a weekend away to

Chicago during winter break. We made love five times that weekend, Ian. *Five times.*

Did you bring this phone with you on our trip?

Were you texting her when I was in the shower?

When I was passed out in your arms at night, dreaming about you?

And all those times you'd wake in the middle of the night, claiming you couldn't sleep, grading papers under the dim lamplight in the living room while watching reruns of *The Office* on Netflix—were you sexting this woman?

I continue onto the next message and the next, all of them volleying back and forth between the two of you and most of the reading along the lines of:

IT WAS SO GOOD SEEING YOU TODAY

WE SHOULD DO THAT MORE OFTEN ;-)

I THINK I'M OFFICIALLY ADDICTED TO YOU

THIS IS SO WRONG BUT I CAN'T STOP

USUAL SPOT? USUAL TIME?

I HAVE A SURPRISE FOR YOU TONIGHT ...

I WISH WE COULD BE TOGETHER NOW ... SOMEDAY WE WILL BE. I PROMISE.

The messages are vague and generic but infuriating all the same.

I can't tell if this was Ari or someone else. For all I know, this is what you used to communicate with Kirsten. Maybe you were seeing her before you asked for the divorce?

You lied to me, Ian.

My chest caves so deep I can't breathe, but I continue scrolling through the messages, my skin as red hot as my vision, until I get to the last one—a message sent the day before you were killed.

I'M TIRED OF SNEAKING AROUND, she writes.

You responded just past midnight, probably after

Kirsten was in bed. LET'S TALK ABOUT THIS. TONIGHT. USUAL SPOT, USUAL TIME.

I gasp and the phone plummets from my hand. It's late. I'm exhausted, eyes blurry. I've been reading these for hours. Maybe I'm not understanding this? Maybe I misread something? I grab the phone and read the final message one more time.

LET'S TALK ABOUT THIS. TONIGHT. USUAL SPOT, USUAL TIME.

Whoever this woman is, she was likely the last person to see you alive.

11

Kirsten

I SIT in my idling car in the parking lot of Saint Mary's Catholic Church at a quarter 'til eleven Friday morning, watching people head inside in a sea of black. Black dresses. Black suits. Black glasses hiding averted gazes.

It's a somber day despite the sunny, unseasonably warm day we're having. The sun hasn't peaked yet and already it's mid-seventies.

The weather is mocking almost. Or celebratory, depending on how one looks at it.

Perspective is everything.

I flip my visor down and check my reflection before getting out. I don't always wear makeup, but I wanted to look nice today so I made sure to wear waterproof mascara and a simple nude lip color. When I climb out of my car a moment later, I have to readjust the hemline of my skirt as it's ridden up. The dress is tighter than it was the last time I wore it. At ten weeks along, I'm not showing, but it doesn't mean my waistline isn't expanding. If anyone were none the wiser and stared long enough, they might think I ate a big breakfast. Maybe.

I close and lock my car door and gather my clutch in my hands, positioning it in front of my belly. My first ultrasound is in three days and I plan to tell Ian's parents about the pregnancy afterwards—as long as everything looks good.

An older couple pass by and give me the kind of nod and quick "hello" that one might give a stranger at a grocery store. The woman links her arm in the man's and they disappear behind double doors, followed by half a large family and a group of high school kids.

At this rate, I'm going to be in the last row.

I make my way inside as the church bells begin to ring. Eleven chimes.

The priest is standing at the altar. Ian's silver casket is in front of him, sealed shut. An oversized portrait of a smiling Ian stands on an easel beside it, encircled by a wreath of white flowers.

The church is packed.

Wall to wall, pew to pew.

The back of the cathedral is standing-room only.

I squeeze between a man in an olive-green suit and a woman bathed in drugstore perfume as the organ begins to play. From here, all I see are the backs of everyone's heads. I haven't seen Ian's parents nor have I seen Dove, but I'm probably safe to assume they're together, in the front row.

The music stops and the priest begins with a prayer.

Everyone bows their heads.

I steal a quick glance around the room and spot what appears to be David about six or seven rows from the back. He's surrounded by three teenagers—two boys and a girl, all with their heads lowered.

The priest finishes with an amen, which everyone echoes, and the service begins.

Already I'm cataloging all the ways this one is different from Adam's. Adam's wasn't held in a church—he nor I were never affiliated with any religion. I found the nicest funeral parlor in the area and bought him the nicest coffin they had. And I had the funeral director fill the place with hundreds of blue-tinted roses because blue was his favorite color. I figured since it was his life insurance money paying for everything, I wasn't going to be stingy. In fact, I didn't know until two days after he died that he'd named me the sole beneficiary to the policy.

I suppose it made sense. We were both foster kids with no close family connections and we were engaged to be married. Who else would he have left it to? Maybe he meant to tell me but never got around to it. At twenty-seven, don't we all think we're going to live forever anyway?

I should visit him.

I haven't been back to Detroit since I left, and that was two years ago.

Adam's funeral was packed—mostly work colleagues and friends he met studying to be a welder at his community college, but people came from all over for his send out—much like this.

I've always been drawn to men who were charismatic and larger than life the way that two magnets with opposite polarity are drawn together. My body freezes when the connection dawns on me, and I draw in a tight breath of air.

Ian reminded me of Adam.

That's why I was so pulled to him.

My eyes burn, but I don't let a single tear fall. I'll do that later, when I'm alone. I think of that foster mom and her words of advice that day at Mom's visitation. *"Toughen up."*

I can't remember her name or even the sound of her voice, only that she always smelled like boiled potatoes, white bread, and mothballs.

Lifting my head, I focus on the sermon which then leads into the actual ceremony. By the time they get to the reading of the eulogy, my feet are burning. I never should have worn heels. At least it's a nice distraction from the emotional pain of this heavy day.

I decide to focus on that.

Perspective is everything.

When the service ends and the pallbearers carry Ian's casket out one of the side doors to an idling hearse, we dismiss from the back of the church forward—beginning with the people standing.

Eyes lowered, I tuck my chin and follow the line of people as we march down the carpeted aisle toward the line where Ian's parents, sister, niece, nephew, grandparents ... and Dove ... wait to receive everyone.

It's like the divorce never happened.

I'm afraid to look at her hands because half of me expects her to be wearing her wedding ring. And clearly his parents are unaware of the breaking and entering two days ago. I thought about calling them and telling them after it happened, but I didn't want to seem like I was stirring the pot, and I knew they already had so much to deal with. I couldn't bring myself to add their dead son's ex-wife/girl-friend drama on top of it all.

There must be a dozen people in front of me, so I bide my time trying to guess how my exchange with Dove is going to go once I'm up there. Awkward or cordial? It's anyone's guess.

A projector screen behind the altar plays photos of Ian on a loop, and I do a quick scan around the room. Surely I can't be the only one who notices every other picture has Dove in it? Doesn't anyone else find this a bit ... morbid? Tasteless? I know they were together since they were teenagers and she was there for a lot of his big life moments, but this is absurd. It's truly as if we're all pretending they were still married.

Either that, or this is Dove's way of rubbing her scent all over Ian's funeral to spite me, to taunt me the way she did when she drove by twice a day, every day, the way she did when she broke into the house Wednesday.

I think about last night when I had to grab Lucy from the back yard and someone was on the other side of the fence.

What if that was Dove?

I take a few steps closer to the receiving line, my blood running ice cold the closer I get to her. She's standing on the end, to the left of his mother, wrapped in the embrace of the man in the olive-green suit.

When it's my turn, our eyes catch. I'm tongue-tied for a second as I find myself looking at her in a fresh light.

"Kirsten, so glad you could make it," she says. Before I have a chance to respond, she throws her arms around me.

Speechless and incapable of reacting this quickly, I hug her back.

She smells like Ian—like his favorite cologne.

She releases her hold on me, though her hands remain on my shoulders. Her head tilts, eyes bloodshot and glassy as if she's been crying, and she offers me a sympathetic smile that chills me to my core.

If this is another one of her taunts, another one of her attempts at getting under my skin ...

I move along, giving my sympathies to the rest of his family before making a mad dash to my car. It's beginning to sprinkle, the beautiful weather we were having gone without warning. It takes a solid half hour for the rest of the packed congregation to make their way to their cars. They begin to form a procession line behind the hearse, and I observe in silence as Dove climbs into the black limousine with the rest of the Damianis.

I start my engine, flick on the windshield wipers and hazard lights, and find a spot in the car line to the cemetery. My palms dampen against my steering wheel, my hair hot and heavy as it sticks to the nape of my neck.

I think about that hug. That smile. The break in. The figure behind the fence.

And then I wonder what she'll do when she learns about the pregnancy.

12

DOVE

"YOU HAVEN'T SAID two words all day. You doing all right?" Ari asks as we leave the cemetery beneath a shared leopard print umbrella. A blue canopy the color of the sky shields your shiny silver casket from the rain and your parents are being whisked away into the back of the funeral home's limo along with your sister and her kids. "Dove, talk to me."

She puts her arm around my shoulders. I shrug it off.

I can't stop thinking about the text messages, Ian. Even during the funeral service, when I should have been thinking about you ... my mind kept drifting back to that burner phone, wondering who the mystery woman could be and how I could have ever been so naïve as to believe you were the man you pretended to be.

I cried for you today, but they weren't sad tears.

Quite the contrary.

Fortunately, no one could tell the difference.

"Hey," Ari says, stopping short to get my attention. She's the one holding the umbrella, so I'm forced to stop with her. "I know today's been an awful day for you, but don't take it out on me. I'm trying to be here for you."

I lift a finger, unable to look at her. "Please don't make this about you today."

Her auburn brows knit together as she studies me, acting like she has no idea what the hell this could be about. Given the fact that your affair—assuming she is the mystery woman—spanned from at least two Decembers ago, I imagine she's gotten pretty good at pretending.

"I know this is an upsetting time for you, but I'm starting to take it personally." There's a hint of smugness in her tone that makes me want to go off on her, but I won't cause a scene, not here. But only out of respect for your family. Not you.

I've lost all respect for you, Ian.

I grab the handle of the umbrella from her and march back to her car. She traipses behind, keys in hand, getting soaked by the thick droplets that fall from the gray sky. Any other time I'd feel bad. Today I don't. Today I don't feel anything but pissed the hell off.

All I want is to get out of here, away from the cemetery, away from Ari, away from you.

The headlights of her Toyota flash as she unlocks it, and we both climb in, slamming our doors.

Rain begins to pelt the car, so loud I can't hear my own thoughts, but maybe that's for the best. It's funny—it was such a beautiful day when your funeral started. Now the heavens seem to have opened up so you could be buried in mud.

Sticky, dirty, wet, disgusting mud.

"Are you going to tell me what this is about?" Ari asks. I

realize now her hair is soaked, her eyeliner migrating beneath her wild eyes. "I know you're in pain, Dove, the least you can do is let me be a friend to you."

"And what would you know about being a friend?" I realize I'm making assumptions, and it's a strong one. I have no proof that the woman on the other end of the burner phone is Ari, but Noah wouldn't lie about seeing you and Ari together. The fact that it was so recently too and that you died the night that the other woman claimed she was tired of sneaking around with you ... it's all pointing in one direction for me.

"Are you kidding me?"

The air in the car is stifling but Ari doesn't notice, she's too fixated on me. I bet that oversized head of hers is trying to stay one step ahead of me, wondering how the hell she's going to do damage control on this.

"I know about you and Ian," I say.

Her forehead lines with creases. "I have no idea what you're talking about."

"Someone told me about the affair," I say, bluffing.

She slinks back against her seat, arms folded, wielding confidence and so relaxed it makes me want to scream in her face. "Oh, yeah? Care to fill me in on this? Because it's sure as hell news to me."

She's acting. That's what she does. It's what she always did. She never hated you, she *loved* you. That's why she was so mean to you. That's why she was so jealous of us.

Oh my God.

How did I not see this before?

"Seriously, Dove. Whoever told you that is lying," she says in a way that would have been convincing a week ago. Now I see through it. I see through her act.

"Stop denying it. I know someone saw you together."

She laughs and it makes me want to rage, but I contain myself with three deep breaths.

"Let me guess," she says with a smirk. "It was about a month ago. Late at night. A Thursday, I believe. Around eleven PM."

That's oddly specific.

"Trust me, I didn't want to be in that car with him, Dove, but that's the day I found out Kirsten was pregnant and I wanted to confront him about it," she says, which seems plausible. Sort of.

"And why would that be any of your concern?"

"Because I wanted to protect you," she says. She reaches her hand for me before retracting it. "I wanted to see if it was true and when he confirmed it, I told him he better do everything in his power to keep it on the down low because you weren't in a good place. I told him once you found out, it would only push you further into the deep end."

She's rambling, words blurring together, hand over her chest. The smugness in her tone is gone.

"Oh, my God, Dove," she says, her mouth gaping. "I can't believe you thought I ..."

"What do you mean I'm not in a good place?" I ask.

She told you that? Some friend ...

Was she trying to make me look bad? Why would she do that? And if she told you I was in a bad place, why didn't you reach out to me? Why didn't you check on me? You couldn't be bothered to pick up the phone for two seconds and call me, Ian?

Ari hesitates. "Clearly you're not over him."

"Right. We spent twenty years together. You don't get over someone just because they got over you first."

"You still have pictures of the two of you all over your

house. It's like you weren't even trying to move on. Not only that, but sometimes you wear that watch of his or one of those old t-shirts. Once in a while I'll drop by and I'll smell his cologne, like you just sprayed it." Her voice is soft and her head is tilted. I wonder if she smells your cologne on me now. "I know you still love him."

"Not anymore."

She begins to say something and then stops for a moment. "Please, Dove. Don't believe the lie. I met with him once, to discuss the pregnancy, and then never again."

I lean back into the passenger seat, staring at a droplet-covered, fogged-over windshield. Most of the funeral guests have left the cemetery now, scattering to their cars to get out of the rain the second it was over. There's supposed to be a fellowship luncheon at the church, but I don't think it would be a good idea for me to attend. Not like this.

"Who told you this?" Ari asks. "Who saw us together?"

"Noah," I say because he didn't swear me to secrecy and if Ari gets upset with him, it won't matter because the two of them are only friends because of me. It'll be no skin off either of their backs.

Ari smacks the steering wheel, head cocked. "Noah, eh?"

I nod.

"The Noah who is head over heels in love with you."

"What are you talking about?" I shoot her a crooked glance.

"Oh, come on. Don't be so dense. He's been in love with you since the second you walked into that job interview last year. Why do you think he offered you the position on the spot? You had no experience working in a medical office or dealing with insurance claims or any of that."

"We hit it off," I say, recalling the interview that felt

more like two friends getting to know each other than a boss sizing up a potential employee. "And those things are teachable skills."

"Yeah. You hit it off." She rolls her eyes. "You know why Noah and I never worked out?"

Oh, God. She's bringing up the failed date.

"Because you're night and day?" I ask. "Not everyone's compatible."

"No. Because when we went on that stupid date you made us go on, he wouldn't shut up about you. He talked about you all night." She picks at a chipped nail. "And it was pretty obvious any time we were all together that he was consumed by you. He looked at you the way Ian did. Or at least the way Ian did in the beginning." She's quiet for a second. "I couldn't compete with that."

The despondency in her tone is unfamiliar. Ari's never this defeatist, never been one to wallow in self-pity.

"You really think Noah's in love with me?" I ask.

Ari chuffs before blowing a puff of air through her nose. "No. I think he takes care of you and does sweet things for you and pines over you like a lovesick puppy dog because he's a nice guy."

"Maybe he *is* just a nice guy?"

"Or maybe you chose to ignore all his creepy obsessed little acts of kindness because you were so hung up on Ian?"

I let her words digest, mentally playing back moments with Noah and trying to examine them from a different angle.

I get what she's saying.

The radio in the background plays Mazzy Star on low volume. It's a dreary, angsty song that fits this day to a T. Also you hated this band. You once threatened to throw Ari's CD out the window when we were driving down the interstate if she didn't stop playing *Fade Into You* on repeat.

"Dove?" she asks a minute later.

"Yeah?"

"I'm not saying Noah killed Ian," she says with the kind of calm, cautious tone a hostage negotiator might use. "But what if he did?"

"That's ridiculous."

"Is it though?" She squints ahead, over the dash, lost in thought. "What if he was tired of playing second fiddle to your ex? Maybe he wanted you all to himself?"

Noah's too benign to kill someone. He's soft and gentle, mild and calming. Too pragmatic to commit a crime of passion. He doesn't even like to prescribe painkillers to his patients because he's afraid they might accidentally overdose or become addicted. I've seen him suggest CBD oil and all-natural numbing tinctures over codeine and Percocet.

He's not a killer.

"Where is Noah anyway?" she asks. "Why didn't he come today?"

"He offered, but I told him he didn't have to," I say. "He didn't know Ian. They'd never met."

Ari licks her lips. "Yeah, well, if I killed someone I probably wouldn't show my face at their funeral either. I'd probably want to lay low, you know? Pretend like it has nothing to do with me."

"Ari," I scold her with my tone.

"What?" She throws her hands in the air. "We're theorizing here. I'm not saying he did it. I'm saying *what if he did*?" Ari points at me. "And what if he was trying to pin it on me by making you think I was hooking up with Ian?"

"Until we have evidence, I don't want to assume—"

"—you were pretty quick to assume I was sleeping with Ian."

"True," I say. I almost begin to tell her about the cell phone, but I change my mind. The smallest part of me wonders if she's pointing the finger at Noah because he pointed the finger at her. Maybe she's still the guilty one? Or maybe they were in on it together?

After all that's come to light this week, I'm beginning to doubt everything—and everyone.

Ari shifts into gear and pulls onto the blacktop cemetery road before turning toward the highway that loops around Lambs Grove.

"You hungry?" Ari asks.

How could I think about food after the conversation we just had? The unanswered questions demanding my full attention?

"Nah. Take me home," I say.

I need to be alone. I need quiet. I need to think.

And until I know who I can trust, I probably shouldn't be around anyone.

13

Kirsten

I PARK in the driveway Saturday morning after teaching a couple of vinyasa classes at the studio, and I let the car idle for a few minutes before pulling in next to Ian's lifeless Passat.

It looks like he's home.

It *feels* like he's home.

It's a cruel trick of the mind.

When I finally head inside, I expect to be met with the soft click of Lucy's nails against the wood floors and the wet slip of her nose beneath my palm, only the house is eerily quiet.

"Lucy?" I call for her.

Silence.

I head to the living room to check her favorite spot on the sofa, but she isn't there. I run to the master bedroom next, hoping to find her on the bed or perhaps nestled in a pile of Ian's dirty laundry.

But she isn't there either.

I check the bathrooms, the spare bedroom, the office, and even the basement despite the fact that that door was shut all day, but no Lucy.

"Oh my God," I say when I get to the kitchen and find the back door unlocked and her food bowl untouched.

This morning, before I left for the studio, I let Lucy outside and then I poured her some kibble. Her food is still here because I must have forgotten to let her back in. I must have left her outside. Making my way to the sliding door and stepping onto the deck, I call for her as I scan the quiet, leafy yard.

Only she isn't there.

From here I can tell the gate is latched. Either someone saw her out here for hours and snatched her or she found a spot under the fence big enough for her to squeeze through.

Either way, one thing's for sure: she's gone.

With hot tears filling my eyes, I run inside and grab my phone and a notebook, making a list of all the local animal shelters. There are four, two breed-specific rescues, a private shelter, and a city-operated pound. I don't know if Lucy was microchipped and if she was, what are the odds that they would hand her over to me? She'd be registered to Ian.

Or Dove.

By the time I'm finished calling around, I'm no closer to finding her. One of the places suggested calling veterinary clinics on the off chance someone has her and brings her in for an examination.

I flip to a fresh page in my notebook and begin making my list. There are seven vet clinics in Lambs Grove. I'll call them every day if I have to. I just want her back. She was precious to Ian. He loved her more than anything. She deserves to be in good hands.

I call the first clinic, my stomach in knots when the woman tells me a stray dog was brought in after being hit by a car earlier today. It's a thought I hadn't had up until now. I've never been a pet owner and Lucy is the first dog I'd ever been around for any long stretch of time. There are so many hazards, so many tragedies you don't think about when you're not an animal person.

"Nope, it's not a Springer spaniel," she says. "Some kind of pit mix, looks like."

I exhale. "Thank you for checking. I hope that dog is okay."

The woman offers a hopeless sigh into the phone. "Good luck."

I start to dial the next number on the list when there's a knock at the front door. I'm half tempted to ignore it. I'm not expecting anyone and the search for Lucy is my top priority, but if someone is stopping by unannounced, I imagine it could be important.

Placing my pen aside, I grab my phone and head to the door, peeking through the sheer curtain that covers the sidelight.

A man stands on the stoop, his back toward the door, hands dug deep into his jeans pockets. He's in a sweater with a plaid collared shirt beneath it, and a shiny black Ford sedan idles in my driveway. A second later, he turns around and I realize it's David Hobbs—the neighbor I met at Ian's visitation a couple of nights ago.

"David, hi," I say when I open the door. "Can I help you?"

"Hey." His dark brows lift and he scratches at his temple. "So, I think I have your dog ..."

With a sharp inhalation, I place my hand over my heart. "You have Lucy?"

"Found her running around the neighborhood a bit ago," he says. "Thought she looked familiar. Then I remembered seeing Ian walking her around all the time."

"Yes," I say. "Lucy's his ... was his dog."

He points to the idling sedan in the drive, and I see her now, sitting in the back seat all prim and proper, like an obedient dog who would never dream of running away.

With bare feet, I step onto the front stoop and pad down the sidewalk to the car. The instant she spots me, her tail goes wild and she whimpers from behind the glass.

"I wanted to make sure I had the right house first," he says, reaching around me to get the door. Lucy climbs down before barreling to the front door and pushing it open with her nose. She disappears inside like it never happened.

We both exchange a subtle chuckle, and I make a mental note to get a special collar for her, one with my name and number on it, just in case she was to ever escape again, though going forward, I'm going to be extra careful.

"I have no idea how she got out," I say. "The gate was shut."

He shrugs, hands back in his jeans pockets. He looks different, then again I've only ever seen him in suits until now. "Dogs are dogs. It happens. If you'd like me to look at the fence sometime, I'd be happy to."

"Really? You'd do that?" I don't tell him that where I come from I've never met a favor that didn't have a string attached. Then again, where I come from is nothing like Lambs Grove. "I don't want to trouble you."

"Psh. Ian was Colby's favorite teacher. All we ever heard was how wonderful Mr. Damiani was. I'd love to help out in any way I can. Sure you have a lot on your plate right now."

"Thank you, David. Truly. That's very generous of you." I'd turn down his offer if I were in a better position financially. I'm sure it would cost at least a hundred dollars to get someone out here to mend the fence, and with the baby on the way and clients pausing their yoga memberships, my wallet is painfully tight.

He waves away my gratitude. "It's no trouble."

I peek into the window and spot Lucy curled on the end of the sofa, sound asleep. "I hope she didn't give you too much trouble today."

"Nah, she was perfect. Reminded me a lot of our old family dog, Fritz. I let the ex have him since he was mostly the kids' dog and the kids live with her most of the time." His shoulders straighten and he shakes his head. "But that's neither here nor there. We had a great time this morning. Played fetch in the back yard and chased some squirrels."

He rocks on his heels, back and forth like he's not in any hurry to leave. For a moment, I see him not as a friendly neighbor but as a lonely, divorced dad longing for human interaction.

"You want to come in for a minute?" I ask. "I've got some iced tea in the fridge."

With everything going on, I could use a friend in the neighborhood—someone to call if I need something, someone to fill me in on any strange or unusual behavior going on around the house when I'm gone.

David's dark brows meet. "You sure? I don't want to inconvenience you."

"It's so quiet. Some company would be nice actually. This place could use a little more ..." I stop myself before saying, "Life."

David checks the time on his phone. "Yeah. I have to pick up my youngest from the movies in about an hour but sure, we can visit for a while."

Stepping aside, I let David Hobbs into Ian's house. The faint scent of his unfamiliar cologne fills the small space by the front door and he removes his shoes, placing them parallel on the rug.

"This way." I lead him to the kitchen and grab the pitcher of iced tea from the fridge and two tea glasses.

Ian always loved his iced tea in the afternoons.

Coffee before lunch, tea after, that was his way. He always drank the cheap teas too, the kind from the tea aisle at the supermarket. It wasn't until I took him to a proper tea shop and introduced him to a world of flavors that he made the change to more sophisticated options.

"Thank you," David says when I hand him his glass and take a seat across from him.

"So you said you've lived here five years?" I ask.

He takes a sip before nodding. "Bought a house down the street after my divorce. We used to live on Conifer Road, by the brick yard off the highway. Had a big acreage out there. You might have seen it? Big white house with the wraparound porch?"

"I'm not familiar," I say. "I've only lived here a couple of years."

"Oh, yeah. That's right. You told me that."

"You said you're an outsider too, right? Where are you from?"

"Everywhere." He twists the stem of his tea glass between his thumb and forefinger. "Typical Army brat childhood. Went away to college in Miami, which is where I met my ex. She was from here so after we got married and found out we were having a baby, she insisted we move to Lambs Grove to be closer to her family."

"Nothing wrong with planting roots."

He gazes out the sliding glass doors to the back yard, stuck in his own head for a second. "I won't argue with you on that. Family is everything. I couldn't imagine leaving my three, no matter how tired I get of this town." His contemplative tone shifts. "Sorry. I'm in a bit of a mood today. I'm not normally this much of a downer. This town is a great place to raise a family. Clean and safe and friendly. This sort of thing ... what happened with Ian ..."

"I know." I fold my hands in my lap, drawing in a deep breath. "I did a lot of research before moving here. It was supposed to be one of the safest cities in the country."

Silence perches between us for a moment.

"Do they have any leads?" he asks. "I just ... he was such a pillar of the community kind of guy. Respected and all that. I can't imagine he had any enemies. It had to be random, right? Maybe someone passing through? You know, I locked my doors for the first time in years this week."

He shudders.

"The police aren't keeping me in the loop since I'm not next of kin. His parents have promised to call if they hear anything new ..." My voice trails off, along with my thoughts. His parents haven't once called to check on me these past few days, but I haven't called them either.

It is what it is.

"I'm sorry. That was rude of me," he says. "We've only just met and I'm prying into your personal tragedy like it's any of my business. Forget I asked. I'll check the news like everyone else."

"It's okay," I tell him. "I wish I had some information for you, but I'm as in the dark as you are."

He gazes out to the back yard again before rapping his knuckles against the table and standing to leave, his iced tea virtually untouched. "I should get out of your hair. I'm sure you've got better things to do than entertain some nosy neighbor."

I rise. "Thanks for bringing Lucy back. You have no idea how scary it was coming home and realizing she was gone."

"I'm going to take care of that hole for you," he says, wagging his finger. "I just need to run to the home improvement shop on Duff. A little fill dirt, a little sod, it'll be good as new. You going to be around tomorrow?"

"I am."

He heads to the door and I follow.

"I should give you my number. You know, in case you ever need anything," he says.

I don't get the impression that he's hitting on me. He's easily ten years my senior if not more, and he seems like a sincere guy who simply wants to do the right thing, so I oblige and program his number into my phone as he rattles it off. I send a quick text so he has mine.

"You know, it's a shame, what happened. Such a loss for the community," he says a moment later. "Colby's been inconsolable ever since we got the news, not wanting to go to school and all that. The principal sent out an email about having a grief counselor on site all week and I think they're planning a candlelight vigil next week. You're going, aren't you?"

I knew nothing about it. "Of course."

He lingers in my doorway before glancing out at his car. "All right. Well. I'll get a hold of you tomorrow and we can figure out a time to get that fence patched. Let me know if you need anything before then."

"Thanks, David." I lock up behind him.

When I return to the living room I give Lucy a scratch behind the ear, and then I make my way to the bedroom to put away a load of laundry, but somehow find myself standing in front of Ian's side of the closet. Doors yanked, I inhale his familiar scent—cedar and bergamot, leather and suede. Books and paper and pencils and chalk. I run my hand along a row of color-coded wool and cashmere sweaters before stopping at his suit jackets. I pull three options: black, gray, and navy, and I lay them on the bed before sorting through his tie collection.

He loved to dress up.

He said his father taught him that it was always better to be overdressed than underdressed and his mother taught him there was no shame in taking pride in your appearance.

As someone who spends most of her days in athleisure and lives for comfort, I can't imagine wanting to dress up for every little occasion, but I always admired that about him. That commitment and discipline to putting yourself together day in and day out no matter what.

I find one of his favorite cardigans—camel-colored cashmere with leather-patching at the elbows, and I wrap it around myself. Drawing in its comforting scent, I dip my hands in the pockets ... only to have my fingertips brush against a slip of paper.

Pulling it out, I anticipate it to be a receipt or one of Ian's 'notes to self' he was constantly writing. I can't count how many times I'd found his to-do lists lying in random spots all over the house. He was almost compulsive about them—making them on a daily basis and stacking them full of the tiniest of tasks. The man loved to stay busy, loved to have purpose in each and every day. He loved to stay organized, to be productive. As hectic as his schedule was, I imagine it's the only way he stayed sane.

Unfolding the note, I scan the writing.

It's not one of Ian's infamous to-do lists.

It's a phone number, small, scribbled in blue gel pen on a torn sheet of white notebook paper.

I don't remember the last time Ian wore this exact sweater or how old this phone number is. This could have been from anyone, at any time.

Still, I save the paper in case.

Maybe I'll call it later.

Chances are it's nothing, but you never know.

14

DOVE

"CAN YOU SIT DOWN FOR A SECOND?" Noah tries to coax me as I pace my sorry excuse for a living room Saturday night. This thing is half the size of our old one, Ian, and our house was small. Not tiny, but small. I always thought it would be temporary, so I tried not to focus on the fact that you take four steps and you're at the TV, you take another four and you're in the kitchen, but I digress.

"I would if I could, Noah." I gather a hard breath into my lungs, hands on my hips.

I found a picture of you in my junk drawer earlier, Ian. It's from our days at Holbrook. We were wearing matching sweatshirts and my face was painted for homecoming. I'm sitting on your shoulders and we're wearing the biggest, dopiest grins.

I ripped it into the tiniest of pieces. I kept ripping and ripping until the shreds were too small to rip anymore.

That picture is gone now, forever.

Like you.

Like us.

"You're worrying me," Noah says from the middle cushion of my sofa. He stopped by unannounced earlier and let himself in with my spare key because I'd been avoiding his calls and texts and he was "concerned for my wellbeing." To be fair, I've avoided Ari's too. I don't know who to trust anymore. I don't know who's telling the truth and who's lying and I can't look at anyone without wondering who they *really* are.

It's like I'm going crazy, a rapid descent into madness.

It probably doesn't help that I haven't taken a single med since Tuesday, but why start now? I'm seeing things I didn't see before, things I couldn't see, things I refused to see. I see it all now. I see all these people—yourself included—for who and what they really are.

"I confronted Ari," I tell him as I shuffle back and forth across the carpet.

"Yeah? Did she deny it?"

"Of course," I say. "She said she was confronting him about Kirsten being pregnant. And the timeline adds up."

"So she met with your ex-husband and failed to tell you about it? A month later he's dead. You don't find that the least bit shady?"

"Of course I do. And believe me, she's not off the hook. Not yet," I say.

"Good. She shouldn't be," Noah is uncharacteristically snarky tonight, tense. Maybe my mood is rubbing off on him. Or maybe he's got something to hide and it's eating away at his conscience.

"Noah, why don't you ever date?" I ask. I stop pacing, arms folded across my chest.

"What?" He's almost laughing. "Where'd that come from?"

"You're attractive and intelligent and educated and successful, and all you do is hang out with Ari and me. Why? Why aren't you putting yourself out there? Don't you get lonely? Don't you ever want to be with someone? Someone other than me?"

He wrinkles his nose, and I think he's blushing. "I don't know where this is coming from."

"Just answer the question."

"I work long hours. And this town is small. Kind of makes dating impossible."

"Difficult," I correct him. "But not impossible."

"I don't understand where you're going with this ..."

"Ari says you're in love with me," I blurt out.

Noah's eyes widen and he sits up, elbows perched on the tops of his knees as he breathes into his hands.

"Of course." He breathes through his fingers, muffling his voice.

"So she's right. You're in love with me." I continue pacing.

"No," he says. "No, Dove. Ari's wrong. I'm not in love with you."

I stop in my tracks. "Okay, then what's your deal?"

"*My deal?*" Noah massages his temples before his gaze flicks up to mine. "I'm gay."

I take a slow seat in the chair beside him, wrapping my head around this revelation that I never saw coming.

"But you dated Ari ..." I say, as if that could disprove this admission.

"That?" he asks. "We were just hanging out. She's the one who assumed it was a date."

No wonder he talked about me the entire time—I was all they had in common and he had no need to impress her.

"We've been friends for almost two years. Why wouldn't you tell us this?" I ask.

His dark brows rise. "Um, because my sexual orientation is no one's business but mine ..."

It's not like him to snip at me, but if this is true, if he wasn't "out," I can understand why he's being so defensive and protective of this information.

"You're right. It's none of our business. It just stings that you couldn't tell us that. Like you couldn't trust us with that information," I say. "We're your friends."

"You have no idea how many times I wanted to." His posture is more relaxed now than it was a couple of minutes ago, lighter. "So many times it was right there, on the tip of my tongue. But you have to understand, Lambs Grove is notoriously traditional. I wanted to get my business off the ground and established before ... coming out."

"You realize what year it is, right?"

"You realize I have six figures worth of student loans and business debts I'm paying on, right?"

"Fair point."

"I realize this is extreme and I'm playing it way too safe, but I've got too much to lose. The last thing I need is that cult group on the north side of town finding out and then picketing at office and scaring patients away."

"That is true." It wouldn't be the first time the cult destroyed a business who dared to defy their rigid belief system. "Ever think about leaving Lambs Grove?"

"All the time," he says, wistful. "If I had it to do over again, I would've set up shop somewhere else. But this was named one of the safest communities and one of the best places in the country to start a business. I guess I should've done more research."

Without saying another word, I wrap my arms around him. "I love you. And I'm glad you told me this."

He laughs through his nose as his arms wrap around me in return. "I love you too, Dove."

It's then that I wonder if he's lying—not about loving me ... but about being gay.

This could very well be an act.

15

Kirsten

DAVID LETS himself in through the sliding door Sunday morning, his brow covered in a thin sheen. "All fixed. No escaping now."

"Do you think that's how she got out?" I ask. "The gap didn't seem that big when I looked at it."

He looks toward Lucy, brows meeting and lips flattening. "You know, I'm not sure. There was maybe six, eight inches? She'd have to really be motivated I think. Didn't look like she'd dug up the ground or anything. You said the gate was shut, right?"

My theory about Dove isn't that far off then. She could have easily let Lucy out that day since there's no lock on the gate—something I've since remedied. But she loved that dog. Why would she let it roam free in the neighborhood? Why wouldn't she have just taken her? Lucy could've been hit by a car or stolen by some creep.

"You want coffee?" I offer David.

He checks the time on his phone before sliding it back into his pocket. "Yeah, sure. I'll take a cup if you don't mind."

"Not at all." I head to the cupboard, reaching inside and grabbing a mug without looking. By the time I'm pouring the coffee, I realize it was one of Ian's favorites. One of those cheesy, giftshop type of mugs that look like a red apple and have #1 Teacher printed on the side.

David notices but doesn't say anything, and he accepts the coffee with a warm thank you before taking a seat at the kitchen table.

A flickering candle in the centerpiece fills the room with the scent of fall—apples and pumpkin spice and fallen leaves. I don't tend to light candles, but one of my yoga clients gave it to me at this morning's 6 AM class. I pretended not to notice the half-scraped off clearance sticker on the bottom of the jar. It's the thought that counts anyway. When I got home, I decided to light it for no other reason than the fact that Ian adored this season.

"Thanks again for fixing that," I say, nodding toward the back yard.

David smiles before sipping his coffee. "Ah, it's nothing. Besides, it gives me something to do. My weekends without the kids get pretty lonely. I'll take any distraction I can get."

"How often do they stay with you?"

"Not enough." He shakes his head. "We've got shared custody. Fifty-fifty. Every other week, that sort of thing." David takes a drink. "Half the time I'm pulling my hair out trying to run a tight ship, the other half I'm beating my head against the wall out of boredom, missing the heck out of those guys."

I chuckle. "You seem like a good dad."

"I'm all right, I think." He takes another sip, giving me

an aw-shucks kind of wink. "You have any kids?"

"No. I mean ... yes," I say. "I'm pregnant."

David sits up straight, nearly choking on his coffee. It drips down his chin and I rise to grab him a paper towel.

"Warn a guy before you drop that kind of bombshell next time, okay?" David asks, but he's in good spirits.

"I'm so sorry."

"I'm just messing with you." He dabs at the spilled liquid.

"Feels good getting that out," I say, inhaling and exhaling. Until this moment, the only person who knew other than Ian was the dental hygienist at a routine cleaning last month. She wanted to do x-rays and I had to stop her. "I haven't told anyone else. Well, Ian knew. But we weren't going to tell anyone until the holidays."

He readjusts his posture, staring at the flickering candle, his thumb tapping on the side of the mug.

"Well, first of all, congratulations," he says. "Having a kid is one of the greatest things you'll ever do. You'll feel things you never thought you could. Emotions you never knew existed. All the corny, cliché things they say about parenthood? All true. You excited?"

"Terrified ... terrified and nauseous."

David laughs through his nose. "My ex had morning sickness with all three. Even had to be hospitalized a couple of times. Wouldn't wish that upon my worst enemy."

"Mine isn't that bad," I say before rapping on the table top three times.

"I'll let you in on a little secret. Everyone is terrified with their first and no one knows what the hell they're doing. If nausea's your only other problem, I'd say you're going to be just fine." There's a docile twinkle in his eyes. "You're going to be a good mom. I can tell."

"How can you tell?"

He's taken aback by my question, like he didn't expect me to ask it, but I'm genuinely curious.

"I didn't have the greatest examples growing up," I confess. "So I worry ... I worry that I won't know what to do or how to act or how I'm going to be the kind of mother this child needs."

Without hesitating, David says, "You're going to have to be. Whether or not you know how to be one is irrelevant. You're all this kid has now." He tucks his chin. "Sorry if I'm being too blunt here. Guess I'm giving you the same advice I'd give to one of my kids if they were in the same situation."

"It's fine." I wave him off. He reminds me of one of the foster dads I had once. His name was Gary and he had a no-nonsense, tough-love approach that I always pretended to hate but secretly loved. "I've never been one for sugarcoating, so you're good."

"You'll figure it out," he says. "You might be surprised at how natural it comes to you. There's something about holding that baby in your arms that changes everything. All the things that mattered before don't matter as much anymore. You'll see."

I rest my elbow on the table and my chin on the top of my hands. The future doesn't seem as murky as it did earlier.

"Not to change the subject, but I couldn't help noticing Dove hugging you at the funeral the other day," he says with a wince. "I take it you two have kissed and made up?"

I roll my eyes. "That hug came out of nowhere, right?"

He laughs.

"All joking aside," I say, "she kind of scares me."

His ornery smirk disappears. "Well yeah. Anyone who

breaks into your house in broad daylight will do that to a person."

I wince, lungs paralyzed as I examine him in a different light. "I didn't tell you about her breaking in."

His expression grows somber. "Yeah. Whole neighborhood was all worked up about it the other day. Word travels fast. Plus it was in the police blotter ..."

I want to ask him what else people are saying, but I don't want to darken an already-dark conversation.

"Is she leaving you alone?" he asks.

I stare into my half-drunk cup of coffee. I don't drink caffeine often and I know I should be careful with the baby and all, so I decide not to finish the rest.

I want to be a good mother.

I want to prove to David, to Ian, to the Damianis and the rest of the world that I can do this.

"She drives past the house a lot. Or she used to," I say, adding, "when Ian was still alive. Honestly, half of me wonders if she let Lucy out the other day. And the night of the visitation, there was someone in the backyard on the other side of the fence. I said something thinking it was the neighbor, but it wasn't him."

"You're kidding me ..."

"We used to be friends, good friends, and she always seemed so nice and normal," I say. "But I took the man she loved. And now she's doing things, things normal people don't do."

David's fingertips form a peak, which he presses against his nose as he digests this information.

"I never knew her that well, but my interactions with her were always pleasant," he says as if he's giving a statement to the police. "That said, how well do you really know anybody?"

"True."

"I've always believed that you should judge someone by their actions," he says. "Because people will tell you anything you want to hear, and most people can put on a good show, but what they do, especially when they think no one's looking, tells you what kind of person they really are."

"I couldn't agree more."

"Let me ask you this, if it isn't Dove behind this, if she isn't the one harassing you, is there anyone else?"

"I don't really know anyone else in this town. Dove introduced me to one of her friends. Ariadne Salonikas. We didn't hit it off, but it's not like she hated me so much she'd go out of her way to mess with me."

"You sure about that? You sure she's not doing Dove's dirty work?"

I shrug before surrendering a slight laugh. "I'm not sure about anything anymore."

He lifts his palms. "I'm playing devil's advocate here. Trying to get you to think outside the box a little bit. Examine all possibilities."

I pick at a thread on one of the placemats. "Back in Detroit, where I'm from, I dated this guy for a few years. His name was Derrick Patterson and he was ... not the kind of guy you'd want your daughter to bring home, let's put it that way. Anyway, we had this tempestuous relationship. Fire and ice. Fights almost every day. The day I met Adam was the day I broke up with Derrick. Adam hadn't asked me out, and already I decided that there were better people out there for me, that I deserved someone like Adam—even if Adam had no interest in me."

"Wait. Who's Adam?"

"He was my fiancé." I inhale. "He passed away a couple of years ago."

"Okay." His brows meet. "Continue."

"So I was working at this autobody shop, running the office, and Adam was a welder. Long story short, by the time we started dating, Derrick was long gone ... or so I thought." I pause, eyes squeezed tight for a moment. "He'd been stalking me. Adam too. He'd leave notes on my car. Move things around in my apartment. I ended up moving several times because he kept getting in no matter where I lived. He slashed Adam's tires once. I could go on and on ... but when Adam died ..." I glance down at my hands and find them trembling. "It was so sudden, so unexpected. He was leaving a bar one night and someone jumped him in an alley." I swipe at a tear that falls down my left cheek. "There were no cameras, no witnesses. His wallet and phone were taken, so the police said it was probably a mugging, but I know, deep down, that Derrick was behind it. He had to have been."

"And do you know that?"

"I don't know." I shake my head, gazing out the glass doors behind David. "Derrick was crazy. And he was angry. So angry with me." I wipe away another tear. "He told me once that the best way to get revenge on someone was not to hurt them, but to hurt someone they loved."

"Sounds like something out of a mafia movie."

"Yeah. Well, he'd seen them all."

"Is there any way that any of this is that Derrick guy? Maybe he followed you here? Saw you with another guy?"

"He's in prison," I say. "He got locked up for drug possession a few years ago."

"You sure about that?"

"They gave him a five-year sentence, and that was almost two years ago."

"Most prisons are overcrowded and underfunded. They

let a lot of guys out early these days for good behavior. Some of these assholes don't even have to serve half their sentence. If you ask me, the system's all kinds of screwed up, but that's a discussion for another day."

All the relief I felt moments before has been replaced with something I haven't allowed myself to experience in years—fear.

If Derrick got out early for good behavior, it's entirely possible that he's behind Ian's murder.

Rising, I clutch my cold coffee, carry it to the sink, and pour it down the drain. "I'll see what I can find out first thing Monday. Maybe reach out to his parole officer."

"You know ... a lot of people in this town brag about not having to lock their doors at night," he says. "And there's a reason you don't see any home security companies setting up shop downtown. But I kind of think you ought to look into getting something ... just to be safe."

"Those are expensive. All the cameras and locks and sensors. Thousands of dollars, right?" I only know because I looked into it back in Detroit, when Derrick kept getting into my place.

"They make DIY security kits," he says. "They're not terribly expensive. A few hundred bucks for a basic system. You have Wi-Fi, right?"

I nod.

"Great," he says.

"I wouldn't know the first thing about hooking up any of that stuff."

"I'm sure I could figure it out. Can't be that hard." He stands, as if it's time for him to go. It also serves as a reminder of how alone I am—how alone I'm going to be mere minutes from now. "Just think about it and let me know."

16

DOVE

GROWING UP, your parents always had a family dinner on Sundays. Your grandparents would come from Greenville and your aunts and uncles and cousins would drive in from their corners of the state. Your mom would cook a feast fit for Easter or Christmas and all of you would celebrate nothing more than the fact that you were together.

I envied that.

But I loved it too, especially when I became a permanent fixture in the Damiani mix.

But here I am, at my own mother's house Sunday afternoon. There's no laughter, no familiar faces sitting shoulder-to-shoulder around a packed dining table. No joy. No togetherness. Just a ticking kitchen clock and the distorted sound of The Gameshow Network on low volume from some other part of the house.

It's crazy. This place looks exactly the same as it did the last time we were here together. You always used to joke that coming to my mom's was like stepping back in time to 2002, everything all hunter green and burgundy and golden oak galore. The same cow motif stuffing every corner of the kitchen. The same lighthouse oil paintings lining the hall walls.

"Mom, it's me," I call out, removing my shoes by the back door despite the fact that it's never been a house rule. The scent of Virginia Slims, Febreze, and White Diamonds perfume clouds the air, so I know she's around here somewhere.

I hoist my packed duffel bag on the kitchen table and trek to the living room.

"Hey," I say when I find her passed out in the recliner, mouth wide open and her orange tabby cat curled up in her lap.

She stirs before blinking awake and when she sees me, she sits up in the chair, sending the cat darting off.

"Dove. You scared the hell out of me," she says, finger-combing her chaotic brown waves into submission.

It wouldn't be coming home if I didn't get a classic Cathie-Ann greeting. She's nothing like your mom, there's no warmth in her eyes or joyful hug coming at me.

"I tried to call. Left you a voicemail," I say. "And a text."

She reaches for her glasses on the coffee table, sliding them on before grabbing her phone, like she has to verify what I just said.

"Can I stay here for a few days?" I ask. I'm trying not to be short with this woman since I'm asking a favor. "Please?"

Mom squints at me. "What's wrong with your apartment? Are they spraying for bugs again?"

"No. I just don't want to be there right now," I say. I don't tell her about Noah or Ari or their allegations and confessions or how I've avoided their calls all day. I don't want to talk about it. I just want to hide out for a bit in my mother's basement. Neither of them will think to look for me here. I just want peace and quiet. I want to think. I can't do that at my place. Not with the cop cars coming and going, the nosy neighbors, and those two blowing up my phone. "It's too hard. You know, being so close to where Ian was killed."

Mom pouts her thin lips before pushing herself up from the chair. "I'm so sorry, Dove. I'm sure that isn't easy for you. Stay here as long as you need."

She doesn't give me a hug, but let's face it, that would be weird coming from her. Instead, she shuffles past me and heads to the kitchen. I follow her, standing back and watching as she fixes a cup of microwave cappuccino.

"Want one?" she asks.

"No thanks."

"Well you need to drink something. You want water? Your brother replaced the filter for me in the fridge, so it's the good kind."

I grab myself a glass from the skinny cupboard and dispense some cloudy ice cubes to go with my "good" water, and then I take a seat at the table.

To my surprise, as soon as the microwave beeps, Mom retrieves her coffee and sits next to me.

"I thought maybe you'd go to the funeral," I say. It's a lie. We all know she's agoraphobic, but she likes it when we pretend she isn't.

Over the years, we tried to help her but she never wanted it. And why would she? All of her husbands, all of her friends, they enabled her. Even my brother. He'd do her grocery shopping and run her errands, anything to earn a ten- or twenty-dollar bill. She never had a reason to want to change. Not even our wedding was motivation enough for her.

"I wasn't feeling well that day," she says, which is the same excuse she's been using since the dawn of time. I can vaguely remember what life was like before she refused to leave the house, though sometimes I wonder if they're false memories my mind created just so I can feel like I had an ounce of normalcy at some point in my life. "I heard it was a nice service though."

"Oh, yeah?"

"Nancy Cotter went," she says. "You know she used to work with Michael Damiani at the bank before he retired."

"That's right," I say, pretending to know who the hell Nancy is.

"She was over here the other day for bridge club, and she told me something about that friend of yours ... Kirsten, is it?"

"We're not friends," I remind her. She knows the story. I'm not going to repeat it. "What'd you hear?"

"Well supposedly Nancy heard this from her friend Dina who works in the loan department at the bank." Mom stops to sip her cappuccino. "I guess Kirsten was late on her last couple of payments."

"Payments for what?"

"Her business loan," she says.

I find that hard to believe. She was always so responsible with her money, frugal without being annoying about it. She said she knew what it was like to have nothing, so she was extra careful so she'd always have something.

"Apparently when she initially came in for the loan, she put down a good chunk of money up front." Mom keeps her voice low, like we're not in the privacy of her cigarette-scented house. "Said it was an inheritance."

"She actually said that?" I ask. "She used the word inheritance?"

Mom's scrawny eyebrows lift and her thin lashes flutter. "That's what Nancy said."

Getting up from the table, I collect my bag.

"Where are you going?" Mom calls after me as I traipse down to the basement.

"I need to make a phone call," I say. When I get to the spare bedroom in the back corner, I toss my bag on the lumpy mattress and dig my phone from my purse.

I can't find Detective Reynolds's number fast enough.

17

Kirsten

"KIRSTEN, thanks for coming in. I'm Detective Reynolds."
A middle-aged woman with a bushy hair and hooded eyes
extends her hand Monday morning. She must be the one
who left the message on my phone while I was teaching the
eight AM vinyasa class. "Sorry to keep you waiting."

There's something gentle and calming about her, which
I appreciate in silence.

I've never loved police. Respected them, yes. But in my
life, they've only ever represented horrible, unspeakable
things, and I've yet to be able to sever that mental association.

"It's no problem," I say, crossing my legs. A shiver runs
through me and I'm wishing I would've brought a sweatshirt. I came straight here as soon as the class was finished
and the last client had left the building. I'm sure I look as
horrid as I smell, but the message on my phone asked me to

come in as soon as possible and I suppose in my frantic state I took that to heart.

She flips a file open in front of her, followed by a yellow legal pad covered in pen scribbles. I try to keep my eyes off the paper. I don't want to come across as nosy despite the fact that I'm desperate for any new information. I haven't seen Ian's parents since the funeral, and of course they haven't called me.

I do find it a little odd that the police officers questioned me the day I reported Ian missing and then it was radio silence after that. It must mean I'm not a person of interest? It's a good thing, no doubt, but it's also frustrating to be left in the dark for so long.

"How's the investigation going?" I break the silence.

She glances up from her notepad and gives me a heart-felt, closed-mouth smile. "It's going."

A vague answer. Typical detective. That's how they were when Adam died. Everything was *yes, no, not at liberty to say at this time* ...

"Any leads yet?" I ask.

"We're chasing a few." She flips to a new page. "Anyway, I know your time is valuable and so is mine, so I'm just going to cut to the chase, ask you a few questions, and send you on your way. Sound good?"

"Sure. Ask me anything." I slick my cold palms together, placing them between my thighs. Her gaze moves to the goosebumps on my arms. For a second, I wonder if she's going to offer me something, a blanket or jacket, but instead she clears her throat.

"Are you pregnant, Kirsten?"

My jaw would probably be on the floor if it wasn't so clenched right now.

I haven't even been to the doctor.

How would she know this?

"I'm sorry ... who told you that?" It's probably not good practice to answer a detective's question with a question, but I'm too distracted by the leaked information to think straight. "I mean. Yes, Detective. I am. It ... it was a secret. No one knew except Ian and me. Or that's what I thought. Who did he tell?"

"I'm afraid I can't share that information at this time." The apology in her voice matches the one in her blue gray eyes.

Of course not.

"I understand," I say, biting the frustrating on my tongue.

"Approximately how far along are you, Ms. Best?" she asks.

"I don't know ... ten weeks I think? I have an ultrasound this afternoon."

She writes something down. "What's your connection to Adam Meade?"

"What does Adam have to do with this?"

"I'd appreciate if you let me ask the questions, Ms. Best." She smiles. Too much. She's too friendly. Too soft to be a detective. Given the gentle history of Lambs Grove, I imagine this must be her first murder investigation—and it shows.

"I'm sorry. Adam was my fiancé. He passed away a couple of years ago. Back in Detroit."

"Cause of death?"

I exhale, knowing how this is going to look. "He was attacked after leaving a bar."

Her chin juts forward, the tip of her pen frozen against her paper. "So he was murdered."

There's no getting around the fact that it looks like I'm

two for two with the dead boyfriends, but I'm hopeful we can get this investigation back on track.

"Did you ever look into that number I gave you last week? The one I found in his jacket pocket?" I ask, trying to switch gears.

"Yes. It was registered to a prepaid mobile phone that is no longer in service. We have no way of locating it or finding out who it belonged to. There's a reason those phones are popular amongst a certain population. They're impossible to track."

"What would Ian be doing with a number to a prepaid phone?" I ask out loud. The first assumption that comes to my mind has to do with Dove, but given the way he spoke about her, I find that difficult to believe. He was over her. As over someone as anyone could be. He said he fell out of love with her years ago, it just took him a while to get past his fear of breaking her heart. He was worried about what it would do to her, that it might set her off, put her in a bad way.

I'd be willing to bet money that he wasn't secretly communicating with Dove, at least not in a romantic way. Maybe her mental health depended on it? Maybe they spoke in secret whenever she was on the verge of a break-down and he left me out of it because he didn't want me to worry. Ian was thoughtful that way, always trying to be everything to everyone.

"Your guess is as good as mine," she says with a casual shrug. "You said you didn't know how old the number was."

"Right."

"It could've been anything. An acquaintance trying to reconnect, a student wanting help with homework, someone he met at the gas station who wanted to detail his car for fifty bucks," she speaks from the side of her mouth.

"We need to focus on the concrete details here. Things we can track and check into."

"Are you able to see if someone's incarcerated in another state?" I ask.

Her head cocks to one side. "I am. Why do you ask?"

I tell her about Derrick. I tell her everything I told David and then some. I give her every last detail, beginning with his psychological and verbal abuse and ongoing harassment and ending with my suspicions about Adam's attack.

I can't tell if she believes me or not, but she takes notes and stops me to ask a few questions here and there. When I'm done, she tells me to wait there, and then she disappears down the hall.

It seems like forever before she returns.

"All right, I'm having someone check into that Derrick Peterson," she says.

"Thank you." I realize after I say that that she isn't doing me a favor so much as she's trying to piece together her own investigation.

"Is there anyone else you can think of that would've wanted to hurt Ian or get back at you or anything like that? Anyone you think we should check into?"

"You're checking into Dove, right? His ex? I gave her name to the officers at my house last week. They said they were going to talk to her. I wasn't sure if she'd been ruled out yet or—"

"—I've spoken to Ms. Damiani personally, yes," she says, her tone unbiased. "But I'd be curious to hear what *you* have to say about her."

"I assume you're aware that she was driving by our house multiple times a day?"

The detective nods. "Yes, that was in your original statement."

"And you know she was arrested last week for trespassing."

She doesn't flinch. "Yes. Also aware of that."

"There have been a few other things around the house, particularly with the dog and the back yard," I say.

"Such as ...?"

I tell her about Lucy running away and the person on the other side of the fence. She takes notes but is nevertheless nonplussed. I realize these might seem trivial and I'm going off nothing more than a paranoid hunch, but she can't deny the picture they paint when everything's added up.

"This is just a theory," I continue. "But what if that burner phone number was Dove's? What if she and Ian were communicating on the side? And what if he told Dove about the pregnancy and she lost it? What if she lured him out there on false pretenses, acting like she was going to hurt herself or something, and then killed him?"

"Do you know how Ian was killed?"

I nod. "They say he was strangled."

"How tall would you say Dove is?"

"I don't know? Five two or five three?"

"Ian was on the taller side. Broad shoulders. Athletic. Six foot two. Do you think it's possible she could have overpowered him?"

Is this a trick question? Anyone can do anything if they want to do it badly enough.

"With Dove, anything is possible." I begin to add, "Maybe she drugged him" when there's a knock at the door and a man appears in the doorway with a slip of paper.

Detective Reynolds takes it from him with a pleasant, "Thanks."

A second later, he's gone and the door clicks shut.

"What is it?" I ask.

She turns the paper toward me, and I find a black and white printout with Derrick's booking photo and fingerprints on it. At the bottom, highlighted in neon yellow, are the words: RELEASED — JUNE 27th.

"According to this, they let him out about four months back," she says, turning the paper back toward her. "For good behavior."

I'm stunned into silence, my body succumbing to uncontrollable tremors.

Detective Reynolds peers at me from her side of the table. "Still want to pin it all on Dove?"

18

DOVE

"HI, LORI," I stand outside your parents' front door late Monday morning. I called in to work and spent the last two hours baking blueberry muffins from scratch—your dad's favorite. I haven't spoken to your parents since the funeral Friday and I thought it might be nice to check on them.

You might have lost all of my respect, but they still have it, and I'm going to hold onto that relationship with everything I have.

"Dove, what are you doing here?" Your mom's greeting is uncharacteristically subdued and she steps outside, pulling the door closed behind her.

I will not be invited in.

Is Kirsten in there?

Is she feeding them lies about me?

"I had the day off," I say with a smile. "Did a little baking, thought I'd stop by and deliver these myself."

I extend the basket toward her, but she doesn't take it. She doesn't even look at it.

"Is it true?" she asks.

"What?"

"Did you break into Ian's house last week? The day before the visitation?"

My jolly demeanor fades.

"We had to find out in the police blotter," she says, a delicate hand splayed over her chest as she gasps.

I wasn't expecting this. I wasn't anticipating having to explain myself here and now. The whole drive here I had visions of the three of us catching up in the formal living room over muffins and coffee, reminiscing about the good old days and vowing to keep in touch going forward.

"How *could* you?" she asks. "And then for you to stand by our side at the funeral like nothing happened? You made a fool of us in front of all of our friends and family."

"I'm so sorry," I say, letting the basket fall to my side. "I ... I had a spare key and I wanted to find his will and—"

"His will is on file with the family's attorney. We could have requested it for you."

Right. Like I was going to ask that of them. I know how it would've looked.

"I know," I say. "You're right. I wasn't thinking."

The door behind her opens and your dad fills the frame, his lips flat as he peers down his nose at me. I've never seen Michael look at anyone that way before, and I know now what you meant when you always said his quiet disappointment was the worst kind.

"Lori, you're getting worked up again. Come back inside," he says. "Dove, you're not welcome back here. Do you understand?"

I spot a flash of tears in your mother's eyes as she turns

away and disappears into the house. Your dad shuts the door and I flinch when I hear the pop of the lock on the other side. It's a final sort of sound and it resonates to the deepest parts of me—the parts that echo with a hollowed emptiness.

In one week, I've lost everything.

I suppose now that makes me a woman with nothing to lose.

19

Kirsten

I LOCK up my office and leave the studio around a quarter past five on Tuesday and wave goodbye to the evening instructor, Pamela. A quick shower at home and then I'll be on my way to the Damianis for that family dinner Michael invited me to last week.

I toss my purse on the passenger seat of my car a moment later, the top gaping wide and revealing a string of connected ultrasound pictures from yesterday's appointment. I plan to take these to Michael and Lori, even give them one if they ask. That said, I have no expectations. Either they'll be elated that their son will live on through this tiny miracle, or they won't. I don't know them well enough to be able to predict any of this.

I'm ten weeks, six days as of today. Healthy heartbeat. Everything looks good.

It takes ten minutes to get home with Lambs Grove's

version of rush hour traffic, and I can't ignore the tiny skip my heart does when I unlock the garage entrance door. Lucy greets me, acting completely normal, and I scan the fully-lit kitchen and living room. With Derrick being out, I'm taking every safety precaution now. I read online somewhere that you should keep your house as lit as possible. People don't like to go where they'll be seen. They like to lurk in the dark, in the shadows, where you don't notice them.

As soon as I determine Derrick isn't hiding anywhere in the house and that all the doors and windows are locked and latched, I jump in the shower and throw on a pair of jeans and oversized rust-colored sweater before stepping into some leather booties. I pour Lucy some kibble and let her out one last time before locking up and taking off.

I make a note of every car I pass on Blue Jay Lane. All have local plates. None of them have Derrick's signature white-blond hair. He always tried to color it, but the darker shades always turned orange and the Crayola-type shades always made him stand out too much, more so than the natural blond.

The day I broke up with Derrick is a memory I'd disremember if I could, but I'll never forget what he said to me: *"I swear to God, Kirsten, the second you find happiness I'm going to rip it away, just like you did to me."*

If it is Derrick behind Adam and Ian's deaths, so far he's made good on that promise.

When I left the meeting with Detective Reynolds yesterday morning, she promised to get a hold of Derrick's parole officer to find out where he's working and to have someone back home bring him in for questioning and to try and establish an alibi.

I'm halfway across town when it occurs to me that Derrick might very well have an alibi, that maybe I'm wrong about his involvement in this. Dove still has the strongest motive out of everyone involved. I can't lose sight of that.

When I get to the Damianis' house, I park in front of Ian's sister's car on the street. The house is lit, soft with lamplight visible through sheer curtains. It looks warm and inviting and not filled to the brim with pain and loss.

Before heading in, I shoot David a text, I THINK I'M GOING TO TAKE YOU UP ON THAT SECURITY SYSTEM OFFER.

David replies with, PROBABLY A WISE DECISION ...

A nice system with multiple cameras and Wi-Fi capability isn't in my budget, but you can't put a price on peace of mind. With Dove's unstable behavior and Derrick free as a bird, I'm willing to slap a top-of-the-line system on a credit card if I need to.

Three dots fill the screen, followed by David's response, I HAVE MY KIDS THIS WEEKEND AND A HUNDRED FOOTBALL GAMES AND TRACK MEETS. I CAN HOOK IT UP FOR YOU EARLY NEXT WEEK IF THAT WORKS?

THAT WOULD BE AWESOME. THANK YOU! I write back. One of these days, God willing, I'll get a chance to return the favor, to do something for him for a change.

I silence my phone and tuck it into the bottom of my purse, ensuring the ultrasound pictures are folded neatly and placed into a side pocket only visible to myself. I'm not sure when I'm going to work this whole baby thing into the conversation, so I'm keeping them out of sight for now.

Climbing out of my car, I scan my surroundings. A

neighbor across the street is hanging fall wreaths on her door, and the brick colonial monstrosity beside it is a vision of purple, yellow, and orange flowers in a hundred different planters.

It's going to be Halloween soon.

Ian asked if I'd dress up with him this year. He said it was his tradition to dress up like a historical figure for trick or treaters. Last year he was Ben Franklin. This year he asked if I'd be his Theodosia as he planned to go as Aaron Burr. He didn't care that the kids more than likely wouldn't know who the heck we were—he wanted to pay homage to one of his favorite historical love stories. Interesting, now that I think about it, to romanticize a romance born of unfaithfulness. Not that he cheated on Dove—but that isn't the kind of love story most people would idealize.

I stand outside the front door and press the glowing yellow button. A soft chime comes from inside and a second later, Michael's broad physique fills the door.

"Kirsten, good to see you." He's dressed in a checkered sweater vest, white button down, slacks with creases ironed down the front and gold-toed socks. "Come on in."

The smell of something savory—pot roast or the like—fills the foyer the moment I step inside the house. A pile of shoes in varying sizes rests on the rug—probably Ian's sister and her kids.

"Everyone's in the dining room," Michael says, waving for me to follow him. I lived in a foster home once where every meal was a formal sit-down type of thing in their dining room. The parents in that house were the worst, but four months later I left there knowing the difference between dinner forks and salad forks and which side the bread plate went on.

I slide out of my booties and trek behind him, my palm

damp against my purse strap. I'm not sure why I'm so nervous. I'm used to people not liking me. I'm used to not being included. It's not like life will cease to go on if the Damianis reject me—reject *us.*

"Hi," I give everyone a wave before sliding my hands in my back jeans pockets. Ian's sister, Claudia, gives me a warm yet wordless acknowledgement. This is only the third time we've met, aside from the funeral.

"Kirsten, won't you please have a seat?" Lori asks.

Ian's niece and nephew, whose names escape me stare at me with the same twinkling blue eyes their uncle once had.

"Hannah, Ethan," Claudia says, "Say hello to Kirsten. She was Uncle Ian's friend."

Friend.

I try not to take it personally.

The kids each mutter a shy greeting before getting into some kind of kicking match under the table. Claudia tends to them while Lori asks if I'd like anything to drink. She offers a glass of wine at first, and I'm so distracted by the newness and strangeness of being here without Ian that I almost forget. *Almost.*

"Water would be great, thank you," I say, taking a seat at an empty chair.

"Of course," Lori says, heading to the kitchen. She returns with a crystal chalice filled with ice water before disappearing and returning once more with a plate of appetizers. She hands the dish to me and I pass it to Michael on my right. My stomach rumbles and I realize I haven't eaten since breakfast this morning.

"Sure you don't want any wine?" Michael asks a moment later as he tops off his stemless glass with a generous splash of red.

If Detective Reynolds knows about the pregnancy, I'm sure the Damianis do as well. No point on saving the news until later.

"I'm glad you invited me here tonight because there's something I wanted to share with you all," I say. Every eye is glued to me and there isn't so much as a clink of a fork against a china plate. "I was waiting. We were going to wait. But I went to the doctor today …"

Lori stands behind Michael, her hands white-knuckling the back of his chair. Everyone is still as statues, barely breathing.

"I'm pregnant," I say, exhaling.

The grandfather clock in the hall ticks. The icemaker in the kitchen rumbles. No one says a thing.

"I'm not quite eleven weeks. It's still early," I continue. "Ian wanted to wait until Christmas to share the news. We only found out about a month ago."

I'm feeding them information, bit by bit, answering their silent questions.

"Well," Michael says an endless moment later. "How about that. A baby."

A baby …

Not exactly the reaction I was hoping for.

I look to Lori and find tears in her eyes, though I can't tell if they're happy or sad or a mix of the two.

"You hear that, Lori?" Michael reaches back, placing his hand over Lori's.

"Wow," Lori says. "It's certainly a bittersweet announcement, isn't it?"

I nod.

Claudia rises from her chair, moving toward me. A second later, she wraps me in an expensive perfume-scented hug. "I'm so happy for you. And I'm happy for Ian. A part of him will get to live on."

Lori dabs at her eyes with the backs of her hands before gifting me with her own hug, this one tighter, longer, like a grieving mother getting another chance to hold her child.

"I have to confess ... I saw you at the pharmacy back in September," she says. "You didn't see me. But I saw what you were buying. I had my hunch, but I didn't know for sure." She places a hand on my shoulder, her palm warm and steady and reassuring as it lingers. "Thank you for sharing this with us and not making us wait. I think we could all use something to look forward to."

Lori smiles at me for the first time. The icy demeanor she once held around me has seemed to have melted. If it weren't for the baby growing inside me, this moment wouldn't be happening, but I choose not to focus on that.

This child has a chance at having grandparents. Actual grandparents that will love it and be a part of its life. I would never dream of standing in the way of that.

"I have ultrasound pictures if you'd like to see?" I reach for my purse, which is sitting by my feet on the rug below.

"Oh, my. Yes." Lori claps her manicured hands together and Michael leans forward.

I retrieve the black and white photos and hand them over. "Not much to see at this stage."

"Oh, it's wonderful." Ian's mother dabs at the corners of her eyes again, grinning ear to ear, not a speck of red lipstick out of place. "Look at this, Michael. Ian's child."

She places a palm over her heart as she carries the connected images to Claudia and the kids. The way she's parading them around would make you think she's a first-time grandmother, but I get it. It's about Ian and his legacy and having a piece of him to hold onto. She has my full sympathies.

"How are you feeling, Kirsten?" Claudia asks.

"I'm good all things considered. A little nausea, but nothing else," I say.

Lori returns the ultrasound images before taking her seat and asking a hundred questions about the baby and the pregnancy and if I've thought of names and what my due date is. I've never seen her talk this much, ever. But I answer her questions as best I can. Claudia serves up dinner while Lori and I chat, and for the next hour, I find my deflated spirit beginning to fill with hope.

For the first time in my life, everything might turn out okay.

At the end of the night, Lori wraps herself in a baby blue pashmina and walks me to my car—something she never would have done before.

"Kirsten, I wanted to have a moment alone with you," she says when we reach the curb at the end of the driveway. A smoky fall breeze blows a wisp of platinum blonde hair across her forehead and the moon makes her blue eyes shine. "Michael and I ... we didn't make an effort to get to know you before. We thought you were ... what do you call it? A summer fling? Anyway, after spending time with you tonight and you sharing this news, I'd like to change that. I'd love to get to know you better. If that's okay with you?"

I can see why Dove loved Lori so much. She's either for you or against you, but when she's for you, she's sweet and maternal, the kind of mom I always wanted. In my mind's eye, I envision Lori as a younger woman, rocking her son to sleep, cheering him on at soccer games, and placing wet washcloths on his feverish brow in the middle of the night. Lori smells like Chanel perfume, a touch of Downy, and an abundance of L'Oréal hair spray, and she has the kind of smile that lights up her entire face—like Ian.

"I'd love that," I say, forcing myself to mentally bury the fact that she initially wrote me off as some fling. We're moving forward, making progress. That's all that matters.

Lori wraps me in her arms again. "Maybe I'll swing by later this week? We could go over some baby pictures of Ian. You know, for fun."

"Stop by any time."

She releases her hold on me and her eyes search mine. "I'd also like to go over Ian's will with you at some point."

"Oh? Okay ..." That came out of nowhere.

"It turns out he didn't update it after the divorce, which is highly unlike him." The corners of her mouth dip at the sides. "He left it all to Dove, so once the baby is here, you'll have to contest that. We'll help you in any way, financially or otherwise. There's no reason why any of it should go to her ... and I found out about her breaking into the house. Kirsten, you should have told us."

"I didn't want to bother you with it."

"Sweetheart, my goodness." She places a hand on her heart, her metal bracelets jangling like distant wind chimes. "If anything like that ever happens again, we want you to call us right away. She has no reason to be over there playing amateur detective and bothering you."

It's funny, now that I'm carrying Ian's child, Lori's suddenly elevated me to Goddess status, treating me like sacred royalty carrying the keys to the kingdom.

"Thank you. I don't think it'll happen again but if it does, I'll call."

"Michael and I are still trying to wrap our heads around why on earth she'd do something like that. We've known her since she was, what, fourteen? Fifteen? It's not like her."

Lori clucks her tongue. "We're just heartbroken over it. As much as we don't want to, we've decided to distance ourselves from her for a bit, for safety reasons. A precautionary thing, you know? And you should too."

"You really think she's dangerous?"

Lori twists the diamond circle pendant hanging from her neck. I never realized how much jewelry this woman wears until now. Ian was always trying to buy me jewelry early on, but he learned quickly that I'm not into that kind of thing. I'd take his time and affection over sapphires and emeralds any day of the week.

"It's hard to say," Lori says. "She's a good person. She means well. But she's had a few bouts in the past where she wasn't quite herself, and let's just say there's a side of her we don't often get to see. I think we're seeing that side right now."

I think back to what Ian told me once, about Dove and her mood disorder and what happens when she forgets her medications. He said it had only happened two or three times over the course of their relationship, that she was always diligent about her pills, taking them like clockwork.

Why would she stop taking them now? And how long has she been off them?

"I'll let you get going," Lori says, rubbing my arm before tightening her shawl over her shoulders.

"Thanks again for dinner," I say. "And stop by whenever you'd like with those baby pictures."

Ian's mother smiles and waves, her eyes glossy in the dark as I climb into the driver's seat of my car and start the engine. I drive home floating on a cloud. I've always wanted a family like Ian's, and now I might have a chance at that. Visions of holidays spent together and my children playing with Claudia's dance in my head the whole ride home.

Eight minutes later, I'm turning onto Blue Jay Lane.

I'm four cars away from the house when I spot a Civic parked out front, tail lights glowing like cherries in the night.

Dove is here.

20

DOVE

KIRSTEN'S GARAGE door begins to rise and a second later her mint green Fiat ramps up the slanted driveway. I climb out, in case she didn't see me. Hands shoved in my pockets, I make my way closer. Calm. Collected. A woman on a mission.

Her driver door swings open a second later and she slams it shut before folding her arms across her chest. Her eyes are wild, her brows pointed.

"What the hell are you doing here?" she spits her words at me.

"I have to show you something," I begin to reach into my purse, but Kirsten gasps, lunging at me and wrestling my bag off my shoulder. I realize now she thinks I have a gun, which is ridiculous. I've never so much as touched a gun in my life.

She tosses my bag out of reach, and it lands on the cracked concrete with a muffled thud.

"O ... kay," I say. I take my time raising my hands to show her I'm unarmed and not going to make any sudden movements.

"You shouldn't be here." Her words are breathy, panicked, and I glance down and realize she's gripping her phone in her shaky hands. I'm not sure when she had time to grab it. Maybe she keeps it tucked into her bra or in her back pocket. I imagine after everything that's happened, she's always on high alert, and I don't blame her. We still don't know who killed you, Ian. It's important to keep our defenses up, to be ready for anything.

"Five minutes," I say. "I need to talk to you for five minutes."

"Leave now or I'm calling the police." She shows me her screen and the numbers 9-1-1 pressed into the keypad. Her shaky thumb hovers over the green 'call' button.

"There's something you're going to want to see," I say, hands still lifted. "It has to do with Ian. And it's in that purse. The one you threw over there."

She squints as she studies me, unsure if she should trust me.

"Look for yourself," I encourage her, nodding toward the bag. "There's a black flip phone inside. A burner. I found it in Ian's office that day I was here."

Kirsten looks to me then to the bag before swiping it off the ground and rifling through it. A second later, she pulls out the black plastic cell phone and examines it under what little moonlight illuminates the driveway.

"How do I know you're not lying?" she asks after flipping it open and staring at the thing like she's examining a relic.

"The arrow keys," I say. "Go to messages then use the arrow keys. Look at the time stamps on those, Kirsten. They start two Decembers ago ... and the last message was sent the night he was killed. He was meeting up with someone. And he never came home."

Her expression hardens as she reads through the messages, one after another. There are hundreds if not more. She won't have time to go through them all, not here, not now.

"Can we talk about this inside?" I ask when I spot a neighbor across the street peeking through their living room curtains.

"This is fake," she says, handing it over. "You're trying to trick me into letting you inside my house, and then you're going to do something."

"I would never."

"I don't know that."

"You're right, Kirsten. You don't." I pause, not knowing how I can convince her that I'm not a threat. Her dark eyes flick between mine before scanning the area, as if someone else is waiting in the bushes to jump out. "There's a book in Ian's office on his shelf that's not a book. It's hollowed out. There's a lock on it. The code is one zero one six. He always kept things in there, valuables and whatnot. I found this phone in there last week. I didn't have a chance to charge it until Thursday. If you want to sit down and look through them all, then we need to go inside. Otherwise Mrs. Higgins across the street is going to call the police, and they're going to haul me away for trespassing and confiscate this phone and we won't be any closer to finding Ian's killer."

She's silent, contemplative.

"He cheated on us both," I say, one hand on my hip. "He's not who we thought he was, and I'll be damned if I take the fall for this."

"Empty your pockets," she says.

"What?"

"Empty your pockets, show me you don't have any weapons on you."

With the burner phone still in my grip, I turn my pockets inside out and lift my sweater before patting down my jeans and showing her that I'm unarmed.

Offering a reticent sigh, she grabs my purse off the ground and waves for me to follow her through the garage. A second later, she produces a shiny silver key to get in. She must have changed the locks.

The house is lit like Christmas, every light and lamp glowing and not a shadow in sight.

She's living in terror. Is this all because of me? Because of last week?

Or is there something she knows that she's not letting on?

Lucy clicks across the wood floor, head hung low. She takes her time coming toward us, as if she's confused. I scratch her behind the ears and her tail begins to wag.

"Here," I hand the phone back as she places my bag on the kitchen table. "I want you to read these and see if you can see something I don't. They're pretty generic, but maybe if you look at the more recent time stamps, something might click?"

Kirsten glares at the screen, eyes scanning, shaking her head every so often before moving to the next message.

"These were mostly sent in the middle of the night," she says. "Two fifteen in the morning. Three forty-two. One thirty. I'm a hard sleeper. A few times I woke up and found him grading papers in the living room, but other than that ...?"

"Ah, yes. The old grading papers and watching Netflix because he can't sleep trick. He used it on me too." I think about the few times I checked on you, Ian. I now know that The Office playing in the background and the stack of ungraded tests on the coffee table were nothing more than props. To think you kissed me goodnight and sent me back to bed just so you could finish jerking it to some strange woman on your cell phone brings a rise of bile to the back of my throat.

"I found a phone number in the pocket of one of Ian's suits last week," Kirsten says, letting the phone fall to her side. "I gave it to the detective on his case. She said it was connected to a burner phone, and tracking down the owner and location would be impossible."

"Do you still have the number?" I ask.

Kirsten treks into the kitchen, tugging on a drawer before producing a slip of paper.

"Oh my God. We have to compare them," I say, pointing to the phone and slip of paper. "See if it's the same number."

Kirsten flips the phone open and pulls up the messages. A second later, her fingers lift to her lips and she takes a step back.

"They match, don't they?" I ask.

Her stupefied gape darts to mine. "Yeah."

"The last thing he texted her was to meet him at the same place at the same time," I say. "That was the night he died. Whoever was on the other end of this is the person who killed Ian."

Kirsten leans against the countertop's edge, elbows angled into her sides and a hand covering her mouth. "I don't understand. If he'd been talking to her since the two of you were married, why wouldn't he date her after the divorce? Why would he go straight to me?"

I shrug. "I don't have an answer for you. All I know is

there's a part of Ian he didn't share with either of us. A part of him he only shared with her."

"You think you know someone."

"Right?"

Her eyes widen. "You should give this to the police."

"Absolutely not. They'll use it as an excuse to charge me with burglary or something, I don't know. And it's not like they can use it as evidence. It's been tampered with, and there aren't any witnesses who can vouch for the fact that I took this from his office that day."

"How'd you get it out of here anyway?"

"I had it in my purse. When they booked me, they assumed it was a personal belonging of mine and kept it with the rest of my stuff." I wave my hands. "Helps that you didn't report anything missing ... since you didn't know he had this."

Kirsten releases a frustrated push of air. "He's such a freaking liar."

Her palm moves to her lower belly, and she rests it there with careful subtlety.

"I know about the baby, Kirsten," I say. She's quiet, tense and still. "It's okay. I was hurt at first but ... whatever. I don't want you to think I would ever wish anything bad upon you or the child, okay?"

"I'm so sorry, Dove." Kirsten's lower lip begins to quaver. "If I could go back, I'd—"

I lift a hand to silence her. "Stop. You did what you did. There's no changing that. We're never going to be friends again, so let's focus on figuring out who the hell was on the other side of this cell phone so the police will get me the hell off their radar."

"Have they officially named you a suspect?"

"No. But I'm pretty sure I'm a person of interest," I say.

"It's the kind of thing a jury would eat up in a heartbeat, too. Bitter ex-wife strangles husband on their anniversary ... Plus the fact that you're my former friend and now you're carrying his child gives me all the motive they'd need. Oh, and let's not forget the fact that Ian neglected to update his will after the divorce and left everything to me."

"But if you didn't do it, if they can't prove it with DNA evidence ...?"

"I don't know what world you're living in or if you've never watched an episode of Dateline in your life, but juries have convicted people with less evidence than that." I drag my hands through my hair, feeling the grit between my fingers. I can't remember the last time I washed it. God, I must look insane. "So will you help me? Will you get on board with this? Because I didn't kill Ian. And I don't think I can prove that alone."

"I don't understand why you need my help. All you have is this untraceable burner phone that you can't prove belonged to him. That has nothing to do with me."

"Because I need someone on my side here, Kirsten," I say with a huff. "Someone who believes me. You believe me, don't you?"

"What about Ari and Noah?"

I hesitate before responding, but given the fact that she doesn't speak to Ari and she's never met Noah, I think I'm safe to share this with her.

"Noah claims Ari and Ian were sneaking around together," I say.

Kirsten gasps. "Do you think the woman on the other end of the phone is Ari?"

I shrug. "I have no idea. I confronted her about it and she denied it. Then she turned it around on Noah, claiming Noah is in love with me and obsessed and implying he wanted Ian out of the picture. I talked to Noah about it and —" I can't tell her about Noah being gay. I promised I wouldn't tell a soul. "Let's just say it's not Noah. He isn't interested in me like that."

Assuming he's being honest with me.

A wild theory hits me out of nowhere. What if Ian and Noah had some kind of secret relationship? In all my years of being with Ian, I never once doubted his sexual preference for women, but some men are masters at putting on airs. What if the two of them had a secret fling? What if my getting the job at the clinic had nothing to do with hitting it off with Noah and everything to do with my relationship to Ian?

What if that's why the last message Ian received from the other person mentioned they were tired of sneaking around?

"I have to go," I tell Kirsten. I need to think about this some more, and I need to get out of here before Kirsten pries the theory out of me. It's ripe and on the tip of my tongue, and it wouldn't be hard.

"What? Why?"

"I'll explain more later. There's something I need to check into." I retrieve my purse from the table and show myself out.

On the drive home, I think about Noah, about his confession and the text messages, about all the things I told him about Ian. He knew our anniversary date. He knew I was upset about Ian and Kirsten moving in together. If Ian refused to go public with their relationship after all this time and if Ian told Noah about the pregnancy, that might certainly have set him off.

It's strange, too, how Noah showed up in Lambs Grove out of nowhere. He doesn't have family ties here. He grew up in Michigan. He claims his research brought him here, that everything he read led him to believe this would be the best place to start a dental practice. But what if none of that is true? What if he met Ian online and moved here hoping they could finally be together?

My stomach churns and I slam on my brakes, stopping outside the Baptist church on Vine Street. Stumbling out of my car, I hunch over near some overgrown hedges, dry heaving. When the sensation finally passes, I return to my car and take a few sips of room-temperature water from a bottle I find on the floorboard.

Before I peel away, I whisper a silent prayer. "Please don't let it be Noah."

21

Kirsten

I STARE at the rickety ceiling fan above the bed, unable to stop thinking about the text messages Dove showed me tonight. At first I thought it was some kind of trap. I was certain she wanted to lure me into the house and strangle me the way Ian was strangled, but once I could see she was unarmed, once I read the text messages for myself, I decided to take a chance.

There was something different about her. More life in her eyes. Or maybe it's determination. Desperation? Or perhaps this is how she is when she's off her meds ...

Detective Reynolds didn't tell me Dove was a suspect, but Dove is convinced they're going to pin this all on her. I have to admit the most damning motives could be tied to her and a judge and jury wouldn't think twice about it.

I close my eyes, but my body refuses to sink into the soft pillow-top mattress. I can't get comfortable. I can't stop the thoughts barreling through my mind at top speed. Flinging off the covers, I trek to the kitchen to take a prescription nausea pill my new obstetrician gave me yesterday. She said it might knock me out until my body gets used to it, but she wasn't against using it to help me get to sleep. She compared it to Benadryl, assured me it was safe.

I chase the tiny pill with a glass of tap water and make another pass around the house, triple-checking doors and windows and locks and lights.

When I'm done, I return to the bedroom and crawl back under the covers with Lucy, but not before shoving the small chest of drawers in front of the door for the tiny peace of mind it'll bring.

Maybe tomorrow I'll ask David if he can get me a gun—but first, he'll have to teach me how to shoot.

22

DOVE

THERE'S no way of knowing whether Kirsten is home because every light in your house is alive Wednesday night, but I knock on the door regardless. The sound of Lucy's barking makes its way through the wooden door, followed by the faintest sound of careful footsteps. A second later, the door swings open and Kirsten stands on the other side of your glass storm door in black yoga pants and a pink sports bra, one hand on her softening hips.

For the briefest of moments, I think about her changing body, how beautiful she'll look pregnant, and how much you're going to miss all because you were a selfish, cheating, lying asshole.

Your loss, Ian.

"Hi," she says, her brows twisted like a question mark.

I realize it's late. I realize it's dark. I realize it might freak her out showing up here unannounced this time of night.

"I stopped by a couple times earlier today. You weren't home," I say.

"You could have called."

"I'd rather not," I say. "Can I come in?"

"I don't know, Dove ... it's kind of late, don't you think?"

I realize it's almost ten o'clock and more than likely she's teaching a five AM class at the studio, but she wasn't here the last time I stopped by or the last time, and this isn't something that can wait.

"Ian had this ... authenticator device," I say, squinting. "It was silver. About this big." I cup my fingers into a 'c' shape. "He kept his passwords on it. At first he bought it during that cryptocurrency craze a couple of years ago, and then he started using it for everything else, email, banking, that sort of thing."

"Okay. What are you getting at?"

"I tried logging into his email earlier and it asked for a keycode—which means I can't log in without the authenticator."

"I've never seen him use anything like that, ever. I wouldn't even know where to find it," she says.

"Right. But I do."

She begins to say something and then stops, opening the storm door and letting me through. I head straight to the guest room at the end of the hall, making a beeline for the top right drawer of the white lacquered nightstand. Reaching in, I shove a few things around until my fingers graze the cool slick of polished metal taped to the back.

God, you're so predictable, Ian. Even when you're not.

"Got it," I say. "Can I use your laptop?"

Kirsten leaves, returning a minute later with a light-as-air Apple laptop. We take a seat on the edge of the guest bed

—which hasn't been used in years since you used to hate it when people invaded your personal space. I always thought that was an interesting contradiction since you were such a people person, but now it kind of makes sense. You only wanted people to see the outward, charming version of yourself, never what existed behind closed doors. Not the version of you with secret chambers and hiding spots.

I laugh to myself. Or am I laughing at myself? Either way, it's funny how I used to think you were quirky that way. Turns out you were just a jerk.

Kirsten taps in her password and I fire up the authenticator. The little symbol along the top shows it's connected to your Wi-Fi. I enter the passcode, which surprisingly isn't one zero one six—our anniversary. It's one two one eight—your birthday. A second later, I'm in, and a list of your accounts populates the tiny screen next to encrypted passwords covered with asterisks.

"Okay, let's try this one first," I show Kirsten your first email address, an old Yahoo account you've had since the dawn of the internet. I don't think you'd be dumb enough to use that one, but you never know. She signs in and the authenticator spits out a code that we use in place of your password. A second later, we're in.

We scan your inbox, mostly junk, with a handful of chain emails from your aunt in California.

"Next," I say, placing the authenticator between us. Within a minute, we're logged into a Gmail account I didn't know you had. But judging by the scarcity of your inbox, it looks like you only ever used it for coupon codes and Netflix free trials.

The third account we try is another new-to-me address: histprof4477 at yaya mail dot net.

History professor? Ian. You were a high school history teacher.

Big difference there, buddy.

A second later, Kirsten gasps as she angles the computer toward me. "Dove, look."

The screen is filled with hundreds of email chains, conversations passing back and forth between you and aLLTHEHEARTEYEs at yaya mail dot com.

My heart ricochets against the inside of my chest, my vision shakes, and I shove down the urge to dry heave so I can focus on the task at hand. Reaching over Kirsten, I run my fingers along the track pad, moving the cursor to the first email, which is dated two days before you were killed.

I'M TIRED OF SNEAKING AROUND. TWO YEARS IS LONG ENOUGH. I WANT TO BE WITH YOU. THE REAL YOU ... IN PUBLIC. WHO CARES WHAT PEOPLE THINK? I'M OVER IT. I LOVE YOU MORE THAN I'VE EVER LOVED ANYONE IN MY LIFE AND I'M DONE SHARING. LIFE IS TOO SHORT TO LIVE OUR LIFE FOR OTHER PEOPLE. I WANT THE LIFE YOU PROMISED ME.

"DOVE, you said Noah saw Ari with Ian, right?" Kirsten asks.

"Yeah?" I don't think we're on the same page here.

"Look at that email address. Starts with an A and ends with an S."

She's right. It does. But I read the email in a different context.

"Maybe I'm reading too much into that," Kirsten says,

tugging on her lower lip as she re-reads the message. "It's a stretch."

My mouth is dry and the words rest on the edge of my tongue, begging to be said. I need to tell her my theory about Noah. If I'm right, it means solving this entire case. If I'm wrong, it means breaking a promise to a trusted friend—and more than likely losing my job if and when he finds out.

I think back to the last few days, how infrequent my interactions with Noah have been. I thought maybe he was giving me space given what happened over the weekend and all the pointing fingers, but maybe he was giving me space for his own benefit? Maybe he was lying low? Waiting for the dust to settle? Acting casual?

I didn't sleep more than twenty minutes at a time last night, and by the time I woke up, I was still fixated on my Noah theory, so I called into work. I left a voicemail on the receptionist's phone, knowing she'd pass it along and I wouldn't have to talk to him personally. I don't know that I can look at him nor do I know if I want to be around someone so coldblooded.

"My ex is out of prison," Kirsten says a minute later, before I have a chance to let it slip about Noah. "You know the one, right? Derrick?"

"The crazy stalker?"

"Yeah. Him. I thought maybe he had something to do with this," she says. "But after seeing these texts and emails ... this isn't his MO. He's more of a break-your-knees-with-a-baseball-bat, bash-in-your-windshield type. This would be too much work for him. Besides, Ian and whoever this chick is have clearly met up several times if they have a usual place and usual time."

I click to the next message, an outbound note from you talking about your picnic under the stars and how amazing it was. You never gave me a picnic under the stars, Ian. Then again, we did our dating in broad daylight. We didn't have to sneak around. How convenient I must have been for you. A normal marriage, a normal house, a normal wife, a normal life. I was covering for you and didn't even know it.

"How the hell do we find out who this is?" Kirsten asks, clicking on the next message. The sender is talking about the flowers you sent. I try to think back to a recent time when Noah might have received flowers at the office, but I'm drawing blanks. You must have sent them to his home.

I rub my eyes, blowing a hard breath between my lips.

I'm exhausted. Mentally. Physically. Emotionally.

Everything is a blur. I'm not sure I'm capable of thinking straight anymore.

"Jesus, Dove. What's wrong?" Kirsten places her hand on my arm. "Are you okay?"

I haven't taken my meds in a week now. Maybe this is part of the withdrawal. Insomnia. Excitability. Irritability. Racing thoughts.

Or maybe this is all your doing, Ian.

"I should probably get home and get some sleep," I say, crawling off the bed. The floor is unsteady beneath my feet. "Can you go through the rest of those and let me know if you find anything we can use?"

"Of course." Kirsten scoots off her side of the bed and walks me to the front door. "Take care of yourself, okay?"

Friend of the Year right there.

There are little pockets of time when I forget why I was mad at her. Then there are moments when it comes crashing down on me like maelstrom waves.

Squinting over my steering wheel a moment later, I drive back to my apartment through empty streets, past darkened houses, trying to decide if I'm going to call in to work again tomorrow.

It isn't until I'm lying in my bed, face scrubbed clean, the taste of mint toothpaste on my tongue and a sleeping pill working its way through my system that I decide to go in.

Noah can't know that I'm onto him.

I need him to think he's in the clear.

23

Kirsten

I RUN home after the eight AM class Thursday morning to take Lucy on a walk. She's been cooped up, and this time of morning is the best—and safest—time to take her out. Everyone's going to work, which means the streets are filled with people in cars. People (witnesses) are the best deterrents. People and sunshine.

I'm not one hundred percent sure Derrick was the one who killed Ian, but the fact that he's out and perfectly capable of finding out where I live these days means I'm back to looking over my shoulder.

It's the past all over again.

I leash Lucy and take her out through the front door, only when I turn to lock up, I spot a piece of folded paper stuck under the exterior handle. It's probably a pizza delivery flyer or someone running for city council, and I almost debate crumpling it up and tossing it in the trash, but my curiosity gets the best of me.

Lucy tugs at the leash, anxious to get going.

"Just a minute, girl," I say, unfolding the paper.

It's not a flyer.

It's not a political solicitation.

It's a message. To me.

DIE BITCH.

The thick black marker and erratic handwriting give it the look of a sick prank. Do people really do this kind of thing? Is this someone's sorry excuse to try and scare me?

I lock the door, shove the note into the side pocket of my yoga pants, and double check to make sure my phone is on me.

Dove came by last night. She stayed until maybe eleven and I let her out the front door, but I didn't stay and watch her leave. I locked up behind her and went back to my laptop to keep digging. This morning when I left to teach my first class, I left through the garage and it was still pitch dark outside—I didn't once think to look at the front door.

This letter could have been left at any point between last night and this morning.

I'm halfway up the block when I spot David's car pulling away from a yellow two-story with preened boxwoods and a soaring oak.

He gives me a wave, and I stop on the sidewalk, waving him over. A few seconds later, he pulls off to the curb, window rolled down.

"Morning, neighbor," he says. Lucy runs up to him, rising on her hind legs so he can reach her for a quick pet. "Everything all right?"

"Can you get me a gun?" I ask.

His jovial mode vanishes in an instant. "Excuse me, what?"

I lean in.

"I need a gun," I say, almost whispering. "For protection."

"And I look like a gun guy to you?" He runs his hand over his steering wheel, face pinched as he stares over the dash. "I mean. I have a couple handguns for protection, but I can't just give them to you."

"If I apply for a permit to carry, it takes thirty days to get approved and I don't have thirty days. I need something now."

"Are you in danger? Did something happen?"

"Dove's been coming over," I say, biting the inside of my lip.

"Ian's ex-wife?"

"No. The other Dove that lives around here."

"Is she bothering you? If she is, you should call the police right away."

"Actually, she's not. She's, um, she found some things. Some evidence. And we're working together to figure some things out." I realize I'm being vague, but I can't tell him too much.

"What kind of evidence?"

"Messages."

"What kind of messages?" he asks.

"Texts and emails. Romantic things, mostly," I say. "I thought maybe Dove made these up, like maybe they were part of some elaborate scheme of hers because ... you never know ... but the timestamps are on the server. You can't fake those. I think these are legit."

"Just ... be careful. This woman has every reason to hate you. She broke into your house for Pete's sake. What if she's setting you up?" Fatherly condescension colors his tone. "Do the police know you two are working together?"

"They wouldn't understand. Quite frankly, I'm not sure

that I understand myself. It's just that she's so damn convincing. When she's around, it's like we're old friends and I believe everything she says and then when she's gone, I'm second-guessing whether or not this is all part of some sinister plan she's weaving to get back at me."

"Jesus, Kirsten." He lifts a hand. "Sorry. Pardon my French. I ... I don't think it's a good idea."

"Can you get me a gun or not?"

"I've got an old pea shooter in the attic somewhere. It was my granddad's. I don't think it has a serial number on it and it probably hasn't been shot in fifty years, but it'd be a good deterrent. Ninety percent of the time, the threat of the gun is all it takes to stop someone."

"Something's better than nothing."

"I'll bring it by later," he says, giving Lucy one last scratch behind the ear. He drives off with a wave and I don't have a chance to thank him. Or mention the letter someone jammed in my door overnight.

We continue on our walk, stopping at the elementary school a mile away to turn back. We're a few houses away from home when I realize something looks amiss, and on closer inspection, I realize why that is.

The back gate is wide open.

The gate that I'd padlocked shut after the other week.

24

DOVE

"HEY, STRANGER," I call from my desk when I spot Noah's white lab coat go by my open office.

The shuffle of his sneakers against the thin carpet stop and he appears in my doorway a second later. "Dove, hey. Feeling better?"

"Much."

Noah tucks a patient file under his arm. "Glad to hear it."

"Why are you acting so weird?"

He makes a face. "What are you talking about?"

"I feel like I haven't seen you all week."

"Thought you wanted some space," he says.

"When have you ever given me space?" I wave my hand and cluck my tongue. I'm probably overselling my faux good mood, but I can't pull back, not now. I'm in too deep.

Noah looks like he's about to say something, but instead he steps inside and closes the door behind him. "Is everything okay? I'm being serious. You're not ... you ... lately."

I laugh. "Are we ever really ourselves? I mean, one minute we're down and out and the next minute we're all *heart eyes*."

Allthehearteyes at yaya mail dot com ...

Noah's almond gaze explores mine, though his expression is impossible to read. He's somewhere between horrified and flummoxed if I had to guess.

"In all the time I've known you, I've never heard you talk like this before. I've never seen you act this way." His lips press flat for a moment. "I think you should take another day to pull yourself together. Come in when you're feeling more *yourself*."

"Have you ever dabbled in online dating, Noah?" I ask. "Or any of those apps where you swipe right or left?"

He pauses, shifting his posture, debating whether or not to engage in this conversation. His brows meet and he sighs. "Yeah. Back in college. A little. I don't know what that has to do with anything or why you feel the need to ask me about this when I've got three patients in the waiting room and one in my chair."

"Have you ever hooked up with a married man? Like a man married to a woman?"

Noah whips around to double check that the door is closed all the way before rushing toward me. "Dove, what the hell? I told you that in confidence. And no, I've never dated a married man. And I would never. But I know guys who have. You'd be surprised how many married men like to hook up with other guys on the side."

"Right. I'm sure I would be surprised." I roll my eyes.

"But I'd never do that. Why are you asking this? Does this have to do with Ian? Do you think he was ...?"

"Funny you go right to Ian."

"Now you're just reading into it." He lets his arms fall to his side, the thick file paper slapping his pant leg. "I assumed you were talking about Ian because that's all you ever talk about."

"Is it, Noah?" I mean, I'll admit I talked about you quite a bit after the divorce, but I could sense the annoyance in Noah's tone and that grated look on Ari's face, so I tempered it down after a while.

In my mind's eye, I can picture Noah speaking to Detective Reynolds, filling her in on how "obsessed" I was with you, how much I "hated" Kirsten. Hell, he has access to my computer password. He could even let her know that it's our anniversary. In fact, Noah has everything he could need to set me up to take the fall for this.

"What are you getting at?" he asks, checking the time on his wrist. "Because whatever it is, I don't have time for it."

"You were in love with Ian, weren't you?"

Noah's face washes in scarlet and he tries to respond, only nothing comes out.

"I knew it," I say, rising from my chair.

"You need help, Dove," he says. "And until you get the help you need, you can't be here."

"Are you firing me?"

He scoffs. "I should fire you. You're accusing me of sleeping with your ex, which I assume also means you're accusing me of killing him."

Noah's eyes water. Stoic, calm, compassionate, sensible, pragmatic Dr. Noah Benoit is wounded by my words.

"Leave this office." He speaks through gritted teeth. "*Now.*"

25

Kirsten

"YOU DOING OKAY? I bet you're all kinds of shaken up, aren't you?" David says when he arrives Thursday night. I texted him earlier today, when I saw the gate swinging wide open after my walk with Lucy. "Geez, it's like one thing after another. We've got to get you out of here."

I could move back to the little place above my studio, but it's a modest five hundred square feet and I'd have to move again once the baby comes. Plus, as odd as it sounds, there's safety in being surrounded by all these neighbors. My only neighbors at the studio were the businesses and offices that filled the storefronts below, most of them only open from eight to five during the week.

"Yeah. I'm okay now," I say, though my head hasn't stopped pounding since it happened. Nothing like a good old-fashioned tension headache to make this day that much more enjoyable.

I stayed outside until the cops arrived this morning. At

first the officer who arrived acted inconvenienced by this call—until he saw that the padlock had been clipped off with some kind of industrial-strength tool.

He took a report after performing a perimeter check and inspecting every crevice of the house inside and out. No footprints. No fingerprints. No neighbors at home who saw anything. He said he'd pass the information on to Detective Reynolds in case it had something to do with Ian's investigation, and he gave me his cell number in case I needed anything.

His personal cell number ...

"Okay, so I brought you something," David says, pulling up a chair at the kitchen table. He reaches into the back waistband of his pants and pulls out a small handgun. It almost looks like a toy cap gun, the kind one of my mother's boyfriends bought me at the dollar store when I was five or six. She ended up throwing it out when I went to bed that night because she couldn't take the snapping and popping and giggling that followed. "Like I said, it's old. Might not even work. But it's yours to use until you get one of your own."

"Thank you, David." I take the pistol from him and examine the sides before checking out the way it fits in my hand. It's lighter than I thought it would be and small enough to hide about anywhere.

"I should have time to get that security system put in for you next week. Haven't forgotten," he adds.

"I'm so sorry I keep throwing these things at you. I swear I'm not usually this needy," I say. "You came into my life at a very vulnerable time."

He waves his hand. "Nah. Don't sweat it. It gives me something to do. Keeps me busy. It's like having a fourth kid and not having to wipe runny noses or sit through four-hour dance recitals."

I smirk. "Well hopefully someday I can repay you."

Before David has a chance to respond, there's a knock at the front door. Lucy barks. The both of us startle in our seats.

"You expecting someone?" he asks.

"No." I get up and tiptoe across the living room, pulling back the curtains enough to peek outside where Dove's gray Civic is parked on the street. "It's Dove."

"She just ... felt like dropping in?" David scratches at his temples.

"She doesn't like texting," I say, keeping my voice low. "She's afraid anything she says can be misconstrued or used against her."

David's eyes grow wide but whatever he's thinking he keeps to himself.

Dove knocks again.

"You going to get that or you going to pretend you're not home?" David asks.

"I should probably get it. She only comes by when she's got information."

"You want me to stick around?" he asks.

I debate his offer and quickly surmise that it wouldn't hurt. "Just don't make it obvious."

David nods. I shove the gun in the back of my waistband and cover it with my shirt before getting the door.

26

DOVE

"I WASN'T GOING to tell you this, but—" A tall man appears from behind Kirsten as she answers the door, and he peers down a half-bent nose. There's something familiar about him, though I can't place him with this overflowing, whirring mind of mine.

"Dove, hey," Kirsten says. "Come on in."

I'm surprised it doesn't take twenty minutes of coaxing for her to let me in this time, though that probably has more to do with her fancy new security guard.

"You know David Hobbs, right?" Kirsten asks. "Lives in the yellow house up the street?"

"Oh." I extend my hand. "That's why you look familiar. I'd seen you around, but I don't think we ever formally met. Dove Damiani."

"Good to meet you." His grip is tight and he smiles. He has gentle eyes, but the way he stands next to Kirsten makes me believe like he's not here to shoot the shit and be buddies. Fortunately we're on the same page.

"I was hoping we could talk about something I came across earlier today," I say to Kirsten. I refuse to talk about any of this in front of anyone else. I don't know David. I don't know how trustworthy he is or what he'd do with this kind of information. I glance to him before looking back to her. "Privately."

The two of them exchange looks—which I don't appreciate—and then they begin to speak over one another.

"Yeah, uh. I'll be outside fixing that ... hinge for you," David says.

"Great. Thank you." Kirsten steps aside and David heads outside. I know she still doesn't trust me and maybe this David guy has put the fear of God into her now that we've been spending time together. I'm sure the whole town is talking about me, painting me in certain lights. I don't blame him for being wary. I'd be the same way if I weren't me.

The second the door is closed, I say, "You can't repeat any of this."

She turns to face me, hands on her hips. I resist the urge to look down to her belly. It's beside the point.

"Noah—my boss—last weekend when I asked him if he was in love with me, he ..." I tell Kirsten my theory, leaving no detail uncovered. And when I'm done, her gaze is fixed on the floor and she's stunned into silence. "And the way he was acting at work today. When I asked him if he'd ever hooked up with Ian before, he kicked me out of the office and threatened to fire me."

Kirsten's bronze complexion turns a shade lighter and she shuffles to the living room to sit down.

"I think I'm onto something," I say. "And those emails ...

the talk about not living your life according to someone else's standards or whatever ... about not sneaking around anymore ... it only makes sense, right?"

"I mean ... yeah." She hides her face in her hands, elbows resting on her knees as she breathes deep. "But the problem is we have no proof. And I don't know how we're going to get it."

"I have a key to Noah's place," I say. "He's at work."

"Dove. Don't." Her stare pierces through me.

"I don't want to, but what if it's the only way?"

"Then tell the police your theory, but for the love of God, didn't you learn your lesson last time? And what if you get caught? You want to go to jail again?"

"Maybe I'll go over there tonight and apologize. See if I can get back into his good graces."

"That sounds like a better plan."

I readjust the strap over my shoulder and eye the door. "That's all I wanted. You can tell your friend he can stop pretending to fix that hinge on your garage door."

With that, I'm gone.

I call Noah on my drive toward the west side of town, but he doesn't answer. Given our heated exchange earlier, I don't want to pop by unannounced and run the risk of putting him on the defensive right off the bat.

"Noah, it's me," I say in my voicemail. "I'm so sorry about earlier. I was wondering if I could stop by tonight and apologize in person. You're right. I'm not myself lately. Call me."

I hang up and head home to wait for his call. When I pull into the parking lot of my apartment, I spot an unmarked police car.

Weird.

Heading up to my place a minute later, I stop halfway

up the stairs when I spot Detective Reynolds standing outside my door.

"Hi," I say, slowly climbing the rest of the steps.

"Ah. So you really *weren't* home. Thought maybe you were avoiding me." She winks.

"I was visiting a friend. You could have called."

"I was in the area," she says, nonchalant. "Mind if I come in for a minute so we can chat?"

"Not at all." I fish my key from the bottom of my purse and unlock the door, letting us both in. The place is a mess—especially for someone who doesn't have a lot. Piles of unfolded laundry are heaped along the edge of the sofa, and takeout boxes and water bottles litter the coffee table. Nothing I can do about it now. "So, what's this about?"

"What have you been doing at the victim's house this week?" she asks. There's no compassion in her voice this time, no sympathy.

Heat flashes through me but I do my best to appear unruffled. "Did Kirsten call you?"

That traitor.

"No," she says.

"So you're having me tailed." I cross my arms to hide my shaking hands.

I knew it.

"Standard procedure," she says.

"Kirsten and I are ... doing our best to move forward," I say. "There's nothing insidious going on, if that's what you're getting at."

Detective Reynolds exhales, looking like a woman who's had the longest day ever. "I've been doing this a long time, Dove. Probably longer than you've been on this earth. Don't lie to me. It's not going to end well for you if you do. Trust me when I say you want me on your side. And believe me when I say I want to be on your side."

"Ian cheated on us," I say. "Both of us. I went over there to show her proof the other day. I thought maybe we could work together and try to figure out who it was, but—"

"—and you know this how?"

"That day I was at Ian's house last week." I don't use the word "broke into" because are you really breaking in when you have a key? "I found a burner phone in his office, in this book safe thing on his shelf."

"You stole evidence from a crime scene?" Her rushed tone scolds me like an aunt slapping a child's hand as they reach for a red-hot stovetop.

"Do you want to see it or not?" I cut to the chase so she can save her lecture. Reaching into my bag, I produce the black flip phone and hand it over. "The messages are pretty vague. There are no names or identifying information, but the last one went out the night he was killed. They were supposed to meet."

She inspects the phone before flipping it open and navigating through the apps until she gets to the messages.

"We can't use this now," she says, "not officially. But I'll see what I can do. Maybe there's something I can glean. But don't get your hopes up." Her gaze flicks to mine. "And Dove? For the love of God, walk a straight line. Stay out of trouble. Keep your nose clean. You understand?"

27

Kirsten

THE SCONES ARE STILL warm when Lori stops by with them mid-morning Friday. She makes a second trip to her car to grab a clear plastic tote with a purple lid. I make a pot of coffee and grab a few things off the counter, shoving them into the junk drawer when her back is turned. I'm glad to see her, but I wasn't expecting her. Though in her defense, I did tell her to stop by whenever she wanted ...

"You didn't have to do all this," I say.

"Don't be silly." She swats at me, clucking her tongue. "This is a welcome distraction. Bittersweet of course, but welcome."

She pops the lid off the tote and reaches in, retrieving a matted teddy bear the color of caramel. He's missing an eye and wearing a red bowtie. "This was Ian's first teddy bear. For three years he wouldn't go anywhere without it. We once left it at a hotel and thought we could swap it out for a new one, but he noticed. Michael had to call and convince them to overnight it back to us. Thank heavens they did."

Lori places the bear gently aside, next to the basket of fresh scones, and reaches in for a layette set.

"He came home from the hospital in this." She spreads it on the table, running her hand across the aged baby blue fabric covered in white ducklings. "Can you believe he was ever this tiny?"

A soft musty smell fills the air, mixing with the sweet, bakery-fresh scent of the scones, and it makes my stomach bubble. I step away to pour our coffees, grateful to pull in a clean breath. Lori has moved onto the next item—one of Ian's old "binkies."

I wonder if I'll be that mom ... the one who keeps everything. The one who cherishes each and every memory, no matter how small.

"What do you think you're having?" she asks when I hand her a white ceramic mug. I made sure it wasn't one of Ian's teacher mugs because I thought that might be a bit much. "I knew right away with Ian. I had a gut feeling it was a boy."

"I haven't given it much thought to be honest," I say. And it's true. I read an article once about a woman who didn't want kids and found out she was pregnant after a one-night stand. She said after the initial shock wore off, she was overcome with a bathing warmth—the physical incarnation of unconditional love, and she went on to describe this otherworldly bond unlike anything else she ever felt. It was magical, the way she talked about it.

I've yet to experience anything like that.

Deep down, I worry I never will.

But I think back to what David said—it doesn't matter if

I can or can't be a good mother, I don't have a choice. I'm going to have to be.

Lori sips her coffee, before wincing. "Oh, sweetheart, you don't happen to have any sugar, do you? The kind in the yellow packet?"

"I think we do?" I say, biting my tongue when I realize I said 'we.'

She doesn't flinch, thank goodness, and I head to the cabinet over the coffee maker to find some.

"Do you take creamer? I should have asked before I poured." I locate two yellow packets of artificial sugar and bring them to her along with a spoon from the silverware drawer. But before she has a chance to respond, there's a knock at the door.

"Who could that be?" she asks over Lucy's background barks.

"Sorry. I wasn't expecting anyone. I'll be right back." I hand over the spoon and Splenda and head to the front door where I find Dove.

Shit.

Last time I was with Lori, she told me she was keeping her distance from Dove and advised me to do the same. But that was before the phone, before the email, before Dove's theory about Noah.

Dove knocks again, harder.

"Is it one of those door-to-door people?" Lori asks from the next room. "They can be so persistent sometimes. You want me to handle it?"

She appears at the threshold between the kitchen and living room, stopping in her tracks when she stares out the picture window and recognizes the car parked out front.

"Good God. What is she doing here?" Lori asks, voice hushed. Her eyes are narrow and she's hunched over, her hand on Lucy's collar as she tries to get her to calm down. "Don't answer."

Dove knocks again. "Kirsten, I know you're home. Please open up."

I look to Lori, knowing she wants to hide and ignore Dove, but Dove never stops by unless she has information. Last I knew, she was going to try to talk to Noah last night. I assume this has something to do with that. Maybe she found some evidence?

"I'm so sorry," I say to Lori. "Give me one minute."

I step outside and shut the door behind me. Dove startles, taking a couple steps back on the small front porch.

"Lori's here," I say. "Make it quick."

Dove's attention grazes my shoulders as she looks to the door, the tiniest hint of longing in her eyes. I'm sure it hurts being snubbed by Lori, but we don't have time to focus on that.

"Did you go to Noah's last night?"

"He wouldn't call me back." She shakes her head. "I went home and Reynolds was there."

"What? Why?"

She turns to peer up the street before checking the opposite direction. "Apparently they've been following me. They know I've been coming around, and naturally they thought it was worth checking into."

"What'd you tell her?"

"That we were trying to move forward," Dove says. "She didn't buy it, so I had to show her the phone."

"And?"

"She said she can't use it as evidence, but she's going to look into it. If someone bought it with a credit card, we'd have a name. You and I don't have the means to look into that kind of thing. Anyway, not going to get my hopes up, but I wanted to give you an update."

I sigh. "I wish you'd text me these things."

"Why? So they can be misconstrued and used as evidence someday?" Her eyes are wild and she's speaking so fast I can hardly keep up. "I've got to go. I'm sure I'm being watched."

With that, Dove hurries back to her car and within seconds she's gone.

I head inside, where Lori is seated at the table, sipping her coffee.

"What was that about?" she asks.

Taking the seat beside her, I debate whether or not to tell her about the phone, but then I think that as a mother, I'd want to have all the information available to me. Ian was her son. She has every right to know.

"Dove found a burner phone in Ian's office last week, when she ... broke in," I say.

"What's a burner phone?"

"One of those prepaid phones where you pay by the minute. They're untraceable. Disposable."

Her thin blonde brows inch together. "Oh?"

"There were text messages ... between him and someone else," I say. "We've been trying to figure out who that someone else is."

I expect shock to register across Lori's face, but she gives me nothing but a stoic poker face. "And you're sure she found this phone in *his* office?"

"We hacked into his email accounts—one that neither of us knew existed—and found some emails. The dates correspond with the text messages," I say. "He was seeing someone else while he was with her. And he continued seeing them up until the night he was ... taken from us."

Her hands cup the white ceramic mug and she gazes into the distance, focused on one of the sweeping oak trees that anchor the backyard. "I don't know that I'd believe anything Dove says."

"Really?"

"She's a sweet girl. But troubled. Very troubled." She takes a calm sip of coffee.

"What do you mean?"

Ian had told me that Dove grew up with a "batshit crazy narcissistic drama queen of a mother," an absentee alcoholic father, and a brother who couldn't stay out of juvie and subsequently jail—but she seemed to thrive in her adulthood. There was nothing about her that I ever perceived as troubled.

"I mean, there's a reason the police are focusing their investigation on her."

I lean back. "I wasn't aware of that."

It makes sense now that they'd be following her, that they'd confront her about coming over here.

"How do you know that phone wasn't a fake? That the emails weren't fabricated?" Lori asks.

I don't tell her that everything seemed convincing at the time, that my gut wholeheartedly believes Dove.

"Ian would have never cheated on anyone. We raised him to be a good man, a good husband and partner." She folds the baby blue layette and places it back in the tote. I've upset her despite the fact that she doesn't believe a word of this. "Forgive me, Kirsten. We'll have to finish this another time."

"Lori ..."

She secures the purple lid on the plastic tote. "I'll leave this here if you don't mind."

"I didn't mean to upset you."

Lori turns to me on her way to the door. "It isn't you, sweetheart. You did nothing wrong. I wish Dove would stop meddling, is all. *That's* what upsets me. I hope to God she isn't out there spreading these terrible lies."

Lori shows herself out, and I look out from the window as she pulls away. I'm sure it isn't easy, hearing these post-mortem rumors about your beloved son, but I certainly didn't expect her to pack up and show herself out. It's nothing more than a reminder that we're still strangers, that I still know very little about Lori Damiani.

And then a wild thought crosses my mind ... what if Lori knew about the affair? What if she's trying to protect her son's reputation by not coming forward about it? I don't know her that well, but I do know she's a mother who would do *anything* for her son.

Anything.

28

DOVE

I WAKE Saturday morning to find Noah and Ari sitting in my living room. I had to double up on my sleeping pills last night to get some sleep, and I must have been sleeping so hard I didn't know anyone else was here.

"What's this?" I ask.

The two of them exchange looks and Ari rises, clearing her throat. "An intervention."

I scoff, rolling my eyes as I shuffle to the kitchen to start the coffee maker.

"When was the last time you took your meds, Dove?" Noah asks.

I scoop the grounds into the top of the machine before filling it with tap water. After the divorce, I couldn't afford one of those fancy, automatic timer ones like you had, Ian.

"Are you eating?" Ari asks as she moves toward me slow and gentle, the way you might approach a caged tiger. "It's only been a week and look at you. You're wasting away. Your clothes are hanging off you."

I glance down. I hadn't noticed, but I realize now she isn't wrong. I tug at the waistband of my flannel pajama bottoms and pull them up over my protruding hip bones. I never had protruding anything when we were together, Ian. You said you liked me soft. You said skinny girls disgusted you—but obviously you changed your mind when you met Kirsten, like you changed your mind on the whole wanting kids thing.

"Are you sleeping?" Noah asks, appearing behind Ari. He studies my face, probably shocked at how dark the circles under my eyes have become. I had the same thought when I looked in the mirror yesterday. It's like they came out of nowhere.

I'm cornered in this tiny excuse for a kitchen. I wouldn't be able to walk to the living room without squeezing through these amateur interventionalists.

"Dove, we love you," Ari says. "But we think you need help."

The coffeemaker spits and sputters, taking its sweet time. I turn my back to them, my fingers tapping out a rhythm on the Formica counter as I wait. A song fills my head—Ocean Avenue. It always makes me think of you, of cruising around in your Eclipse back in high school. You said we were going to move to San Diego someday, that I could be a realtor and you could be a cop and we'd live by the beach.

We were young then. Idiots who didn't know anything about anything. And you made a lot of promises you never kept.

I'm realizing that now.

Every hour, I remember another one, and another one.

You promised me a trip to Paris.

You decided to spend that money on a master's degree instead—saying if you made more money down the road you could take me to Paris *and* Rome.

You promised you'd get me a bike so I could go biking with you on Saturdays in the summer, but you claimed you were waiting for a sale at Diego's Bike World. You wanted me to have the best one. None of those Walmart ones you wheel off the rack and push to the register. Funny how that sale never happened.

Now I wonder if you ever went biking or if that was all a ruse so you could spend a few hours away from me on the weekends.

"Let us take you to the hospital," Ari says. In all the years of knowing her, she's never sounded so gentle and lamb-like.

"That won't be necessary." Finally my coffee is done percolating. I pour it into a mug with a stained bottom that I dig out from under a pile of dirty dishes in the single basin kitchen sink.

"You've been through so much these last couple of weeks," Noah says. "It's taking a toll on you, and we want to help. Let us be there for you instead of accusing us of being the bad guys here."

Bad guys.

What are we, ten?

And they were the ones pointing the fingers at each other, need I remind them?

Taking a sip of coffee, I turn to face them. "Oh my God. You guys are in on this together."

Ari's jaw goes slack and Noah takes a step back. They deserve an Oscar, these two.

"Get out of my apartment," I say. "Now. And leave your

keys. If you come back, I'll have you arrested for trespassing."

"Dove," Noah says.

"Out." I point to the door.

"Please don't do—"

"*Go,*" I say louder, harder.

They scramble toward the door, stepping into their shoes and gathering their things. Ari wrestles the key off her ring and Noah places his on the key hook on the wall.

"Please think about this," Ari says. "We know you're not yourself, and we want to help."

"We just want you back," Noah says.

I lean against the counter, legs crossed at the ankle, drinking my coffee as I wait for them to leave.

They're trying to gaslight me. They're trying to make me think I'm crazy, that I need help, that I'm not capable of piecing together exactly what they did.

Nice try.

29

Kirsten

"KIRSTEN, I'M GLAD YOU CALLED," Detective Reynolds says on Monday as I drive home for lunch.

I thought about Lori's strange behavior from Friday morning all weekend, mostly whether or not I was reading too much into it.

"Derrick Peterson," Reynolds says. My heart tumbles at the sound of his name. "We've got an alibi."

Oh, sweet Jesus.

I exhale and release my tight hold on the steering wheel.

"Confirmed it with his employer. Even got him on camera, working the nightshift at some tire factory outside Detroit," she says.

"And you're sure?"

"One hundred percent."

I'm relieved to know it wasn't him, but it won't make me look over my shoulder any less. I don't think I'll ever shake the feeling that he'll come back for me one of these days.

"Dove told me she gave you that prepaid phone," I say. "Have you had any luck?"

Reynolds is quiet on the other end for a beat. I'm sure it's hard for her to wrap her mind around the fact that Dove and I are working together on this. "We're still checking into it. I've got some desk guys combing through thousands of transactions from all the stores in the area that sell those kinds of phones. It's literally like looking for a needle in a haystack. If they paid cash—and chances are they did—it'll be a giant waste of time. But we won't know until we find something. *If* we find anything at all."

"I see."

"We could find something today or we could find it tomorrow. Maybe a month from now. Maybe never. Just don't hold your breath," she continues. "And speaking of Dove, is she bothering you? I know she's been coming around there lately. I wanted to make sure she's not pulling any stunts."

"We're trying to move forward," I say, which is the very same thing Dove claimed she told Reynolds last week. But I don't care if Reynolds believes me or not. It's the truth. We're moving forward ... in our own way.

"Okay then," she says. "If anything changes with that, you let me know right away."

"Of course." I end the call with Reynolds and pull into my driveway. It's then that I realize I haven't seen or heard from Dove in almost three days.

Something's not right.

30

DOVE

MY MOTHER'S basement sofa is as old as she is and gives off an odor of dankness and must. I wish I could say it's good to be home, but I'd be lying. I always hated coming home, even for visits, even with you by my side reminding me we didn't have to stay that long, that we just had to make an appearance. It's one of the reasons we always hosted her at our house for birthdays and holidays after we moved to the little ranch on Blue Jay Lane.

Some people think of their childhood homes and their insides turn to nostalgic goo.

I think of my childhood home and want to vomit.

With its nicotine-stained ceilings, cat hair covered furnishings, and junk-cluttered kitchen, it's not the most hospitable of places, but this home is so much more than that.

This home represents my alcoholic father beating the shit out of my mother in front of my brother and I when we were barely out of diapers. This home represents growling stomachs and going days without running water when Mom got behind on the bill. This home represents junk food and zero curfews and weekends without an ounce of parental supervision as my mom would be holed up at the Elks Lodge, dancing and drinking with her single, middle-aged friends until close.

You rescued me from that, Ian.

We were fourteen when you asked me out and we became inseparable from day one. You had your school driving permit and my house was on the way, so thanks to you I no longer had to walk to the bus in the morning. In the evenings, you'd take me to your house where we'd hang out in your clean, bright, happy-smelling basement watching TV and snacking on microwave popcorn as your mom asked us both about our days. I'd have dinner with your family and your dad would drive me home around eight.

I lived for those hours with you and your family, for that sliver of wholesome normalcy it provided.

I flip through my mother's satellite channels in the basement family room as one of her cats rubs its face all over me, demanding attention. I gently shove her away, settling on the local news.

For thirty minutes, they talk about the weather four times. Not once do they mention you. It's like no one cares anymore. There are no updates. The shock has ended. Everyone has moved on. One day you'll be forgotten, Ian. An archived news article saved on microfiche at the Lambs Grove Public Library. And I think you kind of deserve that.

The front door opens and slams, rattling the entire house, and that could only mean one thing: my brother's home.

I've managed to avoid Slade for years, but now that I'm

laying low at my mother's, it's kind of impossible. According to the papers on file with his parole officer, he lives here, but Mom says he spends most of his time at his girlfriend's house. Mom talks about his girlfriend's kids like they're her grandkids and to be honest, Ian, it freaks me out, but I can't say anything or it'll start World War III and I kind of need a place to crash.

After Ari and Noah showed up Saturday with that bullshit excuse for an intervention, I decided I needed a change of scenery. I swear that apartment was growing smaller by the day, like the walls were moving in, crowding me and my thoughts. And it's only a matter of time before Reynolds shows up unannounced again. I don't like that. Why can't she just call? I've been nothing but cooperative with her. It's not like I wouldn't come in if she asked me to.

"Dove," Mom calls down the stairs. "Come upstairs. Time to eat."

I mute the news, toss the cat-hair encrusted blanket off my lap, and trudge upstairs—but only because I'm hungry and Mom is a lot of things, but she's never been a bad cook.

I find Slade at the kitchen table, Mom dishing out his plate and serving it to him like he's some kind of helpless man child. And she wonders why he can't do anything for himself at his age ...

"What's up, Bird?" he greets me using the obnoxious childhood nickname he gifted me when we were in grade school. I once gave him a black eye after he convinced my entire fourth grade class to refer to me by that nickname and only that nickname. It wasn't long after that when Mom took me to a shrink who diagnosed me with a behavior and mood disorder. "Long time no see."

I love how casual he's acting ... sidestepping the fact that I've been blatantly ignoring him for years.

"Dove, here's your plate." Mom hands me a thin piece of mismatched china and points toward the lineup on the counter. It looks like she's cooked for an army, but I'm not complaining. I haven't eaten real food since I don't know when.

"Sorry about Ian," Slade says.

I whip around. "Are you? Are you sorry?"

"Dove," Mom scolds me with her voice. "Can we have a nice sit-down dinner, the three of us, with no fighting? It's been a long time since we've been able to do this. Come on."

I dish my plate and take a seat across from my brother. He looks bigger than the last time I saw him. Pumping iron in the yard will do that to a guy ...

"Is that a new tattoo?" I use my fork to point to a drawing on his forearm that looks homemade.

"Yeah, you like?" He rolls up his sleeve a little more.

"Makes you look real hardcore," I say.

He smiles and nods, not picking up on my sarcasm. Still an idiot, I see.

Mom sits between us a second later. "You know it's Aunt Bette's birthday this weekend. Maybe we could all stop by? Grandma's having a little thing at her house on Sunday."

"I'm probably going to be busy," I say. Aunt Bette is a bitch. I'm sorry, but she is. Even you agreed, Ian, and you pretty much liked everyone. Or at least you always pretended you did. I'll never forget the time Bette pointed out in front of a Thanksgiving table full of family members that I'd gotten my period and needed to go change. Later on, I overheard her telling another aunt that her daughter didn't get her period until she was much older—that I must have started mine so young because I was "fat."

I wasn't fat back then. Chubby maybe. Not fat.

"I'm working Sunday," Slade says with a mouthful of food.

Mom says nothing. She simply sighs.

We finish the rest of our dinner in our family's trademark strained silence, and when we're done, I volunteer Slade to help me clean the kitchen because I'll be damned if he's getting out of here without lifting a finger.

"*Bitch*," he mouths to me when Mom gets up to go to the next room. A minute later, the sound of Wheel of Fortune plays from the living room TV.

"I'll wash, you dry," I say, filling the sink with warm water and squeezing a generous dollop of blue soap into the stream.

Slade exhales, and I expect him to snap back at me with some comment about not telling him what to do, but to my surprise, he grabs a clean dish rag from a nearby drawer and flings it over his brawny shoulder. Despite all of our differences, I think there's a part of him that misses me and he knows deep down this is as close to quality time as we're going to get.

"So where are you working these days?" I ask him, but only out of my own curiosity.

"That oil and lube place off First Ave," he says.

"The new one with the fifteen-minute oil changes?" I place the silverware in first, letting it soak on the bottom, and then I grab a dirty plate.

"That's the one."

"I didn't know you knew how to change oil."

He chuffs. "It's not hard to learn. And you try getting a job with a felony on your record."

"I'm not judging you. Why are you being so defensive?"

"Because I know what you're thinking."

"You couldn't possibly." I hand him the plate. He dries

it with zero care and precision and shoves it, still wet, into one of the cupboards.

"You know, one of the guys I work with told me something about Ian the other day," he says.

My hand scrapes against a knife, and I yank it out of the water to make sure I'm not cut. "Oh, yeah?"

"Yeah." He takes his time, his lips twisting like he's about to share some juicy gossip. I don't read into it too much though. My brother has always been a pathological liar. And anyone he rubs elbows with probably isn't the most reliable of sources. "There's this guy, pretty young. Nineteen I think. Just graduated from high school this past spring. He said he heard Ian was hooking up with one of his students. Some girl."

I'm half laughing, half choking on my spit.

You're a lot of things, Ian, but a child predator? You were obsessively professional. You'd tell me about the way some of the girls would look at you and try to bat their lashes to get out of a bad grade or two, but you always treated everyone the same and you never crossed any inappropriate boundaries. In fact, you were on an investigative committee a couple of years ago when the science teacher was caught sexting with a freshman. You took that role very seriously. You then proceeded to take a post-grad class about that very thing – how to spot the telltale signs of a student/teacher relationship.

"You believe this guy?" I ask, handing him another plate.

"I mean, I've only known him a few weeks."

"What else did he say?"

"Nothing really. We were standing around the break room last week and the news was on. They were talking about Ian and he just said *oh, that's the teacher that used to hook up with students.*" Slade shoves another half-dried plate in the cupboard. "It was the way he said it. Like it was some kind of casual, known fact."

"A lot of girls had crushes on him. It was probably a rumor."

"Yeah. Ian was such a damn goody two shoes. I can't imagine him doing something like that," Slade says.

I think back to the messages, re-reading them from memory but in a whole new context.

What if it wasn't Noah you were sneaking around to see?

What if it was one of your students?

"What's this guy's name? Your co-worker?" I ask my brother.

"Why?"

"In case I want to ask him some questions." I hand him a freshly washed spoon.

"His name is Carter," he says.

"When's he going to be in next?"

"The kid just started a few weeks ago. He doesn't need some crazy chick showing up bothering him at work."

"Tell me when he takes his lunch," I say. "I'll make it worth his while. Yours too."

"One to one-thirty. He's off tomorrow, but he'll be there Wednesday," he says. There's nothing my brother won't do for some quick cash. I make a mental note to stop at an ATM. "Just be cool about it, okay?"

"Of course."

31

Kirsten

"OKAY, SO TAP THAT ICON THERE," David says Tuesday night. "You should be able to see all your cameras now."

The screen is black.

"Well that's not right," he says, placing my phone aside. He heads to the counter, next to the control center. "Says it's not connected to the internet."

I glance at my phone. The Wi-Fi symbol is gone, replaced with three cell bars. "Ah. Wi-Fi must be out."

He's been here for hours installing everything, arranging and rearranging camera placement so there isn't a single corner of this house that won't be covered ... inside and out.

"Let me call and see if they can reset the router or something." I look up the customer service number for the internet provider and press the green button. It rings three times before I'm greeted with a recording that states their help line is closed for the day and will reopen at seven AM tomorrow. "Great. They're closed."

David looks up from the command center. "Well shoot."

"I'm so sorry," I say.

"It's not your fault." He straightens his posture before shuffling over to the pizza box. I ordered delivery pizza for us earlier so he'd at least get some dinner out of this whole thing. He finds a cold slice of pepperoni and mushroom and takes a bite. "I can come back tomorrow night and finish up. It's a matter of connecting the system to Wi-Fi and making sure you can log into it from your app, then you should be golden."

David finishes his pizza before checking the time on the microwave clock.

"Hey, before you go," I say, "Dove stopped by last night. She told me the craziest rumor."

"Yeah? What now?" He chuckles as he slips his shoes on by the back rug.

"Someone told her Ian was ... sleeping with one of his students." I cringe. The thought of it sickens me, but to say it out loud almost makes me physically ill.

David's humored smirk fades and his hands go to his hips. "Really?"

"She heard it from someone who heard it from someone else," I say. "For all we know, it's a rumor. I'm sure people are saying all kinds of things."

"Yeah. People love to talk around here. Got to take it with a grain of salt and all that."

"Dove's said she's going to do some more checking around," I say.

"Of course she is." He chuckles again, his hand resting on the back doorknob now. "Really takes herself to be quite the amateur sleuth, doesn't she?"

The fact that he's humored by all of this gives me an ounce of relief I didn't have before. I don't want to believe Ian is capable of doing anything like this and it would appear I'm not alone in my beliefs.

"I think she wants to prove her innocence more than anything. Sounds like the police are focusing on her with their investigation."

His jaw sets and he hesitates before lifting a flattened palm. "Now, Kirsten, you're a grown woman, and I hate to tell you what to do, but if the police are focusing on Dove, it's probably for a good reason. And I think you ought to stay away from her from now on."

I appreciate his fatherly advice, I do. And I realize how easy it is to cast Dove off as some deranged lunatic. But my gut tells me she's onto something.

"Yeah, you're probably right," I say, but only because I don't want him to worry. "Two of your kids go to the high school right?"

He nods.

"I know this is a lot to ask and probably not the kind of conversation you want to have with them, but do you think you could ask if they've ever heard anything like that?" I offer an apologetic wince. "If we had some names, maybe the police could check into them?"

"So you believe Dove? And you believe the rumor?"

"I believe it deserves to be looked into."

"All right." He exhales, his shoulders heavy and sinking. "I'll ask them and let you know what they say."

"Thanks, David."

"Let's hope there's no truth to any of this or you'll find me raising hell at the principal's office first thing tomorrow."

We exchange goodbyes and he shows himself out. I lock up behind him before letting Lucy into the back yard one last time for the evening. When she's done, I secure the house and head back to my room, but not before stopping at Ian's office.

Scooting his leather chair away from his desk, I take a seat and glance around, though I'm not sure what I'm looking for. A leather notebook rests on top of a pile of papers on the left rear corner, and I reach for it.

It's a gradebook, each page covered in his penciled handwriting.

There are hundreds of student names in here, and I trace my fingertip over them, reading each and every one. It could be any of them. Or it could be none.

Dove's theories have been all over the place. First it was a mystery woman. Then it was Ari. Then it was Noah. Now it's a high school student.

Maybe David's right.

Maybe she's trying to throw me off her scent.

Maybe she's up to something.

32

DOVE

"HI! Are you here for an oil change?" The overly bubbly bottle blonde receptionist at Slade's quick lube place greets me with a crooked grin.

"No. Is Carter available?"

She turns to check out the window behind her, where cars are hoisted on jacks and power tools are causing all kinds of ruckus.

"I think he went to lunch. He should be back in a bit."

"Where's your breakroom?"

"Oh, I'm sorry. It's for staff only. There's a guest area over there with coffee and a vending machine and—"

I don't let her finish. Within seconds I'm trekking down a tiled hallway lit with fluorescent lights, and I stop when I find a door that says EMPLOYEES ONLY. The door opens with a light nudge and a handful of young guys in gray uniforms with oil-stained hands glance over at me in choreographed unison.

"Which one of you is Carter?" I ask.

A guy who looks vaguely like Ed Sheeran adjusts his hat. "That'd be me. Why? Who are you?"

"I'm Slade's sister," I say. "You have a minute?"

One of his colleagues punches him in the arm and laughs. "Dude, what'd you do?"

Another one says, "You're in trouble."

Carter shoots them all dirty looks and follows me out to the hall. "What's this about? I'm trying to eat my lunch."

"Follow me." I lead him outside, away from the packed waiting room and the intermittent sound of drills and the front desk phone that won't stop ringing off the hook. "Slade said you graduated earlier this year."

His pale orange brows connect. "Yeah ...?"

"He said you heard Mr. Damiani was sleeping with some of his students."

His mouth inches at one corner and he glances at the passing cars on the busy road behind me. "Well, yeah. It was kind of common knowledge."

My stomach drops, but I remind myself that rumors are just that. I don't want to think you would be capable of doing such a thing, and right under my nose no less. It seems like in these sort of cases people always say, "The wife had to have known! How could she not?" And in a roundabout way, she becomes almost as guilty as the husband.

I will not take the fall for this, Ian.

"I find it hard to believe that it would be common knowledge and not one person would take that information to the principal or superintendent," I say.

"Okay. Maybe common knowledge is the wrong way to put it. I just know that pretty much all the girls had crushes on Mr. Damiani. He was the most popular teacher in school. His classes always filled up—girls mostly. And they'd have competitions to see if they could get him to flirt back. I watched them do it once."

"And did he flirt back?"

Carter shrugs. "I mean, sometimes. Yeah?"

I decide that a nineteen-year-old might have a very different definition of flirting than me. "How so? What kinds of things did he do?"

"I don't know. He'd smile and laugh and joke with them."

"That doesn't sound like flirting to me. That sounds like being friendly."

"Like one day this girl wore a really low-cut top and went to his desk to talk to him during a quiz. She bent over, you know, so he could see down her shirt. And I saw him look." Carter licks his chapped lips. "And there were always girls in his classroom before school and after school. Some of them would pretend like they needed tutoring, and they'd get permission to spend study hall in his room if he had an open period."

None of this sounds scandalous—save for you looking down one student's shirt.

Maybe it was a reflex and you weren't thinking.

Or maybe you're a sick pervert.

"A couple years ago there was this girl, I don't know her name because she was a couple grades below me, but she was hellbent obsessed with him. She put her panties in his desk drawer once."

These are still nothing more than rumors. I can't do anything with this information.

"Where'd you hear this?" I ask. I need to get closer to the source.

"A friend."

"What's his name?" I ask.

"It's a she. And I'm not telling you. I'm not a rat." He shuffles on his feet and chews the inner corner of his lip. I wonder if this girl is someone he's trying to get with and he's worried this'll ruin his chances.

"Your friend isn't going to get in trouble," I say. "And they don't have to know that you and I ever spoke. If they told you this, I'm sure they've told plenty of other people. If this rumor is so rampant at your school, I could've heard it from anyone, really."

Digging into my bag, I produce a messy handful of twenties. I'm sure a hundred-dollar bill would have been more impressive, but my funds are rather limited these days.

"Sixty bucks," I say. "Just give me a name."

He stares at the crumpled bills, lips pursed. "You swear you won't tell her?"

"On my life."

Carter swipes the money from my hand. "Her name is Shawna. She works at the Dairy Freeze. Real tall. Long brown hair. She's working tonight. I think her shift starts at four."

━━━

I PARK outside the Dairy Freeze a half hour early. I don't want to chance missing this Shawna girl, and I'm hoping she arrives early enough that she'll give me a couple minutes of her time before she heads in.

Cars enter and leave and file in the drive-thru lane, over and over, again and again. This was always one of the more popular ice cream places in town because of their dirt-cheap prices, but we never came here because you hated soft-serve, Ian.

I rest my head back on the headrest and take a deep breath. The radio plays softly in the background—some bullshit Celine Dion song from the nineties. I'm unsure of how I got to this station, but I'm too focused on the task at hand to care about changing it to something better.

You used to do the best Celine Dion impression.

It was uncanny.

Looking back, I'm inclined to believe that *you* were nothing more than an impression, Ian. An impression of a normal human being. A mask you wore to cover up the real you.

Several minutes pass when all of a sudden a red Dodge Neon with rusted doors pulls up next to me. Before I have a chance to register anything, a girl with legs up to her neck and dark hair down to her ass climbs out, slams the door, and trots up to the back entrance of the ice cream shop, tying a blue apron around her waist.

Scrambling to get out, I manage to catch her before she disappears inside.

"Shawna," I call out, jogging behind her.

She stops, spinning on her sneakered-heel. "Yeah?"

"Hi, I need to talk to you."

"No thanks. I don't know you." She turns, shuffling her way closer to the building, head angled in a way that she can still see me from her periphery. A second later, she reaches into her back pocket to retrieve her phone.

"It's about Mr. Damiani," I say. "Your history teacher."

Shawna stops, sighing as she turns to face me again. "Are you a cop?"

"No," I walk closer to her, though I still maintain a safe distance in hopes it'll make her less wary of me. "My name is Dove. I'm his ex-wife."

Her eyes scan the length of me, but the expression on her face is unreadable.

"Someone told me you might know something." The clock is running, her shift starts in three minutes, and I'm going to have to be more specific. "I know about the rumors ... that Ian was sleeping with students ... I was told that you might have more information about that?"

"Even if I did, I'm not telling you."

Little brat.

"You have no idea how important this is, Shawna. You might have the information that could help us find Ian's killer."

She stands across from me, steel-faced and arms crossed. I catch a flash of her phone screen and see that it's cued up to dial 9-1-1. She thinks I'm crazy.

Join the club.

"I can't tell you," she says.

"Of course you can."

"The girl he was sleeping with ... she's one of my best friends. I wouldn't do that to her." Shawna's voice is low, unsure. She wants to tell me. A little more coaxing and she might. "Her old man's a psycho and her mom is ten times worse. Mr. Damiani's already dead, so it's not like he's going to take the rap for it. I think it's best we act like it didn't happen."

"No!" I don't mean to scream at her. "That would be the worst thing we could do."

Shawna cocks a hand on one tilted hip, giving me a stare like I have no idea what I'm talking about.

"Your friend is the victim here," I say. "If this is true."

She rolls her eyes.

"Please reconsider," I say. I dig into my purse for a few moments before realizing I'm out of cash. Though I don't know what the going rate is for friendship betrayal these days. "Here."

I find a receipt and a pen and scribble my number.

"If you change your mind, call me," I say. "Or text. Or whatever. Just please think about this and get back to me."

To my surprise, she takes the paper and shoves it in her back pocket. "I'm gonna be late now. Thanks."

So much attitude.

Was I like that at that age, Ian? I don't remember having the nerve to be so sassy and disrespectful.

Regardless, I return to my car, fingers crossed so hard it hurts.

33

Kirsten

"OKAY, NOW OPEN YOUR APP," David says Wednesday night. The Wi-Fi was restored earlier today, and he returned about an hour ago to finish installing the security system. "See where it says Camera 01? We're going to rename that to Kitchen, but tap on that."

I press the icon and tap on Camera 01. A moment later, a grainy black and white real-time video fills my screen. I spot the two of us. David smiles and waves at the camera.

"Let's check the others, real quick," he says. "I want to make sure every last one of them is online before I go."

We go through them all, one by one. He's painstakingly meticulous about it, stopping to adjust a few of the cameras until they're in the perfect position.

"Hey, did you ever get a chance to talk to your kids?" I ask.

"I did."

"And?"

"There might be some truth to those rumors." His gaze rests at my feet and he looks as if he's going to be ill. "I still find it hard to believe Ian would've done what they're saying, but I talked to Colby and ... I've got a name."

I clamp my hand over my mouth. "Why didn't you tell me this sooner? We've been sitting around here messing with cameras and—"

He lifts a palm, slow and steady. "Because I didn't want you getting all worked up ... like this."

Switching gears, David shoves his phone in his pocket before stepping into his boots by the back door. "Bastard's lucky he's already dead."

"Where are you going?" I ask as he mutters under his breath.

"To the police. Going to give them the name," he says. "You want to come?"

It's not right David spent his entire night helping me and now he's got to deal with this, so I decide there's no way I'm going to sit back and kick up my feet. Besides, I want to know the name too. I want to see the look on the detective's face when he presents her with this information. There's a chance she's aware of the rumors, that she's been checking into them unbeknownst to us, but the look on her face will tell me everything I need to know.

"Yeah. Give me a second to grab my things. I'm going with you."

34

DOVE

MY MOTHER'S basement TV flickers, lighting the dark, damp space. A prime-time talent show competition fills the silence, though I'm not paying attention. I've been staring at my phone, which hasn't left my side since talking to Shawna earlier today.

I've tried to wrap my head around this rumor every which way I can, Ian, but the image of you with a high school student refuses to take shape. I can't believe it. I don't want to believe it. But for some reason ... a part of me almost does.

It's wild how you can spend decades with a person and not know anything about them in the end. It isn't my fault though. I don't blame myself in the slightest. You were the illusionist. You were the conman. You were the puppeteer behind the persona.

The credits roll on the talent show. One of the judges, an Instagrammer or influencer with a celebrity husband, rushes up on the stage and wraps her arms around a crying young girl. I can't tell if her tears are happy or sad or why it matters, so I click off the TV, toss the blanket off my feet, grab my phone, and shuffle back to my basement bedroom.

Growing up, my room was upstairs, on the main level. After Mom's third husband moved in and I went off to college, he convinced her to "put all my shit" in the spare bedroom of the basement though it isn't an actual bedroom. Not legally. There are two rectangular windows to let in light, but they're too small for an adult body to squeeze through should there be a fire. After Barry moved out eight years back, Mom left everything down there. All my boxes. My mementos and memories. Trophies and photo albums. Dried corsages and prom dresses wrapped in plastic. Teddy bears and diaries. Everything reeks of basement dankness now, of cold must and earthen mold.

I asked you once a couple of years ago if we could come get everything and store them at our place. You said what would be the point of moving them from one basement to another? Now I wonder if you knew we weren't going to be together forever, if you were sparing us the time and effort and energy and a lazy Sunday afternoon.

As much as I hate to admit it, I'm probably going to spend the rest of my life second-guessing all those little things you said and did.

I head to the basement bathroom and wash my face. The flickering bulb above paints unflattering shadows on my face. The woman staring back in the mirror has the darkest circles, the deepest frown lines. Exhaustion sinks into my bones the more I look into her eyes, so I finish up and trek back to my musty room at the end of the narrow basement hallway.

Crawling beneath the cold, damp covers, I check my

phone one last time ... only to find a text message arriving in that exact instant.

It's a local number, one that isn't preprogrammed into my phone, and the message contains two words.

A name.

COLBY HOBBS.

I sit up in bed, teeth clenched as nerves send tremors down my spine. Why does that name sound familiar? Within seconds, I'm googling the name. The results are scarce and scattered: Linked In profiles, archived news articles, mentions in a few obituaries. Impatient, I pull up Facebook next and type in the name.

Seventeen results populate the screen. I start at the top —a young man from the UK. The second result is a woman in California, a forty-something mom of five. The third result is nothing more than a blank profile. No picture. No identifying information. But number four? It's a girl. A teenage girl. Fluorescent-white grin. Shiny, sandy blonde hair. Clear, tan complexion. Crystalline blue eyes and far too much mascara fanning out her long, dark lashes. I scroll down her page a moment later.

And then I gasp.

Lambs Grove High School.

Holy shit, Ian.

I flick through her photos as fast as I can process them. She's a cheerleader. She has a decent-sized circle of friends, all pretty and lanky with big white smiles and flat-ironed hair and summer-painted tans. I absorb every ounce of information I can glean from her photos. She drives a little red car—a newer model Chevy, four doors with a customized plate. She works part-time nannying after school for a local family with twin second-graders. She went to a Chainsmokers concert last year in the city and loves the trendy angst of Billie Eilish.

There must be hundreds of photos. Everything public. Her profile is an open book, like she wants the attention, she wants people to see her carefully curated teenage life where everything appears to be happy and exciting and perfect and jealousy-inducing to her peers.

I'm halfway through her pictures when I find one of Colby, her arm around the shoulders of an older man. They're grinning into the camera with cheek to cheek matching smiles right down to the shapes of their cupid's bows. There's something familiar about him so I pinch the screen, zooming in then out, eyes squeezing and opening, desperate for a fresh perspective so I can place him.

"*Hobbs*," I whisper out loud. "*Hobbs* ..."

Oh my God.

The man that was at Kirsten's last week ... that's David Hobbs. He was one of our neighbors. Were you messing around with his high school daughter, Ian?!

"No, no, no." I scramble out of my bed, leaving my phone amongst the crumpled covers. With my hands lacing through my messy hair, I pace the small confines of this makeshift bedroom, mouth salivating and stomach twisting with the threat of rising bile.

I'm going to be sick.

Within seconds, I'm sprinting to the bathroom where I land on my knees against the cold, porcelain tiles. A minute later, I'm wiping my mouth, my stomach now empty but still as unsettled as it was before.

Kirsten mentioned once last week that David had been coming around and helping her with a few things around the house. In all the years we lived together, Ian, we'd only ever seen David Hobbs in passing.

Why would he start coming around so much now that you're gone?

I push myself up from the cold, hard floor and drag myself to the sink, cupping my hands under a stream of running tap water and rinsing my mouth.

Did David find out about you and Colby?

And did he do something about it?

Did he kill you for touching his teenage daughter?

I splash a handful of water on my face, my thoughts beginning to clear as I piece together what this could mean.

Kirsten.

I need to get to Kirsten.

Something tells me she's not safe.

Kirsten

"WHAT'S THE NAME?" I ask, fastening my seatbelt as David backs out of my driveway. His hands are wrapped tight around the steering wheel, positioned at ten and two as he checks the rearview. "The name Colby gave you."

His jaw flexes and his gaze narrows on the road ahead as we accelerate down Blue Jay Lane, toward the Lambs Grove police department. We should be there in less than five minutes, but curiosity is eating away at me by the second. I want to google this girl. I want a face and a name—not that it would make any of this more sensical.

I'm having a hard time believing this isn't some rumor started by some bored high school kids. Ian was nothing but ethical, a true professional in every sense of the word. He was always on time. Always volunteered when needed. Had a shelf full of various teaching awards. Stayed involved in some of his students' lives well after graduation—always happy to write letters of recommendation or mentor those whom he inspired to go into the teaching field.

Not to mention, Ian doesn't look like a predator. I know it's naïve of me to assume they all have a certain look to them, but what thirty-something, well-dressed, well-mannered, well-spoken, and well-educated man would prefer the company of a teenage girl over that of a woman? What man would risk it all for something so dangerous and wrong? Why would a man with *everything* to lose, put it all on the line?

Maybe it's a sickness.

"David?" I ask again, because clearly he didn't hear me the first time. "What was the name of the student?"

"Oh, sorry," he says, shaking his head. He flicks on his right turn signal. "Hannah Brown."

I slide my phone from my purse and type the name into a search engine, along with "Lambs Grove." The results that fill the screen a half-second later are less than encouraging. Upon first glance, there isn't anything that's going to be useful here. No articles, no photos, no links to social media. The name is too common to be easily connected to any one particular account and the fact that there were no hits linking Hannah Brown to Lambs Grove is concerning. But I refuse to give up.

I pull up Facebook next and enter the same criteria.

No results found.

"Are you sure that's the name?" I ask. "I'm not finding anything."

He glances over at my lap, squinting against the bright phone screen in the dark car interior. "That's what she gave me."

"She?" I ask. "I thought Colby was your son?"

He makes a right turn. "I never said that. You must have assumed."

He's right. I did assume. All the Colbys I've ever known were male. I begin to regret not asking him more about his kids, but at the time, I didn't want to pry. He'd mentioned he had three teenagers—it never occurred to me to ask their names or feign interest in their lives. At least not yet. We were just getting to know one another. I figured that sort of thing would come with time.

David accelerates as the speed limit changes, and I steal a peek at his tachometer. He's going eight miles-per-hour over, which wouldn't be a big deal if our turn wasn't coming up a block ahead.

The stoplight flashes from green to yellow and I hold my breath, waiting for David to slow down and indicate his upcoming turn.

Only he continues to drive.

My palms sweat against the warm backside of my phone and I clear my throat. "I think you missed the turn off back there for the station."

I don't think, I know.

And something tells me he knows too.

"Yeah," he says with a heavy sigh. "About that."

Before I have a chance to realize what's going on, he reaches over and yanks my phone from my hands, tossing it out his window.

The sound of my own scream fills the car and without thinking for a second about how fast we must be going as we hit a stretch of highway outside Lambs Grove, I reach for the door handle and give it a hard pull.

It does nothing.

David laughs.

"I don't understand," I say as tears begin to fill my eyes.

They're thick and hot and they obscure my vision, turning the oncoming headlights into blurry stars in the dark.

He reaches down, retrieving something from the side pocket of his driver's door. A second later, he rests a black handgun in his lap and it's pointed at me.

"You will soon enough," he says.

36

DOVE

THIRTY MINUTES ago I texted Kirsten to let her know I was on my way over, that we needed to talk and that it was urgent. The message showed as delivered but she didn't respond. According to her studio's website, her last class ended an hour ago.

I pull up in front of your house, which is so well lit you can almost see it a mile away. She's been leaving every light on at all times lately so there's no telling if she's home or not —a smart move given the recent circumstances.

Dashing out of my car a second later, I jog to the front door, knocking and ringing over and over like a crazy person.

Lucy barks inside, loud and deep like she's scared, and then she scratches at the door—an old habit you and I could never break her of.

I knock and ring again. And again. And then I listen for footsteps, voices, whispers, anything, but it's impossible to make out anything with Lucy's bark on the other side of the door, the crickets chirping, and the gentle whir of passing cars as they go by.

"Kirsten," I call her name before heading to the garage door and punching in the code—which doesn't work. She must have changed it after I got in a couple of weeks ago.

Crouching, I push my fingers under the small gap at the bottom and shove my weight against it, lifting at the same time. It isn't easy and I'm not sure I could do this without the help of the adrenaline coursing my veins, but I manage to manually push the garage door up its tracks enough to fit my body through. On my hands and knees, I crawl through the two-foot opening.

Her Fiat is parked on the left side, your Passat on the right.

If she's home, it doesn't make sense that she'd ignore me, especially since I texted her to let her know I was coming and I never do that. She would know it's important.

I dust the dirt from my knees and head to the garage entry door and show myself in without bothering to knock. Lucy scampers across the living room when she hears me, tail wagging apprehensively and ears low until she gives me a sniff.

"Kirsten," I call out. "You home? It's Dove."

The kitchen is a bit of a mess. Not dirty. Just stuff everywhere. Plastic sacks and small opened boxes, instruction manuals and hex screws. Upon closer inspection, I realize it's a security system.

"Kirsten?" I yell again before heading down the hall.

The bathroom door is open, the room dark. I check the guest room next, then the office, and finally the master.

She isn't here.

Grabbing my phone, I call her number. It rings five

times before going to voicemail. I shoot her another text, letting her know I'm at her house and asking where she is. Just like the message I sent earlier, it shows as delivered and not read.

I return to the kitchen and take a look around. Her purse is gone. An open box of takeout pizza rests on the counter—strange considering I've never seen her eat anything that isn't organic or Whole30 approved before. Something red catches the corner of my eye, and I glance up to find a camera mounted above the sink, pointed in my direction, recording.

For a moment, I wonder if she's somewhere watching this remotely from her phone. Watching me run around like a crazy person.

And what if she's with David?

What if she and David are in on this together?

What if they're not?

I leave the house and jog down the street to the two-story house with the yellow siding and the manicured shrubs—the Hobbs house. Except for two lights next to the front door, the place is pitch dark.

Heart pounding in my ears, I ring the doorbell, only to be met with silence.

37

Kirsten

ACCORDING to the clock on the dash, it's been twenty-three minutes since David threw my phone out the window and pulled a gun on me. Every second drips by, drawn out and standing still. We're in some remote part of the county, the city lights of Lambs Grove a distant memory at this point.

Gravel pings beneath David's car.

I haven't said a word. Neither has he.

I learned from a young age that when someone's acting crazy, meeting their crazy with your crazy only amplifies the situation. It never makes it better. Going berserk on him won't help my situation, so I try to remain calm and focused, paying attention to any landmarks or county road signs.

A half-moon and two headlights are the only thing illuminating this journey, but we've passed a handful of farmhouses that were distinct enough that I could pick them out of a photo if it comes to it.

Of course, that's assuming I'm getting out of this alive.

At this point, I haven't the slightest idea what David's intention is with me or why he would have any reason to want to hurt me. Until two weeks ago, we were complete strangers. And the kind of kindness and selflessness he's shown to me has been nothing less than authentic.

I keep an eye on him from my periphery, one hand steady on the wheel, the other steady on the firearm in his lap. I've had a gun pointed at me once before—by Derrick. But I knew it wasn't loaded because I'd taken the bullets out when he wasn't looking one day.

I should assume that David's gun is loaded.

The car begins to slow as we climb a gravel hill, and soon he brings us to a complete stop before making a sharp left turn toward a matted-grass makeshift driveway. He flicks his high beams on and a small cabin appears in the distance, maybe thirty yards ahead. Behind it is a lake, still and glistening, its beauty almost mocking the cruelty of this moment.

He parks his car to the side of the cabin, in an area swallowed by darkness and overgrown bushes, and then he kills the engine. "Don't move."

David climbs out a second later, taking long strides around the front of the car, his gaze pointed at me the entire time, and then he opens my door from the outside.

Motioning with his gun, he tells me to walk toward the front door of the cabin. His footsteps are soft against the grass as he stomps behind me, but each step only makes my heart beat harder against my ribcage.

When we get to the front door, he reaches around me to grab the handle, grazing my arm in the process and making me startle.

The door swings open, smacking against the interior wall, and he presses his gun against my back shoulder.

"Go," he says, voice low in my ear.

I step into the darkness, the scent of lake water and abandoned must filling my lungs. His hands tighten around my upper arm a moment later, and he directs me to what appears to be a kitchen chair.

"Sit down and don't move," he says, giving me a push until I'm seated. The tiniest bit of moonlight that spills in from the open-door paints menacing shadows across his face, but I don't have time to revisit old memories and berate myself for missing the signs that David Hobbs is a psychopath—if there were any.

His shadow moves in the dark, striking a match first and then lighting a kerosene lamp that he places on a small kitchen counter—well out from my reach. Next, he closes the door before heading to a saggy, plaid sofa on the other side of the room where a vinyl duffel bag rests atop a small stack of folded blankets and two white grocery sacks.

Whatever this is was definitely planned.

A shiver dances through every part of me, and my thoughts dart to my unborn child. If David has an issue with me, that's one thing. But I'll be damned if I sit back and let him do anything to hurt an innocent baby.

My gaze returns to the folded blankets. I don't see a bed around nor do I see any other doors. This place appears to be some kind of basic fishing cabin. A pump next to the sink in the makeshift kitchen tells me it doesn't have running water and the amount of dust particles circulating in the dim air means this place is seldom used. For all I know, he's the only one aware of its existence.

I could run.

I could bolt out this door.

But where would I go?

We're in the middle of nowhere. I have no phone. No knowledge of which direction to go or how near or far the closest neighbors are. And he would follow, gun pointed at me until I surrendered. And if I didn't? I imagine he'd shoot me.

A man wouldn't go to this much trouble just to let me get off on foot, alive and well.

My lower lip trembles, but I drag in a deep breath, the pungent air cloaking my lungs in freshwater sogginess, and try to center myself until the shaking subsides.

"So what's the plan, David?" I ask, forcing strength into my voice to hide the terror.

He unzips the duffel, reaching in and retrieving what appear to be clear plastic zip ties. Without saying a word, he trudges across the cabin to where I'm seated, crouches down, and secures my ankles to the legs of the chair before fixing the zip ties together. He moves behind me next, gripping my wrists in his strong hands and fastening before securing them to the chair. The hard wood digs into my bones and I'm restrained so tight I'm unable to readjust my position.

My shoulders burn but I push through it, though it's not like I have any other option.

"I thought we were friends?" I take a different approach next.

He snorts before heading back to his gaping duffel bag on the saggy sofa. He places the gun on one of the cushions, and I try not to think about the blankets and the fact that they could mean anything. Maybe he plans to kill me and wrap me in them before shoving me in his trunk? Maybe he plans on camping out here a while and turning the sofa into a bed.

I think back to my interactions with David. Not once did I ever catch his eyes drifting where they didn't belong. He never lingered around more than he had to when he came over. He never made passes or insinuating comments. He never gave me any kind of vibes that he was attracted to me. He was always a perfect gentleman, a friendly neighbor, a kindly, pseudo-father-figure.

"If you wanted to date me, you could have asked," I say, testing him.

He whips around, shooting me a look. "Don't flatter yourself."

He digs around a bit more in his bag before returning to the kitchen table with something in his hands. Reaching for the lamp, he twists the knob on the side and the flame grows bigger, giving off a little more light, and then he begins placing photographs on the table for me to see.

They're of a girl.

Sandy blonde hair.

Wide-set blue eyes fanned with lashes.

"Is this your daughter?" I ask, swallowing the lump in my throat, only to have it return. "Colby?"

He finishes arranging the photos before grabbing one and inspecting it. A bittersweet half-leer claims his lips and he sets it down before taking another one.

"She was sixteen the first time he touched her," he says, his voice equal parts angry and broken. "Took her innocence."

I'm speechless. I truly am. But I muster an apology.

His burning gaze snaps on mine. "Don't apologize for that son of a bitch."

"I ... I'm not ... I mean ... I'm sorry that happened. I'm sorry she had to go through that ... that you as a father had to—"

"You bring a child into this world and you do everything right. You buy all the best car seats and training wheels and give them the best Christmases and vacations and spend your nights and weekends carting them from camps and games and tournaments ..." his words drift for a moment. "You teach them right from wrong. You make sure they're not drinking. Not doing drugs. Not hanging around the wrong kind of people. You make sure they're going to school every day, getting an education so they can have a future." His eyes flash and his hand curls into a fist. "There are a lot of things in this world you have to protect your kid from ... but their teacher?"

He leans back in his chair, the wood creaking beneath his weight, and slips his hands behind the back of his head as he gazes into a dark corner of the room, lost in thought.

"He was her *teacher*, Kirsten. Her *teacher*." His voice breaks, the shock and hurt and anger renewing with each echo and emphasis of that word. *Teacher*. "An all-around respected citizen of the community, all those bullshit awards and newspaper articles and degrees ... and for what? So he could prey on innocent children?"

"It's disgusting," I say.

"She had her whole life ahead of her," he says. "And he took it from her."

"What happened is a travesty, but she can still move forward. Her life doesn't have to be over. She can still build a life." I won't pretend to understand what it's like to be a parent, nor will I pretend to understand where David is coming from.

"She said they were in love." He's snickering now, mocking the sentiment. "Can you believe that? He had her fooled into thinking he was going to marry her someday, that they were going to be together."

I chuff. "Yeah. Ian had a lot of us fooled, I guess."

"And then he had the audacity to demand she get an abortion."

My blood turns to ice water. "She was pregnant?"

His fist clenches and his jaw is set and he pushes a hard breath through his nostrils. "The sorry bastard got my daughter pregnant, then carted her across state lines so she could get one of those pills."

My middle swirls, but I tamp down the urge to lose the contents of my stomach. "W ... when?"

"Does it matter?" he shoots back.

"N ... no." I suppose it doesn't. "There was a Saturday about a month ago that he said he had to go out of town out of the blue, some last-minute educator's conference. It was a couple days after we found out we were expecting. When he came back that night, he gave me a teddy bear. For the baby."

"About a month ago? Sounds about right."

I still don't understand what any of this has to do with me or why he's brought me here, but if I can keep the dialogue open, keep the conversation going like we're a couple of friends, a couple of regular people bonding over Ian Damiani's betrayal, maybe he'll change his mind?

David squints at me. "Did you really not know your boyfriend was running off screwing some high schooler?"

"No. I didn't."

"Bullshit." He rises from his chair, the wood screeching against the floor. "I knew within a week when my ex-wife cheated on me and let me tell you, the conniving bitch did everything she could to hide it."

"I'm so sorry, David. I didn't realize that happened to you."

He swipes his gun off the sofa, returning to the chair.

"Nah. It was for the best. She was a piece of work. Crazy like a fox. Anyway."

David sets his firearm on the table. I'd be able to reach it if I wasn't tangled up in these zip ties.

"He took things from my daughter she'll never be able to get back," David says, knuckles rapping on the wood. "He lied to her. He used her. He stole from her. And her life will never be the same because of him. Her life will never be what it was meant to be. There'll always be this dark cloud hanging over it."

I want to ask him if he thinks he's being overly dramatic here, but no good can come from poking him when he's already reached his breaking point. That said, his anger is absolutely justified, even if his behavior is not.

"By the way, how the hell are you so calm?" His head angles as he studies me. "Figured you'd be screaming your head off about now ... not that anyone could hear you out here."

"Because I like you, David," I lie. Sort of. Up until an hour ago, I considered us friends. "You're a good person who happens to be in a bad place, and I know you're not going to hurt me. You love your kids too much to do this to them."

He's quiet at first, and for the smallest of moments I think I'm getting through to him. If I can work the kid angle, maybe he'll change his mind? He's one of the most dedicated fathers I've ever met in my life. Surely he wouldn't do anything that would hurt them, right?

He rises from the creaky chair and heads over to his duffel bag, retrieving a bottle of Crown Royal and a crystal tumbler. When he returns, he pours himself two fingers of room temperature whiskey and takes it all in one swig. "You don't know a damn thing."

38

DOVE

I'M RUNNING down the Hobbs driveway when a flash of headlights stops me in my tracks and a small red sedan comes to a hard stop past the sidewalk. A second later, the driver's door opens and a lanky girl with a high ponytail and a LGHS sweatshirt on sprints toward the garage door, punching in the code. The car is still idling, the headlights still slicing through the dark.

This must be her, Ian.

This must be Colby.

She's in such a hurry she doesn't notice me standing under the shadows of the oak tree at the end of the drive.

"He's not home," I say, stepping out.

She whips around, her silken hair brushing against what appear to be tear-stained cheeks, and smacks her hand across her chest.

"I didn't mean to scare you," I say, marching toward her. "I'm Dove ... Damiani."

Her eyes widen, glassy and bright in the dark. It occurs to me that she might think I'm here to hurt her—assuming she believes her secret is out now.

"I'm looking for your dad," I say. "I think he's with Kirsten."

Her attention pivots from the ground to me to the door to the street and then to her car. And then, without any warning at all, she bursts into tears.

I don't understand what's happening. "Colby, right?"

Her pretty face is buried in her hands as she nods, sobbing like a child. "I'm so sorry. I'm so, so sorry."

My heart sinks.

So it's true, Ian. The rumors. What you did.

I wrap her in a hug. I don't think about it, I just do it. She has nothing to be sorry for, Ian. She's the victim here. You orchestrated this. You were the selfish monster who took advantage of a young girl who looked at you with stars in her eyes, who trusted you.

She cries against my shoulder, apologizing over and over.

"It's going to be okay," I tell her, my voice muffled against the side of her head. Her hair smells like summertime and candy-sweet perfume—like a young woman whose only concern should be finishing her English paper on time and finding a date for homecoming.

"We have to find my dad," she says.

"Where do you think he is?"

She dries her tears with the cuffs of her sweatshirt. "Probably at the police station ... turning himself in. I can't let him do that. We have to find him!"

I try to contain my shock as I wrap my head around the truth that has eluded us from the moment your body was discovered: you were sleeping with one of your students, her father found out, and he killed you.

"He can't ... oh God," she covers her face. "This is bad. Oh, my God. I can't ... he can't ... you don't understand ... he's going to do something crazy ... I have to go."

She dashes down the driveway toward her idling sedan, but judging by the way she pulled up here like a maniac and her sudden burst of tears the second I introduced myself, she's in no shape to drive.

"I'll go with you," I say, following her. "And I'm driving."

She stops, turning back to look me over, her dark lashes heavy with tears. I'm sure she's wondering if she should get in her car with a stranger who has every reason to hate her, but I would never dream of blaming Colby for your actions.

"You're not doing this alone," I tell her. I nod to her car. "Come on. Let's find him."

When the police first told me you were dead, I vowed to find your killer. I made it my mission to bring you justice. Now? While I don't think murder is ever the best solution to a problem no matter how vile that problem may be, my heart isn't heavy with anger toward David Hobbs.

He was nothing more than a tax-paying Lambs Grove family man who trusted you to educate his teenage daughter.

You betrayed him.

He snapped.

You did this to yourself, Ian, I mean really. What did you expect? What did you think would happen when your secret got out?

I climb into the driver's seat of her Chevy, instantly choking on the overpowering plethora of scents that greet me. A peaches and cream air freshener hangs from the rearview, an open pack of Juicy Fruit gum sits in the center console, and a bottle of Victoria's Secret body spray has leaked on the passenger floor mat. The radio blares some pop song and the heat is going full blast.

Colby slides into the other seat, buckling up, watching me from the corner of her eye.

I dial the radio volume down before shifting into drive and heading toward the police station. We ride in silence and we arrive in record time—three minutes at most.

"Do you see his car?" I ask as we cruise through the guest parking lot. I have no idea what David drives, but I spot a minivan, a Hummer, and a Volvo station wagon.

Colby leans forward, peering over the dash and scanning our surroundings. "No. His car's not here. Is there another parking lot?"

"Not for the public, no," I say, pointing to the restricted lot reserved for police officers and government employees.

She slides a phone from her back pocket and taps her code in two seconds flat. "I'm going to try calling him again."

No sooner does she press the phone to her ear does she drop it back to her lap.

"What?" I ask.

"It went straight to voicemail." She sighs before checking the parking lot one more time. "Last time I called, it rang. It means he's ignoring me. He turned it off."

"Why would he do that?"

"Because he's psychotic when he gets like this." Colby sniffs, eyes wide as she taps out a text message and presses send. "I'm asking my brothers if they've heard from him."

"You know, I can't find Kirsten and she's not answering her phone either," I say. "It's weird that they're both gone and unreachable at the same time, don't you think?"

"Oh, God." She exhales, eyes closed.

"I don't understand," I say. "What would your dad want with her?"

Colby turns to me. "Did she know? About Ian and me?"

"I told her there was a rumor ... about him and a student."

"Was my dad there when you told her?" she asks.

"Yeah, but he was outside."

She bites her lip before covering her mouth with her hands. "Is there a chance she said anything to him?"

"I don't know what they talked about. But yeah. Anything's possible."

"Okay, we need to find him. *Now.*"

"I'm sorry, Colby, but none of this is making sense to me," I say as we pull away from the police station.

"Drive north," she says. "Catch the highway toward Bonneville Heights."

"Where are we going?" I ask.

"My grandparents have a fishing cabin," she says. "It's a shot in the dark, but maybe he's there?"

I floor the gas and take us toward the highway, the Lambs Grove city lights growing dim in my rearview with each passing mile.

My mind spins around the only two things I know for sure right now: David did not go to the police to turn himself in, and Kirsten is missing.

If David killed you, Ian, and if David was worried Kirsten was going to be able to piece things together and make the connection once she had Colby's name, if David had no intentions of confessing, then it would only make sense as to why he would want Kirsten out of the picture.

I hope to God we can find them in time.

But if he wants Kirsten out of the picture, chances are he's going to want me out of the picture too.

I steal a quick glance at the teenage girl trembling in the passenger seat next to me.

Maybe he won't do anything to me if his daughter's there.

He wouldn't make his daughter witness something like that, would he?

Then again, he's already proved he's willing to kill for her

39

Kirsten

"WE'RE all victims of him, you know," I say as David nurses another two fingers of whiskey. He didn't slam this one. He sips it. Slow and steady, careful and contemplative as the kerosene lamplight flickers against us, painting our shadows like motionless ghosts on the cabin walls. "You. Me. Colby. *Dove*."

His stare intensifies, pointing at me with the mention of Dove's name.

"You set her up, didn't you?" I ask.

David lifts the tumbler to his lips, but he doesn't take a drink. "She was supposed to be a diversion, something to keep the police busy. Eventually it would've fizzled out. No DNA evidence and whatnot. Her life would've gone on, no harm, no foul. But then *she* decided to play armchair detective."

"Can you blame her?" I ask. "She thought she was going to go down for something she didn't do, and she knew she was being set up. What else was she supposed to do, sit around and have faith that it would all work out in the end? I'm sorry, but that's never been a reoccurring theme in Dove's life. She's not the kind of person that things tend to work out for."

"She would've been fine."

"You don't know that."

He shrugs, looking like he's about to say something more, but instead he takes a drink. His cheeks puff out before he swallows, and he places the tumbler down with a heavy clink.

"All those times I told you to stay away from her," he says. "You didn't listen. You kept letting her in. You kept listening to her theories. All you had to do was stay away." David faces me. "Can't say I didn't warn you."

"So that's why I'm here? Because Dove got too close to the truth and you were worried she was going to tell me?"

"She *was* going to tell you. And as soon as you heard the name, you'd put it all together. You'd realize Colby was my daughter, you'd start thinking about how strange it was that I was coming around so often, ingratiating myself into your life, and you'd start to get suspicious—and rightfully so."

"So you were only coming around to keep a close eye on the investigation."

He takes another sip. "Of course."

"So when Lucy got out, that was you?" I ask.

He nods. "You left her in the back yard. I did the rest."

"The note in the door was you as well?"

"After you and Dove spent a couple hours together that night, I wanted to plant some seeds of doubt, make you wonder if you could trust her or if she was up to something." He speaks with casualness infused with pride.

"And the busted lock on the gate?"

"It was all me, Kirsten." His hands lift in the air in a sarcastic surrender, and then he chuckles to himself. I wonder if he's feeling the whiskey yet. If I get him to keep talking, maybe he'll keep drinking, and maybe he'll be too inebriated to do anything rash ...

"All right. So you got me," I say. Nerves creep beneath my skin. What I'm about to attempt is risky, but if it works, there's a chance I might get out of this alive. "And while I should be furious with you, I have to say, I'm impressed."

He scoffs.

"I didn't have a dad," I say. "I mean, I did, but he wasn't around. Typical alcoholic wife beater type who knew how to disappear when the child support was due. Do you have any idea how much I wanted a dad like you? A dad who gave a damn?"

"Parenting's the hardest thing you'll ever do. Not everyone's cut out for the job." He takes another drink. "Your kid is born and it's like someone rips your beating, bloody heart out of your chest, and you get to watch it walk around outside of you for the rest of your life. That kind of thing either scares the hell out of you and sends you packing or it makes you a better man, makes you swear on your life you'll never let anything happen to it."

"I want to know what that's like," I say.

His eyes lower to my belly, as if he'd forgotten for a moment that I'm pregnant.

"The kind of love you have for your daughter, I want to know what that's like. That unbreakable bond that nothing can come between," I say.

His temples flex. "Sorry you got dealt a shit hand in the daddy department."

He's deflecting, changing the subject.

"David," I say, my voice as calm as I can manage as I

hold his fiercely intense gaze. "If you let me go, I won't tell anyone about this. We can pretend like it never happened. Ian is ... Ian *was* a monster. He deserved what happened to him. Let me leave. Let me go home. Let me have my baby."

"You mean *Ian's* baby." He snickers, and my heart free falls. He doesn't see this as an innocent child. He sees it as demon spawn.

"I'm so sorry for what he did," I say, my words turning gravelly in my throat as my hope disintegrates. "But it isn't my fault, nor is it the baby's fault."

David gathers a long, slow breath before reaching for the gun. "Stop apologizing for that sick bastard. The only thing you should be sorry for is that you didn't listen when I told you to stay away from Dove."

40

DOVE

"WE'RE ALMOST THERE," Colby says, leaning toward the dash, her phone screen distracting as it lights the dark interior of her car. We've been driving almost twenty minutes now, a good portion of that on gravel. "Turn left onto Lake Spearfish Drive up here."

I glance down at my phone in my own lap, the signal fading in and out. I'm not sure how Colby's phone is still working, but then again, after the divorce, I switched to a cut-rate cell service provider with a dirty cheap monthly plan and this is likely the result of that.

"What's the address?" I ask.

"There is no address. It's a cabin my grandpa built, like, fifty years ago on one of their acreages." She peers out her window. "We're almost there."

I spot a road up ahead, the tiny green sign barely visible with her headlights, and I jerk the wheel to the left. The road morphs from gravel to dirt, rutted and unmaintained.

The car bumps and bounces until smoothing out a half mile later.

"There's a turn off somewhere up here. On the left. It's hard to see at night, so maybe slow down."

I ease off the gas and keep my attention focused ahead as Colby scans the ditches.

With every second, my breath quickens, my heart hammers harder, and my thoughts turn to the worst-case scenario.

If I die tonight, it'll be all your fault.

41

Kirsten

"REALLY, David? You're going to shoot me? Isn't that a little messy?" I realize mocking him isn't my best plan of action, but I've reached the end of my proverbial rope. I've used up all of my tricks.

He says nothing, his attention focused on the gun as he swallows the last of his Crown Royal.

"I swear to God, David, on my child's life, if you let me leave, I won't tell a soul. I'll leave Lambs Grove. I'll pretend like none of this ever happened. You won't have to see me— or Ian's baby—ever again." Fiery tears stream down my cheeks, leaving itchy trails that dry the moment the air touches them.

"Don't insult my intelligence," he says under his breath.

I don't want to die.

I don't want to go out like this.

I don't want to take my final breath never getting to meet the life growing inside of me.

David's mind is made up. It's no use. My words and my tears are wasted with him.

They say when a child grows up in chaos, they learn to control their environments as a means to feel safe. I have no control. I don't feel safe. So I close my eyes and try to imagine what's next. I've always hated surprises, always needed to plan and know what comes next, so if I can imagine my death, maybe it'll take some of the edge off?

I tell myself there's going to be a loud bang. That it's going to happen so fast I won't feel a thing. Then I tell myself I'm going to be blanketed in peace and warmth and then? I'll get to see Adam.

Salty rivulets slide down my cheeks and settle on my lips. I dry the wetness with my shoulder.

Drawing in a lungful of earthen air, I picture Adam in my mind's eye. If I focus on him, on what's to come, I can get through this.

"Okay," I say a moment later, eyes closed tighter than ever as I brace myself. "Just ... get it over with."

I brace myself for the loud bang, the deafening pop, the flash of light that's going to end this madness and reunite me with my beloved Adam.

But the loud bang comes from behind me.

And when I open my eyes, I'm not dead.

I'm very much alive.

"Dad!" A teenage girl stands in the doorway, the cabin door ricocheting off the wall behind it. Two piercing bright headlights shine from behind her, making her appear like some dark figure in the night.

42

DOVE

"GOD DAMN IT, COLBY!" David yells at his daughter from inside the house as I run up behind her. I make it to the front steps in time to see David shoving something into the back of his waistband.

"Dad ..." Colby stumbles toward him, her attention turned to the left as she claps her hand over her mouth.

My vision adjusts enough for me to spot Kirsten tied to a chair, her wrists and ankles bound with plastic zip ties so tight they dig into her flesh, her face stained with tear tracks.

This is the *mother of your child..*

And she's going through this because of *you*.

You did this.

No one else but *you*, Ian.

I realize now that I was nothing more than a beard for you, a loyal and loving wife to make everyone believe you were the man you so badly wanted to be. You never loved me. You used me. And when I couldn't give you what you wanted anymore, you decided to use my best friend.

Time stands still for a moment as I glance around the tiny cabin that reeks of stale musk and lake water, at the wild and fearful eyes that surround me, at this enormous mess you've created—the mess I'm about to clean up for you.

It's impressive really. *Not Teacher of the Year* kind of impressive. No. It's the kind of impressive you can brag about from the fire pit I hope to God is engulfing you in this very moment.

I swear, Ian, after tonight you're dead to me—for real this time.

"Don't do this, you don't have to do this," Colby runs to her father, throwing her arms around him and burying her face against his chest.

An open bottle of whiskey rests next to a dirty crystal tumbler on the scratched kitchen table. On the other side of the room is an old couch, grocery sacks, blankets, and a duffel bag.

"You don't have to do this for me," Colby is sobbing hysterically and I'm hardly able to make out all of her words. "You don't have to protect me. What I did was wrong, and I deserve to be punished."

"Colby!" David snaps at her, his eyes wild and his voice a harsh growl. "Don't say another word."

Kirsten and I exchange looks, as if we're both wondering if we heard that right.

Colby turns to the two of us, her finger pressed into her chest as she heaves. "I killed him. *I killed Ian.*"

I'm speechless.

I had this all wrong.

Judging by the shell-shocked expression on Kirsten's face as our eyes meet, I wasn't the only one.

"Colby!" her father reaches for her arm, but she jerks it away.

"He said when I turned eighteen we could finally be together." She rolls her pretty blue eyes. "Like, actually be together. No more sneaking around. He said he loved me, that he was going to find a teaching job in the city next year when I went to college." Her attention hones in on me. "He left you for me, Dove. He hated himself for cheating on you. He wanted to make things right."

I find it hard to believe someone capable of something so vile would have any shred of a conscience, Ian, but I let her continue. I'm sure you told her all kinds of things that painted you in chivalry, that painted your situation in a more flattering light.

Colby turns to Kirsten. "But then *you* came along. At first he told me he was only dating you as a cover, so people wouldn't be suspicious." She swipes at a tear before folding her arms across her chest, her thin body swimming in her LGHS sweatshirt. "But then I got pregnant ... and so did you."

Colby's eyes are dull, their crystalline brilliance gone and replaced with a flash of something more sinister.

"It was an accident," Kirsten speaks up. "I was on the pill. It ... it wasn't intentional, I swear to you."

"That's not what Ian said. He said you tricked him," Colby says with a fire in her eyes that wasn't there before. "He said you were obsessed with him, that you always flirted with him when he was married. He said you trapped him."

"He lied to you," Kirsten says. "Those are *all* lies."

"He wanted me to take this pill." Her arms cross and

plump tear streams glisten on her creamy cheeks as she stares up at a dark ceiling. "He wanted me to *kill* our *child*. He said he couldn't raise two babies at the same time, that he had to have the one with you first and that if I was patient, we would have a family of our own someday."

My God, Ian. You truly were a monster.

"When I refused ... when I told him I couldn't go through with that ..." her voice gets caught in her throat. " ... he had this look in his eyes ... like he wanted to kill me ... and his hand was wrapped around my wrist so hard as he told me I didn't have a choice ... and then I ... it happened so fast ... I saw my computer charger in the back seat and I grabbed it and the next thing I knew I had the cord wrapped around his neck."

Colby swipes the thick tears from her cheeks and gathers in a hard breath. For the briefest of moments, I see a small part of myself in her. I see a teenager madly, deeply, and irrevocably in love. I see her scared and pregnant—and then I see her ultimately betrayed by the man who hung the moon and lit the stars.

Teenagers are naturally impulsive. They don't think things through. You—of all people should have known that —Ian. Instead you threw caution to the wind, used her for your own perversions, and expected her to behave like a rational adult when you shattered her unstable adolescent heart.

"I'm not a murderer," Colby says, her hands moving to her sweatshirt-covered stomach.

David groans from behind her, head tucked against his chest. "Colby, that's enough. Don't say another word."

My phone vibrates in my hand, a text or notification coming through—and I take it as a sign that I've got service out here now. I remember watching a true crime show once where this girl was kidnapped and she managed to call 9-1-1 by pressing the side button on her phone three times.

Everyone is transfixed on Colby now, no one paying an ounce of attention to me, so I use the opportunity to press the button three times. I don't look at my screen. I don't draw any attention to myself. I don't even know if it worked.

"I'm not a bad person," Colby says, choking up.

"—that's enough." David grabs his daughter and pulls her toward him, wrapping her in his arms until her petite frame all but disappears.

"I killed him in self-defense, Dad," she says, sobbing into his shoulder. "You lied to me. You told me to get some sleep and you'd take me to the police in the morning ... I didn't know you were going to hide him in the woods. You shouldn't have done that! You made everything worse!"

"I was trying to protect you." His chest puffs and his brusque baritone slices through the small space we share, making both Kirsten and I jump.

"By covering it up? By making it look like it was someone else?" Her voice is pitched and incredulous and she shoves herself away from him. "You always told me we had to do the right thing, no matter what. That's what I was trying to do."

"And you don't think that's what *I* was trying to do?" He counters back. "I was trying to protect your future, trying to keep you from spending the rest of your life in *prison,* all because of an impulsive teenage decision."

I glance at Kirsten while David and Colby argued. There must be half a dozen zip ties fastening her to that chair. I don't have a knife or anything sharp that could come close to cutting through those things, and Colby's keys are in her car, which is still idling out front. There's no way I can get her out of here without them noticing.

Seeing Kirsten, so helpless, so innocent in this, being threatened with her life and then listening to a grown man justify his reprehensible actions stirs something inside of me.

An electric jolt rocks my system, followed by the creep of white-hot rage saturating the layers beneath my skin until all I see is red. For a second, everything around me goes black and someone—Colby I believe—lets out a scream so piercing it brings everything back into focus.

When I look down, I realize I'm on the other side of the cabin straddling David, who's lying on his back, one hand cupping his groin and his other arm hovering above his face, trying to block the punches I'm throwing at him. His forehead is gashed, red liquid spilling everywhere.

Colby's trying to tear me off him, but I'm too strong for her.

I'm unstoppable.

A broken whiskey bottle lies on the floor next to us—I must have used it to disorient him before I attacked.

Blood trickles from his nose and mouth as he pleads for me to stop, and my knuckles are raw, painted in red. My body is numb. There's no pain, no awareness of whether I'm hot or cold, shaking or still. The release is all emotional, pure and unadulterated, no longer anesthetized by my medication.

"Dove, that's enough … please stop!" Colby cries from behind me. "Please! You're going to kill him!"

The irony in her sentence is what stops me in the middle of my next left hook.

"What?" I turn to her, laughing. "What did you just say?"

Colby steps backward, unsteady on her feet, her eyes

searching mine. Her father moans on the ground, attempting—and failing—to push himself up.

"Dove," Kirsten says.

I place my hand out. "It's okay, Kirsten. I'm not going to do anything. I just think it's ironic how she's pleading for her father's life when he was two seconds from taking ours."

Colby has backed herself into a corner, and she slumps down, wrapping her arms around her bent knees and making herself small as she fights off muffled sobs. She's a young woman, barely an adult. And at the end of the day, she's also a victim.

Your victim, Ian.

I try to remind myself of that.

I take a step back, staring at the baby-faced murderess in the corner before taking a glance at the bloody heap of pathetic man lying on the ground and finally, I glance at the traitor I once considered a best friend.

"I need a knife," I say to David.

He doesn't answer. Colby cries.

"*Knife*," I repeat louder. "I need to cut her out of those goddamn restraints and get her to a hospital."

I don't know how long she's been here or how much stress or trauma he's put her through, but I've read that those things can cause miscarriages, and I will not have the most innocent life in this room perish because of their selfish decisions.

"In the bag," David lifts a blood-covered arm and points toward the dingy couch along the wall. A second later, I locate a hunting knife from one of the pockets and make my way over to Kirsten, slicing through the zip ties one by one before helping her off.

"Your keys?" I ask David. "Where are they?"

He hesitates at first, and then he gives me a hesitant and breathy, "In the car."

"Come on," I say to Kirsten, nodding toward the head-lights of Colby's car that beam through the open door. I load her into the passenger seat before spotting the back end of David's car sticking out from the side of the cabin, hidden amongst shrubs and trees. A quick jog over and I'm able to grab his keys from the ignition, shoving them in my pocket before returning to the red sedan. David's injuries aren't life-threatening, and I want to ensure they don't try to get away before the police can get to them.

A second later, I'm peeling out of the grassy driveway and pulling back on the rutty dirt road, speeding in the dark of night and hoping I'm going the right way.

Kirsten rests her head against the passenger side window, massaging her wrists.

"You doing okay?" I ask, my hands at ten and two as we veer towards a gravel road and climb a narrow hill. As soon as we glide down the other side, the lights of Lambs Grove come into view in the distance.

"I ... I'm just in shock." Her voice is cracked and breathless. "He blindsided me."

"David or Ian?" I glance down at my phone now that I have a chance. Still no service, which means my 9-1-1 call never went through.

She sighs. "Both."

If we were still friends, I'd feel worse for her. I'd offer her a little more in the way of sympathies. But we're not in that place, and I don't know that we ever will be again. She's a human. I'm a human. And we're getting out of this alive—friendships and commiserations are irrelevant.

From the corner of my eye, I spot her sitting with her hands on the tops of her knees, back straight and eyes closed as she breathes through her nose, like she's trying to calm and ground herself in the midst of all of this chaos.

When I first met Kirsten, she had this quiet gentleness about her. Maybe it was all the yoga she was doing or maybe it was because life had beat her down a bit and she covered it all with that slow, pretty smile, but it took me less than five minutes to decide I liked her. She didn't hesitate to let me in, and soon enough her life became an open book—the tragic kind.

I remember telling her how proud I was of her, but she'd always brush it off, like she didn't deserve any accolades. And then she'd tell me how lucky I was to have the life I had.

It's one thing to like your best friend's shoes.

It's another thing to steal them when she's not looking.

"Thank you, Dove," she says as she sits up, her dark doe eyes on me, but I concentrate on the road ahead. "For saving me." Her palm glides over her lower stomach—where your child grows, the child you'll never get to meet. No. The child who will never get to meet *you*. It's not about you anymore, Ian. "For saving us. You didn't have to do what you did."

"Yes, I did," I say without hesitation. "Someone had to do the right thing for once."

I drop her off at the hospital ten minutes later, helping her with check-in before getting her settled, and when I get back to Colby's car, I call Detective Reynolds.

43

Kirsten

"KIRSTEN?"

I'm lying in a hospital bed, under a paper-thin gown and white flannel sheets, hooked up to half a dozen monitors, when Ian's mom's voice fills the room. I glance away from the wall-mounted TV and the breaking news report covering the nightmare I'd managed to live through last night and find her standing in the doorway, her petite frame partially obstructed with a massive bouquet of cheerful flowers.

"Lori, come on in." I press the button on the side of the bed until I'm sitting up, and then I mute the television.

"I hope it's okay that I'm here." She sets the flowers on a nearby table before rushing to my side. Her eyes move to my stomach before returning to me.

"Of course it is. Thank you for coming. And thank you for the flowers."

"How are you feeling?" Lori brushes a strand of hair

from my forehead, a sweet and unexpected gesture that makes me long for the kind of mother I've never known.

"Exhausted," I say. "But otherwise, everything's fine. The baby's fine. I'm fine. They're keeping me here for observation."

She glances at the TV, where a local reporter is live on scene. The cabin behind her looks different in the daytime —quaint and unsuspecting, the kind of place a dad might go for a weekend of fishing.

"I still can't believe it," I say.

"Mm mm," Lori says, her red lips pressing flat. Her attention deviates for a second, fixated on the parking lot view from my hospital room window. I think about how strange she acted last time, when I'd briefly mentioned the possibility of Ian having cheated. She packed up, couldn't get out of there fast enough.

"Lori ... did you know something?" I ask. "About Ian and Colby?"

Her mouth titters for a second, like she wants to say something but can't find the words.

"It's okay," I say. "You don't have to tell me. I thought maybe—"

"I ... I saw something ... once," she says, her tone flat and her eyes closed. "He was still married to Dove at the time. It was late at night—I had to run out to the twenty-four-hour Walmart to grab a few things I needed for the church bake sale that was going on the next day. Anyway, I saw his car parked behind the abandoned tractor dealership on the north side of town. I drove closer, to check it out, thinking maybe it was someone else with a similar car, but the windows were all fogged. And I recognized the plate."

Lori glances down at her hands, steadying them on the side rail of my hospital bed.

"I so badly wanted to be wrong," she says before exhaling long and slow. "And I hate how I blamed Dove for what happened."

"I'm just glad it wasn't," I say. "She saved us."

Lori takes my hand. "I owe her an apology. And a lifetime of thank yous."

"She'll like that. I know she thinks the world of you."

A warm expression paints her face. "Everything's going to be okay."

She says it in such a way that I think it's intended for the both of us to hear.

"Yeah," I say. "It is."

44

DOVE

ARI AND NOAH arrive at my place around a quarter past two the next day. It's been over twenty-four hours since I've slept last. There's way too much adrenaline still coursing through me to let my body and mind rest, but at least I managed to get a few things done. I also managed to shower, run a comb through my hair, and put on a little makeup—nothing much, enough to make me look a woman with every intention of putting her life back together again and functioning like a normal human being for the first time all year.

Every memento, every photo of the two of us, is currently sitting in the bottom of the smelly green dumpster in the back of the apartment parking lot. Your t-shirts, your cologne, your expensive timepiece—it's all trash now.

"Thanks for coming," I say when I let them in.

Ari comes in first. I brace myself for a lecture or a stare down of some sort, but instead she gives me a hug. "I'm so glad you called. I'm so glad you're okay."

Noah's a few steps behind her. He doesn't hug me—he's never been a hugger. "Yeah, I was worried. We both were. These last few weeks have been ..."

He doesn't say insane.

He doesn't need to.

"Sit down, guys," I say.

Ari takes the recliner and Noah takes the sofa. I stay standing.

"I wanted to apologize for the way I treated you both," I say. "The blaming. The doubting. The accusing. The ... not appreciating you."

"Dove ..." Noah says, his tone more gracious than I deserve.

"No. I owe you both apologies," I say. "I haven't been myself lately ... for a lot of reasons ... and yet you stood by my side until I wouldn't let you stand by my side anymore. So thank you. And I hope you can forgive me."

Ari rises from the recliner, wrapping her arms around me tight one more time. "I'm so glad you're back, Dove. I've missed you."

Her words catch me off guard at first. Or maybe it's the delivery. Like she's talking about someone who's been gone for ages. And then it hits me. I left the best parts of me with you, Ian. I walked out of that house we shared on Blue Jay Lane, a shell of the woman I was before. I was convinced that I was only whole when I was with you, convinced my life was only worth living when I was living it with you.

It took you dying for me to see the light—if that isn't karma, I don't know what is.

45

Kirsten

SIX WEEKS LATER ...

SHE WAITS for me at a high-top table in the back of the coffee shop, one hand cupped around a to-go latte as she thumbs through her phone with the other. Christmas music plays from the speakers in the ceiling and the air is filled with the scent of gingerbread scones and peppermint mochas.

"Dove? Hi," I say when I approach her, wondering if she's as nervous as I am. I haven't seen her since that night when she swooped in and saved our lives, the unlikeliest and humblest of heroes. Some days I swear it everything happened yesterday, other days a lifetime ago.

She glances up from her phone before putting it aside. "Hi."

The last time I saw her, she was dropping me off at the

hospital. Everything that followed over the next few days was a blur. The tests and ultrasounds and doctor's exams—all of which came back normal. Lori's visit. Detective Reynolds stopping by once I was back home to ask me some questions and give me updates. It's been weeks since I've heard anything, but last I knew, in addition to kidnapping charges, David is also being charged with conspiracy to commit a forcible felony for trying to cover up his daughter's crime. He won't see the other side of a prison cell for at least a couple of decades from what people are saying. As far as Colby goes, they're going to try her as an adult, but given the abuse of power and the fact that she was a victim as well, the judge and jury will more than likely go a little easier on her. Not only that, but she's got the whole self-defense claim on her side.

The whole thing is heartbreaking, any way you look at it.

"The place looks a lot different than before," I say as I take a seat. "It's unrecognizable."

Dove peers around the space that once housed her paint-and-sip shop a lifetime ago, a hint of wistfulness in her eyes, and I silently chide myself for not sticking to a more neutral topic of conversation.

"Thanks for coming," she says, sitting up straight like she's about to get down to business. A second later, I notice a large white envelope resting on the table. She slides it toward me. "I wanted to give you this before I left."

"I didn't know you were leaving. Taking a trip?"

"Moving," she says, leaving it at that, a cordial reminder that she didn't come here to rekindle our friendship.

"What is this?" I examine the unmarked envelope before gliding a finger beneath the seal and peeking at the small stack of papers inside. A quick perusal shows several of Dove's signatures covering the first page, only apparently she's gone back to her maiden name of Jensen.

Can't say that I blame her. I wouldn't want to have any ties to that monster after what he did either.

"Ian never updated his will," she says.

"I know."

"So I went ahead and had my attorney take care of everything for you," she says. "Half of it's yours. The estate, the trust, the house. The other half will be put into a trust for Colby's baby."

I don't know what to say so I sit there, mouth slightly agape, fighting the tears that begin to well. First she saved my life, now this. I was never worthy of her friendship, and I'll forever mourn that loss.

"Thank you," I say, re-sealing the envelope and sliding it into my purse. "So much."

The outpouring of generosity I've experienced over the past month and a half has been enough to last a lifetime and then some.

Last month, Ian's parents offered to buy me a place of my own on their side of town—about a block down the street from where they live. They thought after everything, I could use a fresh start, and they want to be as close as possible to help out as much as they can. At first I declined, as I've never been one to take handouts, but they insisted, and ultimately I had to think about what was going to be best for the baby. The way I saw it, I had two options: I could run from yet another tragedy in my life or I could stay in place and plant roots, let my child grow up with loving grandparents and cousins and extended family and have the kind of childhood I only ever dreamed of.

I decided to stop running.

In addition to that, business at Best Life Yoga has never

been better. After the truth behind Ian's murder came to light, the public rumor mill morphed into a sympathy bandwagon and suddenly people were dropping off donations for the baby and signing up for classes and offering an abundance of services and support, even welcoming me into a group for first-time moms.

Everything is still so new, but I think it's safe to say I have a circle of friends now.

"All right. Well. Good luck with everything," Dove says as she slides off her chair and slings her purse over her left shoulder.

I rise. "Yeah, same to you."

She turns to leave, but I call after her.

"Yes?" she asks.

"I wanted to tell you how sorry I am ... for *everything*."

She takes me in like it's the last time she's ever going to see me, her shoulders rising and falling as she takes a cleansing breath. "People make mistakes. And life is too short to spend the rest of your life having them for it. Forgive yourself, Kirsten. Because I have."

Before I have a chance to say anything, she's halfway to the door. The bells chime as she walks out, and I watch from the warmth of the coffee shop as her navy pea coat is peppered in thick December snowflakes.

I hope wherever she's going, it's worthy of the beautiful soul that is Dove Jensen.

DISCUSSION QUESTIONS

1. What was your initial impression of Dove? Did her obsession with her ex-husband and unfaltering love for him make you believe she was guilty ... or innocent?

2. In your opinion, do you think Dove truly believed Ian would come back for her someday or do you think it was something she told herself in order to survive her new normal?

3. What was your initial impression of the dynamic between Dr. Noah Benoit and Dove?

4. What did you think when Dove let herself into her old house with the spare key? If you were desperate to prove your innocence and to find justice for someone you loved—and truly believed you wouldn't get caught—would you go snooping in your former home?

5. First loves and young love is a reoccurring theme in this book. How do you think our first experiences with romantic love shape the experiences that come after? And have you ever

known someone who wasn't able to get over their first love?

6. Aside from Ian's obvious shortcomings and secrets, what do you think drew women like Dove and Colby and Kirsten to be irresistibly drawn to him? What was so special about him? Was it something about him? Or was it perhaps something the three of them had in common? A need or a want that he fulfilled in all of them?

7. What do you think drives good people to do bad things? Specifically, people in Ian's situation? What about David's decision to do what he did? Why do you think they each felt like they could get away with their crimes?

8. In the end, Dove makes a selfless decision involving Ian's estate. What did you think of the journey her character took from the first chapter to the last? And would you have done the same thing? Why or why not?

SAMPLE - THE MEMORY WATCHER

THE MEMORY WATCHER (SAMPLE)

Sunday Tomassetti writing as Minka Kent

DESCRIPTION

Haunted by memories of the daughter she gave up at fifteen, Autumn Carpenter never fully moved on.

She doesn't have to.

Instead, she lives a life of relative seclusion, content to watch from a distance as the picture-perfect McMullen family raises her daughter as their own. Every birthday, every milestone, every memory, Autumn is watching.

Only no one knows.

But when the opportunity presents itself, Autumn allows herself to become intertwined in the lavish life of the picturesque McMullens. And only then does she realize that pictures . . . they lie. The perfect family . . . it doesn't exist. And beautiful people . . . they keep the ugliest secrets.

PROLOGUE

Autumn

I FOUND HER.

It took three years, but I found her.

They call her Grace, and while she may not look like them, she is theirs.

And she is also mine.

Her hair is light brown with a little natural wave, the way mine was at that age, and her dark eyes, round and inquisitive, light up her cherubic face when she smiles.

Her mother, Daphne, dresses her in pink lace and over-sized hair bows and poses her for pictures every chance she gets, plastering them all over social media.

The first night I stumbled across Daphne McMullen's Instaface, I stayed up until four in the morning going through all the photographs and status updates, soaking in and screenshotting every last moment and immortalized memory from the day they brought her home from the hospital to the day she blew out the third candle on her double chocolate birthday cake.

One thousand and ninety-five days I missed morphed into one thousand and ninety-five days I recovered over the course of one sleepless night.

I hook a leg over the edge of my bathtub, mindlessly scrolling through Daphne's newsfeed for the millionth time in the past week. A million times I've seen these photos, and yet it's like the first time, every time.

Steam rises from the water and sweat collects across my brow. I'm in a trance, and I don't come out until I'm prompted by the sound of my roommate pounding on the door.

"You almost done in there?" she asks. "I put that show on that you wanted to watch. I ordered us a pizza too. Should be here soon."

She's so needy, always clinging to me, always telling me her secrets and whining to me about how hard it is to be her. I read her diary at her bizarre insistence, and believe me when I say she has nothing to cry about.

Her car? Paid for.

Her college tuition? Paid for.

This apartment? Paid for.

Her parents? Overachievers with rigorous expectations. Boo-freaking-hoo.

"Yeah," I call out. "I'll be out in a few."

I don't move. Instead, I keep scrolling, dragging my thumb across the fogged screen of my phone, smiling to myself. I examine another photo, then another and another. I'm not sure how much time passes, but my roommate bangs on the door once more.

"You still in there? Pizza just got here." Her voice is timid and meek on the other side of the door. Over the past few years, I've become her life force. She can't go anywhere or do anything or make any decisions without me. But lately she's been withering away, drawing into her shell. She whispers more than she talks these days, and at night I hear her cry through the shared wall that separates our bedrooms, but she won't get help because the last time she needed it, her parents had her committed.

"Getting out now." I try not to groan as I place my phone aside and reach for a towel.

"You said that twenty minutes ago."

Good God, this girl.

I love everything about her life. I love her overinvolved helicopter parents. I love her dorky little brother. I love her adoring nana. I love her little white BMW and the collection of unused designer purses that fill her closet. I love her drawer full of department store makeup and the way her luxe shampoo smells every morning after she showers.

But I do not love *her*.

She has everything a girl could possibly want, and all she does is fixate on the past, on things she can't change. One unfortunate situation happened three years ago, and she refuses to let it go. This girl dwells something fierce. If only she lived a day in my life, then she'd actually have something to dwell on.

Sometimes I'm convinced I was born in the wrong body, to the wrong family.

I should have been born as her.

"Drying off now," I yell, wrapping a plush towel around my wet body. "Be out in ten."

I finish up, scrolling through photos as I slather her overpriced, fragrance-free lotion on my damp skin, and I do a tiny jump for joy when I see Daphne has posted a fresh picture of Grace.

God, this is addictive.

It's like someone dropped an all-access backstage pass to Grace's life right into my lap.

It's bedtime and my Grace is wearing a princess nightgown that stops just above her chubby little ankles. Wisps of hair hang in her eyes and she's dragging a white teddy bear along side of her.

How I long to kiss her forehead, tuck her in to bed, and tell her how loved she is.

Someday, perhaps.

Until then, this will have to do.

1

Autumn

7 YEARS LATER...

PRESS, tap, refresh.

Over the years, Instaface's algorithms have learned that Daphne McMullen's posts are my favorite. Her posts are almost always at the top of my newsfeed. But today they're MIA.

Something's not right.

Scrolling down, I pass *@TheLittleGreenCottage* and *@FitnessJunkie887*. I pass *@JustJustine* and *@Cali-MakeupGuru*.

Scrolling...

Scrolling...

Scrolling...

There's no sign of Daphne anywhere.

This is odd.

There's a tingle in the back of my throat, and every nerve ending is standing on edge. Something's amiss. I feel it all over. Inside. Outside. The core of my bones.

Tapping on the search bar, I type in *@TheMcMullen-Family* and take a deep breath.

No results found.

This can't be right.

Did she block me?

She doesn't even know me. Of course she didn't block me, and I "ghost" follow her. I'm not an "official" follower. Official followers require proof of identification due to Instaface's strict no-dummy-accounts policy.

Just to be sure, I log out of my account and perform the search again.

No results found.

Maybe she changed her account name?

I type in *@McMullenFamily*, *@DaphneMcMullen*, and *@GrahamandDaphneMcMullen*. I type in fifty thousand other variations, all of which lead me to the same dead end.

No results found.

Heat creeps up my neck, billowing to my ears. My throat constricts, and I can't breathe.

Rushing to the bedroom window, I throw back the curtains and slide it open, gasping for air, met with a blast of tepid morning rain on my face that does nothing to calm me down.

This isn't happening. This isn't happening. This isn't happening.

I refuse to believe it.

It makes no sense.

Daphne McMullen has thousands of followers.

She lives for this stuff.

She has so many followers, companies send her free stuff.

She does paid ads for crying out loud.

Why would she just shut it down?

She posted a picture of the kids getting ready for school this morning . . . how could it all just . . . go away like that? With no warning?

My eyes burn, brimming until everything around me is a hazy blur. There's a cry in the back of my throat, readying itself, threatening to burst to the surface if I don't do something immediately.

My knees give out, and I grip the edge of my dresser to steady myself because I can hardly summon the strength to stand. If my boyfriend weren't hogging the bathroom we share, I'd be on my knees in front of the toilet, expelling the shocked contents of my stomach in an attempt to quell the maelstrom inside me.

My gateway to Grace's life has come to a screeching halt. Just like that.

Everything I live for just . . . gone.

"Autumn, you all right out there?" Ben asks from the other side of the door. "I heard a loud noise. Everything okay?"

No. Everything is *not* okay.

I don't answer. I can't. And the bathroom door swings open just as I push myself to standing and clench the lapels of my robe so he can't see what I'm wearing underneath it.

"I'm fine," I say. "Had a dizzy spell. Think I'm coming down with something."

Ben's blue eyes narrow and then relax. He buys it. He buys everything, all the time.

I check my reflection in the dresser mirror, dragging my fingertips through my sandy hair and piling it all into a messy bun on the top of my crown, precisely the way this pretty girl from a gas station yesterday morning wore hers. Gathered. Twisted. Elastic'd. Pulled and yanked into messy submission. I've also managed to scrounge up a sheer white blouse from the back of my closet, and I've slid two chicken cutlet-shaped inserts into my push-up bra. I'm one hundred percent sure Pretty Girl had a boob job.

Everything's hidden under my fluffy gray bathrobe, and the second Ben leaves, I'll stain my lips in bold, electric red. There's a bluish undertone to this particular shade, which I've learned from several fashion and beauty magazines tends to make teeth appear to be the whitest of white. And if there's one thing I've learned in my twenty-five years on this God-forsaken planet, it's that rich people almost always have teeth the color of driven snow.

A cloud of steam floats from the bathroom doorway, wrapping its damp warmth around me and carrying with it a hint of Ben's cologne, which isn't actually Ben's at all. Another man, Dylan Abernathy, wore it first.

I follow his wife, @DeliaAbernathy, on Instaface, reveling in their every documented, picturesque moment like it's my own. And it *is* mine. All I have to do is close my eyes and I'm transported to their serene cottage on the Portland coast of Maine. I breathe in, and I can feel the salty air in my lungs, pulling in the scent of the ocean again and again.

I spotted the cologne in the background of one of her photos once, and I had to order a bottle for Ben. It smells like wet moss and rubbing alcohol, but he insists he loves it anyway.

Sometimes I imagine Delia inhaling Dylan's cologne, her nose buried in the curve of his neck, and when I kiss Ben, sometimes I pretend we're them, my hands slinking up his shoulders the way Delia might do. Our lips grazing. His scent enveloping us in a sweet moment of simplistic bliss. And in those fleeting seconds, I'm Delia Abernathy.

Inside and out. All over. Everywhere.

"You sure you're okay?" Ben's hands slink around my waist and his body presses against my back. The warmth of his lips grazing against the side of my neck follows, and I can almost feel the slight arc of his grin. "You need me to run to the store and get you some meds?"

"No, no. I'll be fine." I glance at my phone, which may as well be useless at this point, and I just want him to leave so I can wrap my head around all of this.

"Just take some time for yourself today, okay?" He lifts his dark brows, searching my eyes for confirmation.

All I do is take time for myself anymore. Losing my job as a medical assistant at Children's Medical Group two months ago has given me more than enough time to take care of myself.

"I will," I say.

"Good." He kisses my neck again. "Because I'm getting off early tonight."

My mind spins, trying to recall what we had planned for tonight.

"My sister's birthday?" His dark brows lift as he attempts to jog my memory. "We're taking Marnie out for dinner? You said you wrapped her gift last night."

"Oh. Right." I force a smile, lying through my teeth. I haven't wrapped his sister's gift yet. I haven't even purchased it. Mentally adding that to my to-do list for the day, I rise on my toes, press my lips against his, and send him off to work with a, "Have a nice day, Benny."

He both loves and hates when I call him that, but it always elicits a smile, and I need him to believe nothing's wrong. At this point, I need Ben now more than ever and for reasons he'll never understand.

Sometimes it feels wrong staring into his unassuming blue gaze and basking in his adoring smile while knowing I chose him the way a woman might choose the perfect pair of shoes from a mail-order catalog.

I saw. I researched. I chose.

But he made it so easy; his social media was a click-of-the-mouse smorgasbord.

Before I'd officially met Ben Gotlieb, I knew everything there was to know about him. Where he grew up (Rochester, New York). Where he attended college (University of Vermont). His favorite band (Coldplay). His favorite food (Mexican). What he did for a living (accountant). I knew he was single. I knew he was the oldest child, which meant he was responsible and dependable. I knew he was kindhearted as evidenced by the abundance of inspirational and motivational articles he'd post on his newsfeed. I knew he was a runner who traveled the country for marathons, collecting medals and stickers to showcase on the rear window of his hunter green Subaru. It took me all of an hour in front of a computer screen to ascertain that Ben Gotlieb was a good man.

As Ben would check in to various pubs and restaurants, I would follow.

Keeping back.

Always watching.

Observing who he was with and which kind of women drew his eye.

And Ben definitely had a type.

The blondes never did it for him. Neither did the brunettes or the redheads. But the ones with the Jennifer Aniston sandy-blonde hair caught his attention every time.

He seemed to be drawn to the girl-next-door types. Low-slung boyfriend jeans and a V-neck t-shirt. Minimal makeup. Cute ponytail. Bookish glasses.

And so I had to become her.

With a phone full of Instaface screenshots of some beauty blogger named *@EmmaLeeFacesTheDay*, I marched into the salon on Vine and Copeland and had my stylist transform my muddy brown strands into *sandy ash blonde* 532. On my way home, I stopped at the optometrist, grabbing a pair of cute glasses with thick, tortoiseshell frames and a non-prescription lens. I ended my day with an extensive shopping excursion at the Valley Park Mall, balancing my overpriced iced mocha latte, which I was determined to start liking, with an armful of shopping bags and a maxed-out credit card.

It took several days and a lot of practicing in front of the mirror, but by the time the following weekend rolled around, I was ready to officially meet Ben.

Stepping into someone else's skin made meeting him that much easier. The way I walked . . . the way I casually traced my collarbone as I laughed . . . the way I let my stare linger on his just a second too long as my mouth curled into a teasing smirk . . . none of that was me.

And yet it *was* me.

"See you tonight," Ben calls out before he leaves our bedroom, and I watch him grab his leather billfold off the dresser and slip it into his back right pocket. Pulling his navy suit jacket over his broad shoulders, he lingers in the doorway, taking me in the way he has since the moment we first–officially–met. I can almost hear him asking himself how he got so lucky. Ben exhales, his gaze fixed on mine. "I love you, Autumn."

"Love you too," I say. And I mean it. Mostly.

I *think* I love Ben. A girl spends two years with someone and she ought to by now. It's just that he said it so fast. We'd only been dating eight weeks when he blurted it out over Chinese takeout–his choice–and a rented DVD–also his choice. And then he proceeded to ramble on about how he'd never met anyone like me, how he couldn't believe how perfect we were together, how it was as if his dream girl had just . . . manifested from nothing and waltzed right into his life.

Two months after that, he asked me to move in with him, and of course I said yes.

That was the whole reason I scoped Ben out in the first place.

He lived in the charming blue bungalow behind the McMullen family.

And I wanted to watch my daughter grow up.

2

Autumn

THE WAY I SEE IT, I have two options: I can crumble to a dysfunctional heap, refusing to move off the sofa and mourning the loss of Daphne's Instaface account while raising a million red flags with Ben. Or I can carry on like nothing's wrong until I figure out what I'm going to do next.

For now, I need Ben. Ben equals access to Grace, even if we're separated by an acre of yard space and a fence.

I'll figure this out, and I'll land on my feet. Always have, always will.

The supermarket is packed for a Thursday morning. Apparently no one in Monarch Falls has anything better to do this morning. The yoga shop must be closed for renovations? Maybe the coffee shop ran out of soy milk? The bakery out of gluten-free cupcakes?

"Hi." To my right, a man's voice cuts through the cereal aisle, and when I glance up, I see a dopey grin with a laser-sharp stare pointed at me.

For a moment, I'd forgotten that today I'm the pretty girl from the gas station. Red lips. Big breasts. Tight jeans. Sexy, messy bun.

It feels good to be her right now, to step out of my burning, twitching, anxious skin. I almost forget about Instaface for a moment. *Almost.*

I smile the way I imagine she would, eyes half-squinting, lips closed and pulled up in one corner. Lifting my left hand, I give a small wave with just my fingertips and push my cart past him. From my periphery I see him turn, and I allow his stare to linger until I turn the corner.

"Excuse me." An older woman with bushy gray hair and a lavender twin set nearly bumps into me with her cart, wielding the audacity to glare at *me* as if our near-collision was *my* fault.

"I'm sorry," I lie. I saw this woman seconds before she saw me. Her attention was fixed on the wall of oatmeal selections before her as she mindlessly pushed her cart forward one shuffled step at a time.

The woman huffs and keeps moving, giving me side eye as if my look today offends her personally.

Typical Monarch Falls old-moneyed bitch.

I wonder how Pretty Girl deals with people like her? Half of me thinks she's probably too oblivious to notice. Or maybe she's too coked up? I could definitely see Pretty Girl with a two-grand-a-day coke habit. Easy.

Up ahead, a mother with a screaming infant and another mother with a squirrelly toddler are blocking the exit of the cereal aisle, gabbing on about something that seems to get the two of them fired up. Maybe preschools or the PTA? Swimming lessons? I couldn't care less. Their faded yoga pants and dark-circled eyes don't interest me.

They may as well be invisible. I don't see a mental vacation when I look at them. I see exhaustion.

I would never want to be them.

"Excuse me." I say with a polite smile, staring straight ahead as my cart is pointed in the direction I intend to go.

The women stop yammering and glance up, gawking at me with the kind of stare that suggests they're contemplating how their life would've turned out had they not married their high school sweethearts fresh out of college and popped out a litter's worth of children before their thirtieth birthdays.

Not that there's anything wrong with that.

It's just not my cuppa.

Not my cuppa . . .

I stole that phrase from a woman on Instaface I followed briefly last year. Her posts intrigued me at first. She seemed well-traveled. And her boyfriend was some Italian model who walked runways all over the world. Anytime she didn't like something, she'd politely say it wasn't her cuppa, and it just stuck. Eventually her boyfriend dumped her, her posts dwindled to few and far in between, and after a while she fell off the face of the earth. I unfollowed her shortly after that, and now I can't even recall her name.

The exuberantly exhausted mothers stop gawking long enough to move their carts and let me through. I don't waste my breath thanking them. People who are inconsiderate enough to block a busy grocery aisle with idle chitchat don't deserve common courtesy.

Rounding the corner, I stop at the end of the gift aisle, fighting the smart ass smirk on my mouth.

Marnie. Marnie. Marnie.

If I wanted to be the bigger person, I'd run to the mall and grab something decent. Maybe a giftcard to Bloomies or

Victoria's – something she might actually use and enjoy. But I'm feeling very, *very* small today.

The image of Marnie's crestfallen face comes to mind when I envision handing her a cheap stuffed bear and a bouquet of dyed carnations wrapped in pink cellophane.

She would hate it.

She would hate me.

But she already does. And she's made her sentiments crystal clear dozens upon dozens of times behind my back. Never to my face. She's spineless like that. Any time she gets Ben alone, she feels the need to opine that he's too good for me, that I'm using him. Ben shuts her down each time, bless his heart, but it doesn't keep her from bringing it up all over again the next time.

Snickering, I reach for a neon green teddy bear with scratchy matted fur, checking the price tag.

$4.99.

And then I think of Ben.

I can't do that to him. He's a good man. He asked me to get his sister a birthday gift, and that's exactly what I need to do, even if it kills me.

Placing the ugly bear back on its shelf, I trudge ahead, moving toward the card aisle. A pastel yellow birthday card with the most generic inscription draws the short straw, and I toss it in my cart before making a beeline for the gift card section.

I know many things about Marnie Gotlieb.

I know she loves to shop-til-she-drops, and I know her favorite things in the whole wide world are covered in images of dead presidents. I know she likes to be wined and dined by various older men she meets through online dating apps. I know she once slept with her college chemistry professor in exchange for a passing grade.

Pretty sure she has some daddy issues going on as well, though I'm not sure how that came to be since their father is Ward Cleaver reincarnate.

Swiping a couple gift cards from the rack, I grab one for a bookstore, because this woman needs to spend some quality time away from a phone screen, and another for a department store to mask the passive aggressive undertones of the first gift card.

Tossing them in my cart, it occurs to me that I told Ben I had wrapped Marnie's gift last night, which means I need to get her an actual gift. Heading toward the bath and body aisle, I grab a few blocks of organic, hand-milled soap from a low shelf, three for twelve dollars, and then I swipe a bottle of honey almond lotion.

I have no idea what Marnie's favorite scents are, nor do I care.

Rounding the next aisle, I stop in my heels when I spot a familiar image in the distance.

Long legs, red-bottomed shoes, glossy red hair and a screaming toddler paint a portrait of a woman I know like the back of my hand but have yet to meet in real life.

Daphne McMullen pushes her filled cart, slowly perusing organic boxes of macaroni and cheese and loaves upon loaves of gluten-free breads. Her hair glides across her back when she moves, and she turns to the youngest McMullen, four-year-old Sebastian, every few seconds to tickle his chin or give him an Eskimo kiss.

If there is a God, this must be his way of apologizing for this morning. He's sorry her account disappeared. He put her in my path on purpose.

My heart thrums and my mouth runs dry. With a tight grip on the handle of my cart, I watch, jaw loose and eyes glued. She's beautiful in person, which tells me what

I've suspected all along: that her Instaface persona is authentic, that Daphne McMullen is exactly who she says she is.

It makes my heart warm, watching her in action with her youngest. Grace is truly lucky to be able to call Daphne her mother.

I chose well.

Sebastian drops something on the floor, and Daphne crouches down to retrieve it, glancing around. My chest tightens, and I turn my head in the opposite direction. I can't stand here and gawk, though if I could, I'd do it all day long.

Behind me, an elderly gentleman clears his throat as if to tell me I'm in his way.

"Excuse me," I say, pushing my cart away.

When I enter the next aisle, I spot Daphne in the distance, making her way to the checkout lanes, so I do the same. Checking the customer congestion ahead, I try and calculate which register she'll choose, and I succeed. Within moments, I've secured a spot behind a round-bellied middle-aged man, who happens to be standing behind Daphne. She doesn't look past him, and she doesn't notice me.

To my back, a woman keeps checking out the other aisles as if jumping to the next one over could possibly save her a lifetime of waiting. She checks her watch, exhales, then glances at my cart. She seems annoyed, whether at this situation or the fact that I'm pushing a full-sized cart for three paper-y items and a few bars of soap. Maybe she's offended that I'm taking up an unnecessary amount of checkout aisle space, and that personally offends her? It's a perfectly reasonable reason to get bent out of shape . . . if you're a miserable asshole.

Two lanes down, a green light flicks on, and a female checker calls, "I can help whoever's next."

The woman behind me scurries off, followed by the hard-bellied man in front of me who nearly topples over the candy display in the process.

People.

This is what's wrong with the world.

And this is why I hate the grocery store: it's a fucking zoo with real, live human animals.

I glance up, readying to take the man's place in line, only my heart drops and my body breaks into a cold sweat when I remember Daphne is standing there, and it takes me a second to realize this is real.

This is happening.

I'm not imagining this.

With my heart pulsing in my ears, I move forward. I move closer and closer still until I'm directly behind her.

If I thought I was star struck before, watching from an aisle endcap twenty feet away . . . that was nothing compared to this.

I observe from my periphery as Daphne chitchats with the checker, some barely-nineteen-year-old kid with acne and auburn hair and a smattering of freckles across his full face. His movements are jittery and uncoordinated, like he's extremely self-aware in her presence, though she's calm as can be. Her skin is the color of bisque porcelain, creamy and flawless, and her golden blonde hair falls around her shoulders in all the right places, shiny and lush.

Four-year-old Sebastian, sits in the front of the cart, kicking his legs and singing some wildly annoying yet equally adorable little nursery rhyme to himself.

"Just a minute, my little love," she says, her voice soft as cashmere and rich as honey as she cups his chubby cheek in her right hand. I think about all the hashtags, and especially her oft used *#mylittlelove*, and my chest expands with warmth. "We're almost done."

Glancing in her cart, I spy things like pomegranates and starfruit, unsweetened almond milk, organic dates, and arugula. These are the foods she'll feed her family.

These are the foods she'll feed my daughter.

It's a far cry from the processed casseroles and frozen, prepackaged dinners and store-brand potato chips I grew up on.

"Two hundred five dollars and eleven cents," the cashier says, clearing his throat after his voice cracks. He pops his knuckles against his green apron and scans the line, avoiding eye contact with the rest of us as Daphne slides her shiny silver debit card through the machine.

Sebastian kicks her again. Harder this time. And she turns to him, leaning down and whispering something in his ear that makes him stop. She makes parenting look like a breeze, and everyone around us is watching in awe.

"Do you have children?" she asks the cashier.

"No, ma'am," he says, clearing his throat again. The color of his face intensifies the longer she focuses her attention on him, and I wonder if she has this sort of effect on everyone she comes across.

Probably.

"I didn't think so," she says with a kind chuckle. "Almost naptime for my little guy."

Checking my watch, I note that it's only ten in the morning. I'm not a parenting expert, and I only worked at the children's clinic for a couple of years, but I'm pretty sure four-year-olds don't take morning naps.

"Thanks so much." Daphne takes the receipt from the red-faced teen, folds it in half, and slips it into her wallet in a hurry. In the process, a twenty-dollar bill falls out, fluttering to the cement floor as her heels click away.

A swift tap on my shoulder from the man behind me pulls my attention from Daphne momentarily.

"You going to give that to her?" A mustachioed Good Samaritan points to the lifeless bill that has come to a stop a few feet before me.

Up ahead, Daphne is almost to the exit, and without thinking, I reach down to grab the twenty before chasing after her.

"Ma'am," I call out, though Daphne McMullen is much too youthful and beautiful for such a common formality. "Excuse me . . ."

Her heels, because of course this beautifully enigmatic creature would grocery shop in heels, come to a quick stop, and she scans the area around her until her gaze stops on me. My hand is outstretched as I move closer, my heart pounding so hard in my chest, I struggle to breathe.

"You dropped this," I say, marveling at how such a simple exchange could knock the wind out of me.

Her lips, shaded in rich mauve, pull into a smile that lights the rest of her face. Smoothing her hand along her flat belly, she saunters toward me, taking her time and meeting me halfway, and I'm amazed at how a person can strut along in heels the same way anyone else would strut along in tennis shoes.

"Thank you so much," she says, her eyes searching mine as if they're vaguely familiar. And they should be. Grace, *our* Grace, has *my* brown eyes. She has *my* wide forehead. *My* round face. *My* muddy brown hair.

I nod, releasing the breath I'd been sheltering and finding myself uncharacteristically incapable of forming a response.

Daphne smiles, releasing me from this moment when she turns back to her impatient Sebastian. Just like that, our exchange is over, and the only mother my daughter has ever known walks away, pushing Grace's little brother in her overflowing shopping cart, loading the organic groceries in the back of the SUV that hauls my daughter from soccer to ballet, heading to the home my daughter runs to after the bus drops her off from school at three fifteen every afternoon.

Returning to the checkout lane in a daze, I retrieve Ben's credit card from my wallet and pay for Marnie's gifts. The cashier doesn't fumble and flit in my presence. He doesn't clear his throat or crack his knuckles. His eyes don't dart around. He only stares at me with dull, vacant eyes, and then he calls out, "Next!" before I have a chance to gather my things.

Within minutes, I'm seated in the front seat of my car, slamming the visor down to take a good look at myself. Or rather, Pretty Girl. My red lips are fading, some of the lipstick smudged beyond my lip line, and my perfectly messy bun has fallen loose in several places, sagging past my crown. I can never get these things to stay in place for more than an hour or two.

I'll never figure out how these women make it look so easy, but I'll never stop trying. After all, they're proof it's possible.

I start my engine and blast the AC. Autumn, the one who does not turn heads or make teenage boys nervous, stares back at me from the rearview mirror, a stark reminder that she was always there, hiding beneath the façade. Being Pretty Girl was fun for all of two hours, but the second I get home, I'm retiring her in favor of Daphne.

Daphne trumps them all.

The years have come and gone. I've followed and unfollowed more people than I can recall. I've tried on a dozen personas purely for fun and neatly placed them back in their box when I was done. I've been inflicted with all-consuming obsessions and morbid fascinations that have dissipated just as quickly as they began, but it's different with the McMullens.

They're practically family.

And they're the only true family I've ever known.

Even if they don't know it.

3

Daphne

MY BLOUSE IS SOAKED clear through, sticking to my skin and sending a quick shiver down my spine. Graham keeps the house at a frigid sixty-eight degrees year round. It's the way he likes it. Never mind the fact that he's rarely home. When he's not putting in fifty-hour weeks, he's sauntering around the country club greens pretending he's in the company of a quiet crowd who silently applaud his perfected chip shot.

Sebastian splashes in the tub, giggling when it hits my face. I drag the back of my arm across my chin before wiping a streak of running mascara from under my eye. Bathing my four-year-old is worse than bathing the enormous, hypoallergenic labradoodle Graham insisted on getting for the kids last Christmas.

"Come on, buddy. Let's get you out." I turn to grab a towel and ignore my son's whiny pleas.

"Daddy lets me stay in longer." He crosses his arms and brings his knees to his chest.

"Now you know that isn't true," I say, leaving out the fact that the number of times Graham has bathed the kids I could count on one hand. I attempt to tuck my hands under Sebastian's arms, but he's got them locked against his sides. "If you get out of the tub now, I'll read you an extra bedtime story later tonight."

I am that parent. The one who bribes. The one who, somewhere along the line, lost all control and hasn't the slightest idea how to get it back.

"I hate when you read me bedtime stories." Sebastian scowls, his square jaw clenched as he finally stands. He is a mirror image of his father: milky, caramel complexion with chocolate hair and clear blue eyes. On his best days, Sebastian is a delicious little boy, all sweet with a smile that could melt the coldest of hearts. On his worst days, Sebastian is a spoiled monster. "I only like when Daddy reads to me."

Refusing to take a four-year-old's insult to heart, I ignore him, draping a towel around his shoulders and hoisting him out of the tub. The sound of giggling girls coming from Grace's room makes me question whether or not they're changing into their school uniforms like I asked ten minutes ago.

Lifting Sebastian to my hip, I carry him to his room at the end of the hall and place him at the foot of his bed where I had the foresight to lay out his clothes for the day earlier. The sooner I can get him dressed, the sooner I can capture an ounce of my sanity before we hit the grocery store together.

"I don't want to wear dinosaurs. I want trucks." He kicks his legs in protest when I try to slide his jeans on and throws his T-rex shirt across the room.

"Dinosaurs look so good on you though," I say, knowing full well only crazy people try to reason with tantrum-prone preschoolers. I slide his leg into one side and ready the other, but he wiggles out and renders the pants halfway inside out. An exasperated sigh leaves my lips as I try once more. "Your daddy picked this outfit."

It's a lie.

But then again, so is every other facet of my life.

Sebastian's face lights when I mention his daddy. I was hoping Graham was going to get to see the kids before they went to school, but he kissed me goodbye before the sun came up this morning and whispered that he'd see me tonight after work.

"All right." Sebastian crawls off his bed and gathers his thrown shirt before handing it to me. "Sorry, Mama."

It's in these still, small moments I find myself falling back in love with being his mother. I think about the sweet hugs, the occasional unprompted *I love yous*, the lit smiles, and picked dandelions that make me think perhaps my son might actually love and appreciate me after all. I remind myself that maybe it isn't so bad – that it can only get better from here.

"Okay, let's check on your sisters." I take his hand and lead him down the hall, following the trail of laughter to Grace's room. The door is half closed, light from her lamp casting a warm glow that spills into the hall.

I smile when I hear my sweet Rose's giggle. And then a metallic snip follows. I storm through the doorway, the door banging against the wall and bouncing back.

"No, no, no, no . . ." My heart stops in my chest as I reach down and retrieve handfuls of Rose's silky blonde hair. Glancing up, Grace is frozen, shears in hand, wicked little smile fading.

I yank the scissors from her hand with a violent pull that startles both of us and sends her falling back on her bed. My seven-year-old Rose begins to cry.

"Rose . . ." I go to her, cupping her sweet face in my hands, my eyes filling with tears as I examine the monstrous haircut Grace saw fit to give her beautiful little sister. Finger-combing the baby blonde tendrils away from her forehead, her bottom lip quivers.

"Grace was trying to make me pretty, Mama," she says, her blue eyes two perfect glassy pools.

"You're already pretty, Rosie. You're beautiful just the way you are." I kiss the top of her head, taking in a deep breath and inhaling the scent of her vanilla-orange shampoo. Her soft locks lie in a pile at our feet, the same hair she'd been growing out since her toddler years with the exception of the occasional back-to-school haircut. It was past the middle of her back . . . until tonight.

"Mommy, I'm sorry." Grace's voice pulls me from Rose, and I turn to face her. Seated on the edge of her bed, her expression shows no remorse. No regret. Her sandy hair hangs limp around her round face, in a constant state of disheveled tangles no matter how much I comb and tug and pull and braid. "I didn't mean to."

"I don't understand, Grace. You're old enough to know better." I glance down at Rose's hair, my anger coming to life by the second. My stomach is knotted, my fists clenched so hard they ache. This week it's Rose's hair. Last week she let the dog run out the front door and I spent an hour chasing it around the neighborhood like a crazy person. Two weeks ago, she dropped eight of my perfume bottles from the top of the stairs to the wood floor of the foyer to see if they'd break. Six of them did. My house still smells like a French brothel.

My hand grips the scissors so hard they leave indentations in my palm, and when I loosen my hold, I realize I've never seen this pair in my life.

"Where did you get these scissors?" I ask, shaking like a woman who's lost all control of her life.

I've taken every precaution to Grace-proof this house since I first suspected there was something special about her. Graham refuses to believe she's anything but perfect, but he doesn't see what I see because he's never around.

There's something off about her.

"Tell me, Grace." My voice is deeper, my stare harder. "Where did you find these?"

Grace sighs, rolling her eyes. "I took them from Mrs. Applegate yesterday. They were sitting in a cup on her desk."

"You *stole* from your *teacher*? From the *school*?" My jaw hangs for a moment until I can compose myself. "We do *not* steal, Grace McMullen. Do you understand me?"

"Yes." Her ten-year-old voice is chock full of resentment as she stares at the garish Hello Kitty poster on her wall.

"Look me in the eyes when you speak to me," I say.

Her lifeless brown gaze snaps onto mine, her jaw clenched.

"Apologize to your sister. And you're giving the scissors back to Mrs. Applegate today along with a handwritten apology. I'll be back to check on you in a minute," I say. "I want you dressed for school. Teeth brushed. The bus leaves in twenty minutes, and your breakfast is getting cold. Move it. Do you understand?"

"Yes." She stomps to her dresser, yanking the top drawer until it almost falls out, and from the corner of my eye, I spot the eight-hundred-dollar cocktail dress I thought I'd lost last year. I'd even gone so far as to blame the dry cleaner, taking our business elsewhere and sharing my suspicions with the girls at the coffee shop one frenzied Thursday morning.

"Why do you have my dress?" I march over, yanking her other drawers open to see what other treasures were waiting to be discovered. Just as I suspected, I find my grandmother's antique, diamond-encrusted timepiece resting in a Strawberry Shortcake pencil box. I fired the last housekeeper over this missing watch. Another opened drawer contains a box of chocolate cupcakes and a half-eaten bag of family-sized potato chips, crumbs scattered and sticking to her winter sweaters. Shaking my head, I mutter her name under my breath.

I'd be lying if I said there wasn't a day that passes when I don't regret bringing Grace home. Our bond hasn't been easy, and most days, I'm not sure it exists at all. Everything about her is a challenge, and most days I don't have it in me to conquer those tribulations. Adopting a baby was a quick-fix. A marital Band-Aid. Another one of Graham's non-negotiable whims. And I was just a young wife, trying to please the only man I'd ever loved, desperately trying to keep him at any cost.

And if there's anything I've learned in my thirty-six years, it's that desperate people are incapable of making good decisions.

END OF SAMPLE - Available Now Exclusively at Amazon

ABOUT THE AUTHOR

Sunday Tomassetti is the pseudonym of a Wall Street Journal, Washington Post, Amazon Charts and #1 Amazon bestselling author (Winter Renshaw/Minka Kent) who wanted an outlet for her passion projects. A thirty-something married mother of three, she resides in the Midwest where you can always find her hard at work on her next novel. She is represented by Jill Marsal of Marsal Lyon Literary Agency.

For more information, please visit www.sundaytomassetti.com or sign up for her newsletter here.

Don't forget to follow her on Instagram and like her on Facebook!

CPSIA information can be obtained
at www.ICGtesting.com
Printed in the USA
LVHW091123070420
652480LV00002B/57